MW01671185

In Search of
the Lady Lion Tamer

By the Same Author

The Last Train to Berlin
Operation Parterre

In Search of the Lady Lion Tamer

GEORGE BLAGOWIDOW

Harcourt Brace Jovanovich, Publishers
San Diego New York London

Copyright © 1987 by George Blagowidow

All rights reserved. No part of this publication may be reproduced or transmitted in any form or by any means, electronic or mechanical, including photocopy, recording, or any information storage and retrieval system, without permission in writing from the publisher.

Requests for permission to make copies of any part of the work should be mailed to: Permissions, Harcourt Brace Jovanovich, Publishers, Orlando, Florida 32887.

Library of Congress Cataloging-in-Publication Data

Blagowidow, George.
In search of the lady lion tamer.

I. Title.
PS3552.L344I5 1987 813'.54 86-25644
ISBN 0-15-144500-1

Designed by Kaelin Chappell

Printed in the United States of America

First edition

A B C D E

In Search of the Lady Lion Tamer

1

I knew the very moment I caught my first glimpse of the gaudy image of the lady lion tamer on the poster that I must find her. The intensity of my determination surprised me. I admitted to myself that the idea was a bit ridiculous. It certainly had its comic aspects. The age of Romanticism had long passed in that spring of 1977. How could I, then, a respected member of Gourmet Internationale, author of short stories published by intellectual magazines, and a Parisian of independent means, consider setting out on a search for a woman whose profession was the taming of circus lions, perhaps an array of other wild beasts?

But I had already seen the lion tamer on the poster, and it was too late for rational behavior. Mine was a compulsion. I had to find her.

Moments before, I had been strolling through the streets of the Left Bank, a footloose and free bachelor, when, in the middle of the rue de Seine, a May downpour hit me. To protect my well-coiffeured gray hair and to keep from dampening my double-breasted Dior suit, I stepped inside the nearest building, which happened to be an art gallery. The only person there was a young woman dressed in a floral chiffon gown, the colors of which were already at war with a purple polish she was applying with great concentration to her fingernails. Seated behind a Louis Quinze desk, she looked about half my age.

It was impossible to see her eyes, since her orange hair covered them as she bent to her task. But her lips, painted the same purple as her nail polish, curved downward in annoyance at this interruption of the Parisian woman's sacred rite of making herself irresistible. *En plus,* she obviously had guessed the real reason for my visit. This thought added to the annoyance she did not attempt to hide.

Fearing that the girl might apply her tongue, now busily following the movements of the tiny brush, to invite me to leave, and not being ready to face that prospect, I decided to act like a customer. A series of framed watercolors was displayed against the wall; the remaining space was covered by cardboard-mounted posters in glassine covers. I approached a bin under a sign that priced them at ten francs—the cheapest in the place—and began to sort through the posters.

When my eyes caught sight of the lady teasing a green lion with a huge red scarf, my heart began to pound and I stopped. It was crazy, miraculous. I had never laid eyes on her before, but now, looking at her delicate profile, I realized that I had been longing for her all my life.

I pulled the poster out and carried it to the window with intense excitement. Feeling as if my hands were holding one of the missing Brandenburg concertos, I examined the portrait more closely. The lady lion tamer posed in golden high-heeled shoes, her long legs covered with black net stockings, her miniskirt not quite covering her pink panties. She wore an open, black vest embroidered with gold over a white lace blouse, and she had short, strawberry-blond hair, an impudent nose, and, what most attracted me, eyes the color of some Alpine lake softened by the haze of a morning fog.

"Monsieur should be careful," said the woman clerk. "You might damage the gravure."

"Don't worry, mademoiselle. I am being extremely careful. Besides, I am going to buy it."

The girl took her time placing the bottles she had been using in the drawer. She agitated her fingers as if she were playing an invisible harpsichord, and approached the counter. Having learned to expect the most extravagant tastes in her clients, she glanced at the poster and, with no emotion whatsoever, picked up a piece of gray paper to wrap it up.

"Ten francs, monsieur, *s'il vous plait.*"

"Wait just a minute, mademoiselle. I want to locate that lady. I would like very much to meet her."

The girl backed away impatiently.

"How would I know who she is?"

I looked at the girl with anger, thinking briefly that she might be lying.

"How would I know where to find her, monsieur? In this place we have thousands of prints depicting all kinds of women: queens, actresses, courtesans, virgins . . ." She looked at me with curiosity. "Were you perhaps in love with her, monsieur, and then she left you?"

"I've never seen her before . . . but you are right, mademoiselle, I must admit I am in love with her."

"But how can one fall in love with someone one has never met?" she asked, smiling with her purple lips and showing her white teeth. "She might not be French! She might not *speak* French! She might not be able to cook a *boeuf bourguignonne* or even a simple *omelette aux fines herbes.*"

"I would cook for her. I grow dill myself for omelets in a special soil mixture, including dried blood and a few drops of ordinary white wine. But I don't want to digress. Where did you get this poster?"

My eyes returned to the image on the print. The lady lion tamer was smiling at me with a touch of irony.

"Oh, many of the posters, monsieur, are bought second hand. This print might have served as an advertisement for a circus, glued to a kiosk, with the name of the circus and the day of the performance pasted separately. The poster looks to me to be at least ten years old."

"Are you judging by the age of the paper?"

"No, by the shoes the lady is wearing. These were in fashion a decade ago."

I lit a Gauloise, ignoring the sign, *"Défense de fumer."* The girl came closer to me and looked at the print I was holding. I could feel the pressure of her well-formed breast against my right arm.

"The lion tamer is a good-looking girl, I give you that, but our gallery has thousands of pictures of much more beautiful ladies. Why don't you fall in love with someone I might know?"

"In my fifty-five years I have met hundreds of women. I've been fond of some of them; I've even loved a few, but never before have I been so infatuated as I am with her."

"Is it not always the latest love that is the true and only real love?" she asked.

"My love for her is absolute, forever," I said, deeply inhaling the smoke from my cigarette. "I have always loved her. I have always been in love with her. During sleepless nights, I have dreamed of her. I have wanted her. Now that I have seen her image, my passion for her is unbearable. I would crawl on my hands and knees all the way around the world until I find her."

"That would seem to be the most difficult way," she said, and the pressure of her breast against my arm intensified. "Those are beautiful words, monsieur. But what if you find her and she does not return your love?"

"Oh, that is impossible," I said, smiling like a teacher hearing complete nonsense from one of his pupils. "The kind of love I feel for her is too contagious. It will sweep her off her feet, envelop her in a blanket of happiness, carry her, carry both of us, toward the bliss of discovery and the search for absolute beauty." I even laughed for a moment. "It is impossible that she would not fall in love with me."

"Men often err in searching far for the bliss etcetera that you have just described, monsieur." She looked into my eyes. "I am the niece of the owner. One day I will inherit this place. I have a fiancé, but . . ."

She was a tall, good-looking girl, and I was conscious of a pleasant-smelling perfume on her body. "I cook over two thousand dishes well, and I would not mind—"

"Sorry, mademoiselle. It is too late."

She raised her shoulders slightly and shook her orange coiffure, as if to say that everyone is entitled to the folly of his choice. She turned and wrapped the poster quickly.

"Ten francs, please."

I handed her two five-franc coins.

"Monsieur, in case you do not find her, will you come back to see me? I don't know you at all, but I am ready to follow you anywhere, even into the lion's cage."

"I promise, but I am convinced that I will find her."

At the doorstep I turned back. "One day you will find your own lion tamer and then, mademoiselle, you will know what life is. You will live. The rest is just existence." And, whistling the allegro of Vivaldi's *Concerto for Divers Instruments,* I went through the doorway. As I stepped outside, the sun broke through the dark clouds and lit the wet streets.

I rushed toward the boulevard Saint-Germain so that I could call Bernadette, my mistress. I always spent Thursday evenings with Bernadette, and, since this was a Thursday and it was four o'clock in the afternoon, she would be leaving her home at that moment for our rendezvous at my apartment. I did not have the courage yet to tell her about my new love, so I planned simply to cancel her visit.

The telephones were located in the basement of the post office. I asked for *jetons,* and the usually unfriendly middle-aged clerk smiled at me.

"What has happened to you, monsieur?" she asked, handing me three *jetons.* "You look like a different man. I always had the impression that you were a tired, bored man. But now . . ." Smiling, she unobtrusively opened the top button of her blouse. "You sparkle with life, with hope."

"Yes, yes, I am different. I have begun to live."

She was an attractive brunette, I saw now, with dark eyes that smiled.

"Could you enlist me as one of your students?" she asked, touching my hand with her fingers. "I would like to live a little."

"I wish I could," I said, moving away. "But you are a beautiful woman. You will live."

My call to Bernadette was answered by her fifteen-year-old daughter, who told me that *Maman* had left about half an hour before and that she shouldn't be too late for her visit with Monsieur.

The unavoidable visit loomed, a potential disaster. We had started our affair some seven years ago, two years before Bernadette's divorce. She was an artist, and I had met her when my publisher suggested that I try a children's book, an adaptation of Aesop's fables, instead of the short stories that always received good reviews but did not sell. In a week's time we had become lovers and, though I had other mistresses, I kept seeing Bernadette regularly, being fond of her sensuous body and her *joie de vivre.*

As I was leaving the post office, I noticed two *aubergines* (meter maids) in their uniforms the color of eggplant. They were writing a ticket. The gravity of their task engraved itself on their faces in a disdain for the unknown car-owner and for the world in general. But when they noticed me they stopped to smile at me, and one of them dropped her ticket book into the gutter. As I moved on down the boulevard Saint-Germain, the women doing their *leche-vitrines* (window shopping), or just strolling, turned their heads to look at me. And the Parisian ladies driving along the boulevard slowed their cars to gaze at me.

I checked my appearance quickly in the mirror in one of the store windows, but I could find nothing strange or unusual in my wardrobe. The ladies' attention and their smiles embarrassed me, and I walked faster and faster until I was running; yet I could not help hearing female voices: "*Voilà*, a man in love, real love!" Or, "How I envy the woman he loves!" Or, "I would give anything to be loved by him!"

As I passed a school building, several girls, still putting on their navy blue blazers, were leaving. I was a familiar figure to them, and in previous encounters they had called me "*Monsieur Pompes Funèbres* [Mister Funeral Home]." But now the girls stopped and several of them waved at me. One of them called me "*Monsieur L'Amoureux*," and the others echoed that call.

I was happy to reach my apartment house at last. As soon as I opened the door I knew that Bernadette had arrived, for the odors of garlic, marjoram, bay leaf, and fish told me that a *bouillabaisse à la Marseillaise* was being prepared.

The table, all set with a bottle of Tavel in the middle, confirmed my guess. Bernadette liked to drink Tavel with her bouillabaisse.

She came to greet me dressed in a smart white silk blouse and elegant black skirt. Around her neck was a single strand of pearls.

I abhorred women dressed in anything but black and white, and Bernadette dressed to please me.

"Wandering about as usual, my dear Maje?" she asked. For some reason unknown to me, she did not like my first name, Jan, preferring instead to shorten my family name, Majeski, to Maje.

"Doing research on your next novel?" She smiled and kissed my forehead. "Interviewing all the attractive females you can find?" The aroma of the spices from her cooking lingered in her clothes. I stepped back.

"I don't know how to tell you this, Bernadette, but I fell in love today."

"That is a fascinating beginning, my dear Maje," she said, sitting down on the sofa next to a pile of books and records.

I began to pace the floor, not an easy thing to do, since books, albums, and pots of growing herbs were scattered all about. I lit a cigarette and, clenching it in my mouth, continued to talk.

"I saw her picture on a poster with a lion. A lady lion tamer. I fell in love with her."

I looked at Bernadette, whose skirt was raised a little so that it did not quite cover her knees. For an instant I experienced a feeling of sadness that I would never touch or kiss them again, one by one, every *tache de rousseur* (freckle) . . .

"Oh, how interesting! A lion tamer," Bernadette exclaimed. "Then you went and found her in the circus. She was in a cage with twenty-three lions, all of them roaring with anger. Nevertheless, you made your declaration of love, the lady believed you, and therefore you made passionate love to her on the back of a ferocious beast. End of chapter one."

"I don't like your—"

"Will you excuse, please, your for-the-lion-tamer-abandoned mistress, so she may attend to the bouillabaisse for a few moments?"

"But I want to—"

"I can hear you in the kitchen, or you may join me there, if you like."

She picked herself up and rushed to the kitchen. I followed her. Bernadette did not believe in taking short cuts when cooking for me. She made her soup stock from the fish heads, instead of using water as so many cooks in Paris do nowadays. On a large tray she laid out chopped onion, leeks, garlic, ten spices, seven kinds of fish, and an orange. The fish stock was boiling and she began straining it.

"My love for her is like a fresh breeze of hope, it's the strongest feeling I have ever experienced in my life."

"Does she love you, too?" Bernadette asked, putting the onions and leeks into the large pot with the soup stock.

"She will one day, I am sure," I said, focusing my eyes on the movements of her hands. "Where did you get the garlic?"

"Marcel brought it yesterday from Provence, fresh from his mother's garden." She smiled, perhaps because Marcel was her ex-husband who, nevertheless, knowing his former wife's culinary interests, never failed to share with her the good things he was able to get in the country. "And she told you that one day she would love you?"

"Of course she will. Are you sure you are adding enough bay leaves?"

"They are fresh from Perpignan, and quite aromatic. I don't want them to dominate the flavor of the soup, Maje. Of course she will love you forever, you say?"

"I will love her forever, so there is no question that she will love me in return. Should I cut the orange peel?"

She nodded. "Cut it from the top. It is more flavorful there. This will be a bouillabaisse that Venus would be proud to serve her Vulcan. You should have invited her."

"Whom? Oh, you mean my lion tamer?"

"Of course, Maje, your lion tamer." She began to add the chunks of fish to the soup.

"But I have not found her yet."

"I guess I had better cut this langouste in two pieces," she said, motioning to me to hand her a pair of scissors hung neatly on a hook on the wall. My kitchen, unlike the rest of my apartment, was always in perfect order. I kept it immaculate.

"Is she alive or dead? Maybe you are in love with a ghost?"

"I don't know anything about her, but I hope she is alive. She *must* be alive! Her image was so appealing . . . her image on the poster. I will show it to you."

"In a little while. Now you may serve the wine. The bouillabaisse will be ready in just eight minutes."

In the dining room I tasted the wine and filled each of the two crystal glasses half full. Then I unwrapped the poster to admire once more the image of my lady love. That sadness in her eyes. It reminded me of someone else, but of whom? Pondering it, my mind summoned up the images of boys. Boys? Bernadette's entrance with a Limoges tureen of steaming soup interrupted my thoughts.

Both of us ate our meal in silence. Tacitly, we knew that any conversation, and especially one on such an exciting subject as my love for the unknown lady lion tamer, would be an unwarranted intrusion on the delights of Bernadette's superb soup. After the meal we both lit cigarettes, and only then did I tell her how I had found the poster by chance and how I had fallen in love.

"I knew all my life that I would find real love one day. It's ironic, though, that my love is for a woman for whom I must search. I don't know why destiny is punishing me so severely."

"*Toute proportion gardée* [Everything considered], you should not complain, Maje. You are very lucky to have found true love. All France will envy you."

"But will you help me to find her, Bernadette?"

"Of course, my dear Maje. What else is a mistress for?" Then she looked at me for a moment. "By the way, I'd like to mention it, if you still would like . . ."

"It would be a little unfair to the lion tamer lady. Don't you agree?"

"You are right, of course. How tactless of me to suggest it. *Quelle delicatesse du sentiment* [What delicacy of feeling]! I adore you."

I looked at her as she stood up and began to pile up the empty plates. Her bosom was full and well formed. And I was reminded how I especially enjoyed making love to her after a bouillabaisse . . .

"I have something in mind that might work," I said, getting up. "We could hang the poster up over the bed and while we made love, I could look at the lady lion tamer on the poster."

"Oh, what a glorious idea!" she exclaimed. "Why didn't it occur to me?" She put the dishes and plates back on the table. "Where would you want it?"

"I think in the *salon*. The walls there are bigger and the light much better than in the bedroom. We could hang the poster over the couch."

Bernadette took off her shoes and brought a hammer and some nails from the kitchen. She stepped up on the couch and held the poster against the wall. "Do you like it here?"

The late afternoon sun lit the poster, and the lady lion tamer took on an incandescence. Her eyes had a mysterious glow. But didn't I know this woman from somewhere before? I concentrated hard and a blurred recollection of this person surfaced, trailing with it—oddly—names I had known in my youth: Michal, Kurt, Bogdan. . . .

"How do you like it here?" Bernadette asked again. "My arm is getting tired."

"It won't do, I am afraid. The location is all right, but the poster is too small for me to see that far away."

"You could use a magnifying glass," she said, stepping down.

We looked at each other in silence.

"A magnifying glass would be too inconvenient."

"Why don't I enlarge the poster?" she asked. "I have my paints, brushes, and paper here. I could do it in no time. You would want her life size, I assume?"

I nodded. The idea pleased me. In a few minutes Bernadette had cleared the table, placed on it a huge sheet of white paper, and, looking at the poster as I held it, began to draw. I watched her work with approval.

There was a ring at the door. Unhappy at the thought of an interruption, I went to open the door to Marcel, a small, wiry man with bushy brown hair, dressed as usual in his rumpled brown suit.

I was not surprised to see Bernadette's ex-husband. It was Marcel's habit to drop by whenever he knew that we were preparing a special meal. And since he had contributed his mother's fresh garlic today, it was only natural for him to come to taste our bouillabaisse.

"You are too late, Marcel," I said, walking with our guest into the dining room. Marcel kissed his ex-wife on the cheek and went straight to the kitchen, reappearing in a few minutes with a bowl of bouillabaisse.

"I am sorry I wasn't here on time," Marcel said. "Bouillabaisse is best right after it has been cooked." He sat on a chair and balanced the plate on his knees. "But that damn traffic. What are you up to?" he asked, looking at Bernadette at work.

"We have a new excitement here," Bernadette said, smiling. "Maje has fallen in love with the lion tamer on the poster he is holding. I am enlarging the picture. He wants to see her—"

"Excellent bouillabaisse," Marcel said. "What kind of orange peel did you use?"

"Valencia," Bernadette told him.

"I thought so," Marcel said, continuing to eat the soup. "It would have been better if you had used an orange from Provence."

"I agree," I said. "But they are so hard to get."

"The next time, tell me," Marcel said. "I will try to get it for you. That's a superb idea to fall in love with a woman on a poster, or a drawing on the wall. Since love to me is the enjoyment of ego for two, a poster instead of a woman makes it easier. Very creative. Congratulations, Jan."

Bernadette was working to recreate the red scarf.

"That red is too pale," I observed.

Marcel got up, still holding the soup bowl, and approached the table where Bernadette was working.

"Jan is right," Marcel said. "You should deepen the shade."

"Of course, I agree," Bernadette said. "But I don't have the right shade."

She stopped working, and the three of us looked at the freshly painted scarf.

"The color on the poster is that of the red in the *tricolore*," Bernadette said.

"Poor Jan," Marcel said, continuing to eat, standing up. "We won't have the right— But let me think, Jan, you must have the *tricolore* somewhere. Why don't you cut the red part off it and superimpose it over the area now painted in this faded red?"

"That's a terrific idea," I said. "Thank you, Marcel."

I rushed to the bedroom where I kept the *tricolore* under the bed. It was quite dusty, but the color was a rich red, exactly that of the scarf on the poster.

Marcel took out a pocket knife that included many gadgets, among them a pair of miniature scissors. Putting his now empty bowl on the floor, he approached the table to measure the size of the scarf on the painting. He then began cutting the fabric.

"Where is this lion tamer?" Marcel asked. "She's not bad looking."

"We don't know," Bernadette said with a sigh. "We hope to find her."

"Will she come to live with you here?" Marcel said.

"What a question, my friend," I answered. "I could not possibly live anywhere but Paris."

"Of course, of course," Marcel said. "How stupid of me. Where did you buy the poster?"

"On the rue de Seine."

"I think I know the place," Marcel said. "In the cuisine of love there is a dish for any taste. I might look up that poster shop myself."

After another hour's work, Bernadette was finished, with Marcel's assistance. They hung the painting over the couch.

"How do you like Bernadette's handiwork?" Marcel asked, hitting the last nail with the hammer.

"Splendid, thank you," I said.

"Without you, Marcel," Bernadette said, "it would have taken us at least an hour longer."

"I'm glad I came by. I have another suggestion," Marcel said. "It might be helpful to you, Jan, to have a mirror across from the painting. You may not remain in the same position all the time, and that way, if you turn you could still see the painting in the mirror."

I liked the idea, and with Marcel's assistance I unscrewed the long, narrow, built-in mirror from the bathroom wall and attached it with large screws to the wall opposite the couch. It required moving two heavy bookshelves and a lot of books and papers from the floor, but it was worth it, I decided. The mirror reflected the painting perfectly.

Marcel adjusted the lamps so they shone directly on the painting, then stood at the door to leave. "I am sorry to have to go," he said. "I wouldn't mind staying around to help you further, but I want to get to the gallery before it closes. In the kitchen of love there are thousands of imitations, but only one true bouillabaisse." With that he left.

"I knew I could count on you and Marcel," I said, kissing Bernadette.

"Would you like to listen to some special music while we make love?" Bernadette asked. "I think you have a record of 'The March of the Circus Clowns,' don't you?"

"Yes, but that would be too distracting."

"Some special perfumes? What do you think, Maje?"

"I was thinking about it, my dear Bernadette, but the only aroma that I associate with her is sawdust. The next time, maybe, you could bring a few sacks and we would spread the lion tamer on the floor and make love there."

"Of course, I'll get some," she said, undressing.

"I'll be eternally grateful," I said, taking off my trousers and dropping them to the floor. Why do I love the lady lion tamer so much? I asked myself, taking off my socks.

"You are so imaginative, my dear Maje," Bernadette told me, her voice soft with emotion. "I don't think that I have ever loved you so much as I do tonight. I am touched, extremely moved by your creativity. There is nothing in the world I would not do to please you, *mon amour.*"

Seeing Bernadette against the background of the green lion, I desired her intensely. Bernadette had now undressed down to her panties and bra.

"Darling, I am concerned your naked body might distract me."

"Sorry, Maje. I did not think about it." Bernadette stopped undressing. "Should I put my dress back on, and perhaps keep the panties on?"

"Yes, that would be better."

"Should I put on anything else? Overcoat, gloves, shoes?"

"No overcoat, darling. The fabric would be too coarse against my skin. However, shoes, gloves, and a hat with a veil would be de rigueur."

"Of course. I understand perfectly, Maje."

And then when she was all dressed up as agreed, I made love to her, concentrating my thoughts on the lady lion tamer, in the end weeping from happiness. Later, Bernadette kissed my hands to thank me for the opportunity of being allowed to please me on such an important day. And, accepting her expressions of gratitude, I begged: "Help me find her!"

"Of course, my dear Maje, of course. What else are mistresses for, but to come to the aid of their lovers?"

Bernadette was a well-organized, enterprising woman. Within a few days she had organized the biggest search campaign in the history of France, perhaps in the whole world.

To start with, officials in the prefectures of all of France were notified, and a reward was posted, offering free meals for a week in a Michelin three-star restaurant. Several newspapers and magazines ran the story of the author who had found his true love on a poster, accompanied by a photograph of the lion tamer and a call for help in locating her. All three television networks carried interviews with me, and channel one interrupted a news broadcast of an interview with the president of the republic to appeal to its viewers to assist me in my search. Another television station put together a special, featuring all the living lion tamers in France, including some already retired. But none had ever heard of or seen the lady lion tamer of my poster.

Thousands of letters poured into my apartment; all turned out to be nothing but false leads. I suffered a great deal. During the nights I paced the dining room, smoking hundreds of Gauloises.

All my efforts appeared in vain, and for a few weeks I was so discouraged that I even considered giving up the entire project. But I realized that I could never be happy again until I found her and learned the reason why she had enchanted me so. I soon renewed my efforts.

But I began to realize that a curious thing was happening to me. Whenever I thought of the lion tamer, the names of my Polish childhood friends would rush to mind. I forced myself to remember my old nursery school in Czestochowa, Poland, where I had grown up. There had been six boys in the class: myself, that is, Jan Majeski, then Zdzislaw Drzwicki, Kurt Eisner, and three others whose family names I could not remember, only their first names: Romek, Bogdan, and Michal.

I began to theorize: Was it possible that the lion tamer reminded me of the nursery school teacher? Or of the mother of one of the boys? But why should I fall in love with a person reminding me of a teacher? Or a mother? In any case, I could remember neither the teacher nor the mothers. In my despair, I decided that the only reasonable way to clear up the mystery was to find my former classmates and learn something of the women *they* had fallen in love with.

I knew that the task before me would be difficult indeed. So many Poles had been killed in World War II that I knew I could not expect to find more than half of my friends alive. The others might be living anywhere in the world. But I was determined to leave no stone unturned. I had to learn the secret of my own love even more urgently than I needed to find the lion tamer herself.

As the freshness of the Parisian spring gave way to the heat of summer and as the hordes of foreign tourists swarmed the streets and parks and boulevards, my dream of finding the lady lion tamer continued to hold me in its grip.

But I avoided speaking of my obsession, even to Bernadette.

In an effort to restore some semblance of normalcy to my life, I took Bernadette for a month's vacation in a small pension in the little village of Saint-Hilaire on the coast of Normandy.

There we filled our days in the enjoyment of gourmet meals enhanced by detailed verbal consideration of each dish we consumed, in swimming in the waters of the Bay of the Seine, in quiet reading, and for me, putting on paper some ideas for future fiction.

Once we had returned to Paris, however, and Bernadette had gone back to her job, I found myself with great blocks of free time during which the mystery of the lady on the poster returned to haunt me once more.

Finally, I could postpone the inevitable search no longer. The only boy from my nursery school I had ever met again after the war was Zdzislaw Drzwicki, who had emigrated to the United States. I had met him years ago in Paris when Zdzislaw had come to visit his American girlfriend, an exchange student at the Sorbonne at that time. Zdzislaw eventually married the girl. We kept in touch for a while, but in recent years our correspondence had ceased. Nevertheless, I still had his address in the United States.

I wrote him right away, informing him about my desperate search for the unknown lady lion tamer, and awaited his reply. It came only a few weeks later. Zdzislaw informed me that he had changed his name to Arthur C. Wick Jr., that he often traveled on business to London, and that he would be delighted to renew our friendship and to try to help me solve my problem. More precisely, he was willing to tell me of his loves.

We met in September at the Hotel Mayfair in London, where Arthur had been residing. After several meetings I was able to record Arthur's story.

2

The lady standing in line two people in front of Arthur C. Wick Jr. was holding a small brown dog in her arms, and she spoke softly in Polish to her little puppy. They were lined up before the philately counter at the main post office at Eighth Avenue and Thirty-third Street in New York City, waiting to buy collector stamps and specifically a new series issued that day, October 17, 1970.

"*Cicho piesku kochany* [Keep quiet, dear doggie]," she said to the animal, "or we will be chased from here." She wore a yellow raincoat one or two sizes too small for her, so that the hem of her pink gingham dress showed at the bottom, making her appear shorter than her height of about five feet, five inches. Around her neck she sported a hand-knitted scarf of wool that looked to be in all the colors of the rainbow, plus a few more, and originally destined perhaps for someone twice her size. One end of the scarf circled twice around her neck and still reached below her knees; with the other end, she was trying to cover the whimpering animal. That did not prevent her from being noticed by the middle-aged postal employee, who told her, "Hey, miss, no dogs allowed here. Didn't you see the sign?"

The lady with the dog turned around and spoke in heavily accented English, "Please, madame, would you be so kind as to buy the stamps here listed on my paper?"

The woman addressed did not seem to understand. She continued to smoke her cigarette, staring with indifference at the ceiling.

"I will be glad to do it," Arthur said, moving forward toward the lady, who turned gratefully to him. She had golden hair arranged in braids and, he noticed, blue eyes the shade of cornflowers reflecting the sun on an August day. "*Z przyjemnoscia, tak* . . . [With pleasure, yes . . .]," said Arthur.

It was raining outside, and here inside the post office it smelled of wet clothing and ink.

"Oh, how wonderful! You are Polish," said the lady, handing Arthur a sheet of paper and a five-dollar bill. "You will do it. You can do it." There was a glint of joy in the lady's eyes. She picked up three heavy packages and began to move away.

"I will be waiting at the main entrance, outside," she said, turning to face Arthur. "So you are Polish?"

Arthur nodded and blushed. He was not quite sure that he should have answered that question affirmatively. True, he had been born forty-seven years ago in Krakow, Poland, as Zdzislaw Drzwicki, but after a time in the United States he had decided to cut off all ties to his native country. He had changed his first name to Arthur, altered his family name by dropping the first three letters and the last letter to come up with Wick, and for good measure, to achieve a real Anglo-Saxon effect, he added a middle initial of *C.* and the *Jr.* at the end.

The first few years after the war, Arthur had lived in Germany and France, first as a very poor, often hungry, student, and then as an unwanted, unemployed, and unemployable émigré. When he came to the United States, he wanted to forget those years and to succeed, hoping to become a business executive eventually. He had a degree from the University of Munich in business administration, but realizing that it would be of limited value in his search for a career in this new country, he enrolled in the evening college at the Graduate School of New York University.

Arthur—that is, Zdzislaw—started his career as a file clerk in the export department of a company producing house paints. This job paid thirty-five dollars a week and offered neither much opportunity to learn nor any chance for advancement. His first name provided lots of fun for his fellow employees.

Anxious to improve his prospects, he tried to find another job by canvassing the employment agencies during his lunch hours. He was asked to fill out application forms in various shapes and colors and was promised that as soon as a position for a person with his qualifications opened, he would be notified immediately. But he never heard from these people again.

Once, on a hot July day, during his second year in America, he came to an agency that had advertised: "College Grads, several openings, career executive potential, knowledge foreign language plus, $60.00+." A middle-aged lady—she wore a lilac dress with deep décolleté that showed her ample bosom, and she was loaded down with costume jewelry—invited him into a small cubicle.

"I have seen you here before," she said, sitting down. Her lips, coated thickly with a brick-red lipstick, curved a bit in an attempt to convey an expression of friendliness. Arthur could hear the traffic moving on Fifth Avenue through the open window behind the lady's back.

"Do you think you are qualified?" she asked.

"Yes, I do," Arthur said, blushing. "I have a degree corresponding to a master's from Munich. I am attending a graduate school of business here, and I speak four languages fluently." This might be a breakthrough, he thought. Now he would get an interview with a prospective employer; he was sure.

"I have been working for a year and a half in an office here. I shall work very hard."

The lady reached over with her heavily decorated hand and closed the door of the cubicle.

"I did not mean professionally," she said, lowering her voice to a whisper and focusing her eyes on one of the many rings on her plump hand.

"You see, you are a fine young man, good-looking, strong, tall, muscular, even with blue eyes. But you are barking up the wrong . . . I don't know how to put it." She looked straight at Arthur.

"These people want young men with American college degrees, of Anglo-Saxon background, so that eventually they can become executives. I am telling you this because I want to help you."

"But I could become—" Arthur began, and regretted it immediately. There was a moment of silence, interrupted only by the distant sound of a fire siren.

"I am sorry, very sorry," said the lady. "You could try in a garage. There are good-paying jobs."

Thus it was that Arthur stopped searching the help-wanted classified ads of the *New York Times* and never bothered to apply to an employment agency again.

As the next step, he tried to reach potential employers by mail. He typed two hundred personal letters, enclosing his résumé. He received seventeen replies, fifteen of which acknowledged the receipt of his letters and promised to keep his résumé in their "active files." Two of the letters suggested an interview. When he visited the first firm, he was told that the opening had just been filled; at the other place, a large metal firm, he had a brief interview with the personnel manager, who made a note on his application form and told Arthur that he would hear from him. He never did.

One day a classmate of his in one of the courses at the university suggested that Arthur apply for the job of junior statistician, which he himself was about to leave. When Arthur arrived for the interview, he realized that he had created a major embarrassment. He saw the vice president of personnel, the vice president of research, and one other executive whose title Arthur did not catch, and none of them took the time to ask him any questions, only apologized and explained why he would not qualify. They handled him with such super courtesy and sweetness that the interview left Arthur with a bitter memory.

As a result, when he received his American citizenship, he filled out the forms and became Arthur C. Wick Jr.

So it was that when the unknown Polish lady asked, he was not sure whether he could say with honesty that he was still Polish, but he continued to nod. "Polish or not Polish, I will get your stamps for you," he said, and watched the lady drag her packages toward the exit, talking softly all the while to her dog. He felt a little angry with himself for speaking Polish to the lady and for getting involved in this whole business of the stamps for her. When he met her outside later, it was pouring, and she was trying to cover the dog and her packages with a little umbrella.

"Here are your—" Arthur wanted to say stamps, but he could not remember the Polish word. "Oh, yes, here they are," he said, reaching into the pocket of his Burberry.

She put the whimpering dog down, trying to hold on to the packages which were slipping from her arms. Her light cloth shoes were drenched. The stamps passed into her wet hands.

"They will be ruined. Let's go somewhere out of this downpour," he suggested. "We'll be able . . ." He moved to pass the stamps to her, but stopped.

They struggled up Eighth Avenue, Arthur carrying the wet packages and shopping bags until they reached a bar. The counter was crowded with men sitting and drinking with their hats on. The place smelled of wet clothing, whiskey, and stale cigarette smoke, while a juke box played a Tijuana Brass tune at full force.

"Sorry to cause so much trouble," the lady said, shaking the water from her raincoat like a baby duck after a swim.

He liked her profile, the small nose, straight forehead, and clear eyes. She reminded him of someone he had known a long time ago in Poland, but he was not sure who. Perhaps it was an actress in a Polish film he had seen before the war.

"Take off your coat, please," he said. "You have to dry out a bit."

She hesitated.

"I have to . . ." she said. "Well, thank you. You are right. The rain will be a good excuse."

He helped her to take off her coat. A slight aroma of carnations emanated from her. They moved to the table, she still holding the whimpering dog in her arms.

"I had to pick up this dog," she said, sitting down, "from my sister-in-law, who is going on vacation. Poor little Zutshek. He will miss her. I had other errands, too, buying sausage, Polish sausage in a special store, then the purchase of the stamps for my uncle in Poland."

She looked around, observing their shabby surroundings with curiosity.

"It is a fancy place," she said. "It's New York after all."

"Fancy? You call it fancy?" he said. "It's ugly, depressing, malodorous."

"For me it is an interesting, strange, exotic place," she said. "I have never been in one like it."

"It's because of the rain that I brought you here," he said. "I promise, the next time—"

"Will there be a next time?"

She appeared very pleased with her outing, assuming the air of a little girl being taken to a restaurant by her father for the first time in her life. As she turned her head to look around, Arthur noticed a sprinkling of freckles on her small neck. She must be in her mid-thirties, some ten years younger than himself, he decided.

Arthur had gone to the post office to buy stamps for his older son Jerry, an avid stamp collector now in bed with a cold, and he had planned to be home in his Westchester mansion early to join his Anglo-Saxon wife Lillian and his other son, Arthur III.

He felt suddenly angry at this encounter with the lady who spoke Polish to her puppy. Arthur was a methodical, well-organized, successful business executive, a man who abhorred any interruption of his plans that resulted in delays, especially for such unimportant reasons as the rain and an encounter with a stranger. He felt silly for having said "next time" to her. Of course there would be no "next time."

Why should there be? Just because the woman happened to speak Polish? For many years Arthur had been avoiding any necessity to speak his native language. Just as he had married an American girl, he had sought out only American friends. He feared that anyone speaking English with a foreign accent might spoil his own hardwon peculiarity of diction. In the first years in America, he had had a lot of problems with his accent. He had studied the problems, even consulted specialists in the field, who told him that he would never lose a touch of foreign accent, and that he would never be able to pass as a native American. He was already twenty-eight years old, he was told, and at that age it would not be possible to learn a new language and speak it like a native.

After consulting many books and listening carefully to other immigrants speak, he decided to acquire an English accent, the way English is spoken in Oxford, Cambridge, or London. In that way, he decided, his own foreign accent would be less noticeable. He worked hard at it and succeeded extremely well. Most of his casual acquaintances assumed that he was an Englishman who might have lived for a period in France or Belgium. Some of his friends even envied his diction. Still, the question about "next time" with the Polish lady had to be answered.

"One never knows. Perhaps."

"You hesitated too long," she said. "You look as if you are already regretting your impulsive promise to take me to a better place. You are even still hiding your identity, so unsure are you—"

"What do you mean?" Arthur asked.

"We have been walking together for a few minutes and talking here for a while, and I still don't know your name."

Before he could respond, a young bartender came to their table to take their order. Arthur ordered wine for her and an extra-dry martini for himself.

"I apologize. My name is Zdzislaw Drzwicki."

"And I am Stasia Wroniecka. My maiden name is Zagorska." She extended her hand and he rose and kissed it. "I am from Lwow," she said.

He looked at her and their eyes met. He had the urge for a moment to kiss her on her mouth and to take her in his arms.

From the television set behind the bar, the broadcaster spoke for continuing rain for the next day.

"I am from Czestochowa, but I was born in Krakow," he said, looking at her breasts, outlined against the black sweater. "No one could pronounce Drzwicki or Zdzislaw, so I changed my name to—"

"Oh, so you are one of those," she said, but without reproach, only patting the dog, sleeping now in her lap.

The bartender placed their drinks in front of them.

"Were you in Poland during the war?" she asked.

"Yes, I was. Anyway, most of that time. I was active in the

underground and participated in the Warsaw uprising as a liaison officer. I was wounded in my left arm."

Stasia brought her head forward, trying to hear better. She appeared not to want to miss any of his words.

"I was twenty then, and I had a fiancée—her name was Genia—who had once saved my life. It was in June of 1944. I took a streetcar in Warsaw. It was very crowded. I had a gun in my pocket. Then the Germans, the Gestapo, surrounded the streetcar and began to frisk all the men for weapons. Anyone found with a gun would have been shot then and there. The two policemen were pushing their way toward me. And then a girl standing next to me looked at my ashen face. She knew why I was so scared. Still looking at my eyes she opened her handbag, and I dropped my gun into it. She saved my life."

Arthur gulped down half of his martini. His hands shook.

"It was a clear, cool summer day. We walked together for a while, talking about nothing. Then in a dark stairway she returned my gun. We started seeing each other. We knew each other a short time, but we were very much in love. Genia was just seventeen. She was killed by a bomb during the uprising. I found out about it only after the war."

A feeling of sadness and warmth engulfed Arthur at the memory of Genia and those times. He used to take her flowers, carnations and roses. They kissed on the stairways, walked in the streets holding hands, talked about getting married. Then it was all over.

"Another of those?" asked the bartender.

"Yes," Arthur said.

When Arthur came to the United States, he had wanted to talk about his war experiences all the time. Everything that he had seen, everything he had lived through, how his father had been executed, his mother deported, how he had been imprisoned and had escaped. But he found his new American friends were not interested. When he spoke to them about the war, they seemed bored. The war for them meant other experiences, entirely different from his. And besides, the war was over. Why should he talk about it?

He looked at Stasia. She was absorbed with his words, and when he mentioned Genia's death, she had tears in her eyes.

"And you?" he asked.

"The Soviets arrested and deported my parents to Siberia. I never heard from them again. My aunt and uncle raised me until my uncle was killed. Then my aunt and I were carted away to work in the fields of Germany, where I was liberated by the Allies. After the war I lived in many displaced persons camps. It was in one of these that I met my husband. We married after we came here, while we were still studying at Brooklyn College."

Arthur began to imagine two poor Polish students living in Greenpoint or some other part of Brooklyn. Stasia, as if she had been reading his thoughts, smiled.

"We had tough times at the beginning. Our first girl was born while Franek was earning sixty-five dollars a week. That was only ten years ago. Now we are doing much better. We have a store where we sell Polish handicrafts and specialty foods. Franek's mother and I prepare many of the foods. You should call at our store sometime. You might like what I make."

"Of course, I would like it very much," Arthur said. Stasia kept her hands on the table, and Arthur, as if he wanted to emphasize his interest in her handicrafts and her cooking, touched them. She did not pull her hands back, and for a moment both of them remained silent. By now the news was over, and the television program gave way to the noisy juke box playing another tune by the Tijuana Brass.

"And where are you working?" Stasia asked.

"I am marketing director for a very large firm that manufactures bathroom fixtures."

"I am not sure what that means," Stasia said, blushing, not from her ignorance of marketing, but because the pressure of his hands on hers had intensified.

"People consider me a super-specialist at creating programs to sell products. I have a Ph.D. in marketing, and last year I received an award as the number-one marketing wizard."

"That's wonderful," Stasia said. "I am active in Polish organizations. In Elizabeth, New Jersey, we have a group, a chapter of the national organization of SPJ. I am the chairwoman of this chapter."

"What does SPJ stand for?" Arthur asked.

"You are Polish and you never heard about us?" she asked. "It stands for Stop Polish Jokes. As you know, these boorish jokes are in vogue right now, and they are demeaning and unfair to us."

"Wouldn't it be better to forget the whole matter?" he asked. "The same kind of jokes are being told in England about the Irish, in France about the Belgians, in Germany about the Bavarians and in Poland about their *milicja* [policemen]."

"It's different here," Stasia said. There was sadness in her eyes. "We came here because we wanted equality and freedom. I don't want to be the butt of the American cinema, television, and radio."

"They'll get tired one day," Arthur said.

"I certainly hope so," Stasia said, getting up. "This conversation reminds me that I promised myself to write a number of letters tonight to congressmen protesting these jokes on television. I must go now, and catch my bus to Elizabeth."

The rain had stopped and they strolled through the wet streets holding hands.

"Are you happy?" Arthur asked as they approached the bus terminal.

"I have my two girls, my husband, lots of work. I have a good collection of classical records of the Polish composers, and I like to listen to their music. I don't have much time to think whether I am happy."

At the entrance to the bus terminal, Stasia stopped. "Now I must say goodbye," she said, kissing him on the cheek. Before he had time to do or to say anything, she moved quickly away and was gone.

Arthur took a taxi to Grand Central Station. He was pleased with himself for not asking Stasia her telephone number or establishing any other means of communicating with her. It was a pleasant, warm encounter—the sound of Polish words, old memories, an attractive woman. It was a one-time, brief meeting and should remain that—a short time spent with a Polish woman that he could even tell Lillian about. Stasia had clear eyes, as clear as the surface of the lakes in the Tatra Mountains, and it was nice talking to her. Arthur was drawn to her very much, and that was the reason he wanted to forget he had ever met her. Not that Arthur was afraid of women. In his fifteen years of marriage, he had had a few affairs. One, with the wife of a neighbor, lasted for several years. Later, on a business trip, he had met a good-looking Californian and made opportunities to see her several times again. But none of these liaisons was serious enough to interfere with his marriage and his family life.

Arthur considered his marriage one of his major achievements. He had met his future wife, Lillian, at a party. She was then a senior at Vassar, the daughter of a prominent banker from an old American family. He liked her, a tall girl, healthy and clean-looking, with a narrow face and a pair of gray eyes. When he met her, he had already received his master's degree in business administration as well as his new name. At the time, he had been assistant export manager of a plumbing and heating concern and was earning over ten thousand dollars a year.

Arthur and Lillian played tennis, and they made an excellent pair for doubles. They also enjoyed swimming. Lillian was majoring in French, and she enjoyed reading Camus and Sartre. Arthur bought all their books and everything that had been written about them. After reading all this material he was able to discuss their work with her. Did he love Lillian? he asked himself. He thought so. She fitted very well into his image of total happiness in his new country.

Her parents were opposed to the marriage and dispatched their daughter to Paris to study, hoping that the distance from Arthur would change her mind. They assumed that Arthur had courted Lillian for her money. On both of these assumptions, they were wrong. Arthur did not care to inherit any money from Lillian's family or to benefit in any way from her parents. And Lillian did not forget him in Paris. They wrote daily, and he visited her during his vacations. They were married a few days after her graduation. Lillian agreed to live on his income, and the first year she also worked in a Wall Street firm as a translator.

Soon after the marriage, Arthur became export manager, then vice president of his company's international division. He tripled the company's sales in a matter of years and became the director of domestic sales. As his firm's profits mushroomed, largely due to his ingenuity, he was named vice president of marketing. Since his income was tied to his performance, it soared into six figures.

Arthur was pleased with his achievements, with his Westchester house and its two tennis courts, with his yacht, and especially with his boys, with whom he liked to watch baseball and play catch on the lawn.

As he was boarding the train, he was still determined to forget the whole encounter at the post office. No, Arthur did not want the lady with her whining puppy to shatter the world he had expended so much effort to build.

As he reached for his monthly ticket in his coat pocket he realized that he still had the lady's stamps and the change from her five dollars.

I'll mail her the damn stamps and her change, he decided, opening his briefcase and pulling out one of his many computer reports. But how can I mail them? he asked himself. I don't even know her address. He began to look at the figures in the reports, but he was unable to concentrate.

It might be that Stasia wouldn't want to mention this encounter to her husband, who might be jealous. It might be better to call her by phone. She must get a lot of business calls at the store. I could ask her whether she would like me to mail her the stamps or pick them up from me at the post office. All I would do is give her the stamps and the money, shake her hand, and bid her goodbye, goodbye forever.

As the train neared the Chappaqua station, he had not yet decided what to do about the wretched stamps. Maybe the best thing would be to forget the whole thing. She can afford to lose the five dollars. I could contribute in her name, or even better, without her name, fifty or a hundred dollars to some Polish cause like, say, the SPJ, and that would put an end to the whole matter. She had such a sad expression in her eyes when she talked about the stupid Polish jokes. He himself had never been irritated by them, had never found them particularly offensive.

At home Arthur continued to wonder what to do with the stamps. It was already late, and he was still debating various ways of dealing with the problem. Pondering his choices, he reviewed his conversation with Stasia in his mind. She had not given a direct answer to his question about whether she was happy. It might be that she was not. But most of all he was disturbed by her reaction to the fact that he had changed his name. "Oh, so you are one of those," she had said. Without doubt she meant one of those traitors to the Polish cause.

During the Warsaw uprising, he had crossed the German lines many times as a messenger of the military units. In his unit, eighty percent of the men had been killed. While volunteering for and going on those missions, Arthur had been aware of the poor odds for his survival. Yet after each mission he had volunteered for the next. His unit was responsible for taking the SS headquarters and killing Olsza, a notorious SS leader. He should have told that to Stasia. Then she wouldn't have said, "Oh, so you are one of those."

He had changed his name because he did not want to be a second-class citizen. He should have told her about Christmas Eve, 1945, just after the war. Wearing the uniform of a lieutenant of the Polish Division, he took an American train from Frankfurt to Bremen, where he hoped to join his mother. He got the necessary ticket and travel permission from an American officer at the Reserve Officer Training Corps office in Frankfurt. The train left at midnight and was scheduled to arrive in Bremen on Christmas morning. At that time there were no other express trains, and the German civilian trains ran irregularly. As it happened, the train was half empty. Arthur was joined in his compartment by two American GIs, who complained at their bad luck in having to celebrate Christmas on the train. When the train made its first stop at Bad Nauheim, a British soldier from the Palestine Division joined them.

The four of them exchanged cigarettes, shared their liquor, talked about Christmas, German beer, and German girls. A half-hour later a tall, muscular military-police sergeant entered the compartment and requested a show of travel documents. When he noticed the word *Palestine* embroidered on the sleeve of the

British soldier's uniform and the word *Poland* on Arthur's, he shouted, "What in hell are you two bastards doing on this train? Get the hell out of here!"

The train was moving fast and the sergeant's breath smelled of alcohol. He opened the window.

Arthur was sitting across from the Britisher. He looked at the sergeant and, without raising his voice, said, "Both of us have tickets and permits validated by the American ROTC. If you—"

"Damn your permits. I'm in charge here," he said, grabbing Arthur's arm. The other two American GIs left the compartment hurriedly.

Arthur freed his arm and got up. The Britisher rose too. "There are two of us and we'll fight you," he shouted.

"You scum of the earth, the two of you," the sergeant shouted back. "It's too bad that the likes of you haven't been wiped out yet."

Confronted by the possibility of violence, the sergeant sobered. "You two SOBs had better get the hell off at the next station, or I'll come back and shoot you."

As soon as the sergeant left, Arthur walked through the other compartments, trying to find an officer who could help them. He spoke to an Army captain in the next compartment who must have heard the shouting and known what it was about.

"The MP is drunk," Arthur told him. "He has no right to evict us. We have valid tickets for this train." The captain looked at Arthur with indifference. "The sergeant is in charge here. It's none of my business."

After Arthur got the same response to further appeals, he was so disgusted that he no longer wanted to stay on that train anyway. He and the Britisher left it in Fulda. The next three days he spent in various unheated German trains and railway stations.

Would Stasia understand why he had changed his name if he told her about that experience?

Arthur felt he needed to talk to Stasia again. She had formed the wrong opinion of him. He would have told her that he wanted to stay in Belgium or France and work, but those countries would not grant work permits to refugees like him. The only work he would have been allowed to do was that of a miner in Belgium. Everywhere in Europe he was unwanted, a refugee and a foreigner. Whenever and wherever he was introduced, he heard the standard reaction to his name: "Oh, you are Polish. How sad."

He could not stand it any more. The borders of the United States were opened to war refugees and he had come, simple as that. He had found the people here friendly; here he was not a tragic figure.

Was it wrong to take on the new identity? Even if it offered better opportunities? It had helped him to forget the past, the bleak war years and the hard times after the war.

The next morning, Arthur did not go straight to the office, but shopped first at Sam Goody's, where he bought records of the Polish composers Chopin, Wieniawski, and Moniuszko. At ten-thirty he called information from a booth at Grand Central Station and got the number under her husband's name. With shaking fingers he dialed the number. He was glad when her voice answered the call.

"It's me," he said. "You know, the man—I have your stamps."

"It's kind of you to call me." There was a silence at the other end. "You could mail them. I will give you my address." She sounded indifferent and unconcerned. It appeared to Arthur that a certain warmth and eagerness was missing from her voice.

"I wouldn't mind bringing them to you personally. I would like to do it. I could come to any place you name."

There was a moment of silence again at her end. Arthur's heart pounded. He was imagining Stasia holding the receiver and perhaps smiling. He began to tremble.

"Yes, in a week if you would like. Next Wednesday I'll be in New York." Her voice sounded uninvolved, like the voice of a stranger. And yet, Arthur thought, they were no longer strangers. Their eyes had met while they had held hands; they could never be strangers again.

"Then perhaps lunch, at twelve noon at the Four Seasons." He gave the address of the restaurant. At that moment, he realized that next Wednesday he was scheduled to be in Cleveland for an important regional sales meeting with his company's two hundred salesmen in the Midwest territory. He was to conduct the meeting. But he did not dare propose an alternate date.

"I'll find it. Thank you," she said, and hung up.

It was too late now to postpone Cleveland. Arthur decided to delegate his sales task to one of his assistants. They should be able to get along without him for a day.

During the next few days, Arthur could not concentrate on his work for carrying on imaginary conversations with Stasia, imagining her smiles and her body. He imagined undressing her, touching her breasts, making love to her. The thought made him quiver with desire.

To prepare himself for the meeting, he bought a few Polish newspapers and an old copy of *Quo Vadis* by Sienkiewicz in Polish. Instead of reading the inventory reports on computer printouts, he read aloud in Polish so that he might speak his native tongue more fluently than he had during their last meeting. At home he listened by the hour to the music of the Polish composers. He even arranged to spend the weekend with Polish friends. His job, his social life, and his family appeared unimportant, even unreal to him. He realized that he had been living the life of an actor, performing a role ill-suited for him. Now he wanted to resume his real identity, to find himself.

Stasia arrived a few minutes late for their meeting. Arthur found the waiting unbearable, and before she had arrived he had finished two martinis.

"So this is the next time," she said, smiling. She wore a navy skirt and a white lace blouse.

"I wanted to see . . . to tell you . . ." Arthur searched for the words. ". . . to say I missed you." Their table was only yards away from other diners. Stasia looked around with the curiosity of a girl scout.

"I was late," she said, "because our meeting with the New York chapter of SPJ took a little longer than usual."

"You look so beautiful, Pani Stasia, more beautiful even than the memory I had of you."

Stasia smiled at him.

"We will do something about it," she said.

"You mean about your beauty?"

"No, no. I meant the Polish jokes," she said. And the expression on her face became serious. "We are organizing a campaign. All the Poles in America will write letters to their congressmen, senators, politicians." She wore little makeup, but she still had a trace of summer tan and her eyes had a glow.

"I could look into your eyes," Arthur said, "and forget the whole world."

The waiter came, a well-groomed middle-aged man with graying hair glued to his head with brilliantine.

"Would you like to order now, sir?" he asked, bowing. There was a trace of foreign accent in his speech.

"I recommend the trout here," Arthur said.

"Why did you switch to English?" Stasia said in Polish. "It is because of people like you, who are ashamed of their native tongue, that we are facing these problems."

Arthur blushed, and so did the waiter. Stasia noticed that the waiter had understood her words.

"*Pan rozumie po polsku* [Do you understand Polish]?" she asked.

"I am a Slovak," the waiter said, nodding. Then in a lowered voice, in Polish, "During the war, I worked with many Poles."

"You don't have to whisper when you speak Polish," Stasia said. The people sitting at the tables near them stopped their conversations. "You should say with pride, 'I am a Slovak,' so that everyone can hear it." Stasia rose, took the waiter's hand, shook it, and kissed him on the cheek. "Thank you for speaking Polish."

Arthur remembered, when he had come to the United States, the first night he was returning home with his sponsor, a Polish sailor. They were walking on Third Avenue, the elevated tracks over their heads, and speaking Polish. As they stopped at the red light, a hobo in a torn jacket and shabby pants with large holes had approached them.

"Shame on you bastards," he said. "Well-dressed stinkers. You shitheads should speak English in public places." Since that time, Arthur had avoided speaking Polish in the streets.

"English is just one of the languages of the many immigrants here," Stasia said, sitting down and taking up the menu. "Polish is as legitimate an American language as English."

Her eyes darkened, and the skin on her neck reddened.

"You are beautiful when you are angry, Pani Stasia."

After she had ordered the asparagus soup and the trout, Arthur added, "I have never met a woman that attracted me so much as you do. Everything you do enhances your attraction for me."

He sat across the table from Stasia, looking at her blond hair reflecting the rays of the October sun. He wished to undo her braids, caress the loose hair that would cascade to her waist. The thought made him want to touch her. He took her hand. It felt warm and gave him a feeling of pleasure.

"I would do anything you wanted me to do to make you happy," he said.

"Make the whole world speak Polish; stop the Polish jokes," she said. "I know you can do it. I know you will." She spoke the words without irony, unsmiling, with the air of a teacher telling her student that he can learn to multiply two times two.

During lunch he talked to her about his student years in Munich, how he had subsisted on bread and milk for weeks on end.

"I lived in a Polish students' home, in a room with three other men. One of them was studying beer production and was thus entitled to a free gallon of the best Bavarian brew every week. He shared it with us. After this diet, it was difficult for me to adjust to American food. It made me sick for the first few weeks. It was simply too salty for me. I had to drink water by the gallon, and for weeks I had a burning sensation in my mouth."

"I would like to cook for you sometime," Stasia said. The statement surprised him. "You must miss Polish cooking."

"I do. I would like to try your dishes very much," he said, pressing her hand harder.

After lunch, they walked in Central Park. The walkways were covered with fallen leaves, and they held hands. He brought her back to the bus terminal.

"Would you like to meet next Wednesday?" he asked.

"Certainly," she said, and smiled.

"I will reserve a room in a hotel, the Hotel Americana," he said. He was surprised at his courage and looked at her for her reaction.

"Do they serve lunches there?" she asked.

"We could order lunch, sure," he said.

"No, please don't order any food," she said. "I will make all the preparations."

Arthur was excited at the prospect of seeing her in a hotel room. The whole of the next week he was not able to work or sleep. He kept imagining making love to her, and the very thought had him all aquiver with desire.

His hands were shaking as he greeted Stasia in front of the Americana. She carried a large valise and three other packages, as if she had planned to spend a month with him, not just a few hours. As soon as they entered the room, she started to explore it with the curiosity of an archeologist discovering a cave loaded with the remains of an unknown civilization.

"It is unbelievable," Stasia said, "but this is the first time I've ever been in a hotel. In Europe it was always the barracks. I traveled once here in the States, but we stayed in a tourist home."

The suite was large, with a double bed. It also had a cocktail table, a couch, and four chairs. Stasia approached the window, and he joined her. For a while both of them admired the view from the thirty-seventh floor. Arthur put his arm around her.

"I have a lot of work to do," Stasia said, freeing herself. "I wish to surprise you, so for a few minutes you could go out, or perhaps, even better, stay in the bathroom and come when I call you."

Arthur obeyed and went into the bathroom. He was sure that Stasia would undress and meet him in a transparent nightgown with her hair loose. For a moment he wondered whether he should undress himself, but since he had not brought pajamas he decided against it. It would be even better to return dressed, since she might want to help take off his clothes. Like a tiger in a small cage he paced the bathroom, his body shaking.

When he heard her say "*Prosze,*" his hands trembled so much that he could scarcely open the bathroom door. Against the light of the window, he saw Stasia standing in a long white dress trimmed with lace around a deep décolleté and along the hem. She wore a pair of gold shoes with high heels. Around her neck was a lapis lazuli necklace, the stones the color of her eyes.

"Oh, you are so beautiful, Stasia," he said, approaching her. He took her hands and their eyes met. She smiled at him.

"Let me put the music on," she said, moving away to a portable Gramophone. In a moment, the tune of a Polish tango filled the room.

"You may dance with me," she said.

Arthur bowed, inviting her. She came into his arms. The light aroma of wild carnations emanated from her. Their cheeks met. The whole world disappeared for Arthur; there was only the dreamlike awareness of beauty, happiness, and Stasia. "I love you, Stasia," he said.

"If you do, this is the right moment to say it," she said, blushing. They kissed, but Stasia did not open her mouth. "Excuse me," she said. "Let me check on the *flaki* [tripes]. I am afraid they might burn." Arthur noticed only then that the table was covered with an embroidered cloth and laid with porcelain-plated china and silverware. In a crystal vase was a bouquet of red and white carnations, and pale yellow candles burned in a crystal candelabra. On a small, portable oven, some dishes were being warmed up.

"We still have time to dance," she said, coming back close to him. They continued to dance cheek to cheek without a word. The aroma of Polish cooking reminded him of his childhood, and he knew the tangoes from his first parties in his high school days. Arthur felt relaxed and safe.

"I am trying to catch up," Stasia said as they sat down at the table and she served the *flaki,* "with the lost time of my teen years. There was no time to go out with boys or fall in love. It was a struggle for me to survive . . . hunger, the labor camps."

"Do you miss Poland?" Arthur asked.

"I do. I remember our happy home with my parents alive, my father's hands on my head . . ." Tears appeared in her eyes. "My father would do anything for me. He often said so."

"Would you want to go back and live in Poland?"

"No. Our home, I have heard, was destroyed, burned to the ground. Besides, that area is now part of the Soviet Union. My old home is gone forever. My real home is here now."

At that moment Arthur wished very much to do something for her. He knew he would do anything to make her happy.

"So you like it here?" Arthur asked.

"In the beginning I hated it," she said with a smile. "Everything in America was bigger: the cars, the houses, the roads, the portions in the restaurants. Everything was more: more salt in the food, more makeup on the women, and much louder music. But I got used to it. I disregard some of the chintz and the kitsch. I value the opportunity to achieve anything you want here, and the freedom and the people."

"I took advantage of those opportunities," Arthur said.

"Except that you have misdirected your efforts," she said.

"Perhaps. Anyway, I am trying to change direction now."

Stasia laughed and put on another record. They danced. He felt her breasts against his body and he began to kiss her neck, her cheeks, her mouth.

"May I take off my jacket?" he asked.

Stasia appeared surprised.

"You look good in your suit," she said, sitting down. "Why would you—"

"Because I love you. It is normal for a man who loves a woman to desire her, too." He knelt down in front of her and began to kiss her hands. "I want to take you to the bed there and undress you, my Stasia."

"Naive idiot that I am," Stasia said, kissing his forehead. "Oh, God, you will never believe me." She laughed. "What a fool I am. I thought you wanted a meal with Polish food. I am *glupia* [stupid]. Forgive me."

"You didn't . . . you don't want to go to bed with me?" he asked.

"I didn't think about it," she said, putting her hands on his cheeks, glowing with the fever of his desire for her.

He had assumed that Stasia had understood the unwritten code of New York dating: if you accept a date in a hotel room, bed is a sine qua non.

"Please, please. I love you," Arthur said.

"I like to be with you. Your touch feels good, but it hadn't even occurred to me to go to bed with you."

"The happiest moment in a man's life must be to love . . . physically, too. I have never made love to a woman with whom I have been so deeply in love as I am with you, Stasia. I want to experience and share that happiness with you, to caress you, to be tender with you."

"Some day, some day . . ."

"Please, Stasia. I want you now. This very moment I want to touch you, kiss you. I could not sleep, eat, work, thinking of the moment when I would feel your warmth through your bare skin against my body." He kissed her hands again. "I beg you, Stasia."

"All right," Stasia said, standing up. "Will you lower the shades, please? I am not sure it will work."

Shivering, Arthur went to the window and began to lower the blinds. Stasia began to undress in silence. He watched as she took off her stockings, her dress and her panties, but kept her slip on. Then she lay on the bed and covered herself with the blanket. Arthur took off his clothing and rushed to her side. With trembling hands, he began to loosen her braids. A mass of silky hair enveloped her body. He embraced her and felt her pubic hair through the silk. He kissed her neck, arms, breasts.

She put her arms around him.

"I love you, I love you," he whispered. He looked up to see her face. Her eyes were opened wide and focused on the ceiling.

"You don't love me," he said, looking into her eyes.

"I don't know, Zdzislaw, Zdzis, but you are very—the most important man in my life. Do you understand?" She pulled herself down closer and curled her body against his, putting her head against his chest. "It feels marvelous to be with you, Zdzis."

He put his arms around her. His desire gone, he felt relaxed and sentimental. "My little Stasia, Stasienka, I love you, I adore you," he whispered, caressing her hair. "I will do anything to make you happy."

"I know you will, Zdzis. I know."

Later on, as they were getting dressed and packing Stasia's belongings, he said, "I would like to join the SPJ, although I'm not sure that it's the right approach to the problem."

"What is the right approach?" she asked. "We are getting some results already." She was wrapping up the crystal vase.

"Some of your activities might backfire. I will have to study the matter, do some research. Give me some time."

He invited her to meet him next Wednesday at the Plaza Hotel and suggested that he make all the arrangements.

During the next week he rented the Grand Ballroom, hired a Polish orchestra, ordered five hundred red carnations and the same number of white ones to decorate the room. Arthur also made sure that they would be served a Polish menu.

"We won't be meeting in the room?" she asked, looking around the huge ballroom.

"Some day, some day," he said, imitating her. "When you say so, I'll take a room again."

Later on, as they danced to the eleventh Polish Schlager of the late thirties, he whispered in her ear, "I think that we should approach the problem with a positive action. Complaining to politicians is a poor and retreating strategy."

She pressed her body closer to his.

"What strategy, then?"

"We must polonize America."

"What do you mean?" she asked, as they waltzed, watching themselves in the mirrored walls.

"Make the United States into Poland, or parts of it, anyway."

"Interesting," she said, her eyes glowing. She pressed her cheek against his. "Tell me more, Zdzis."

"Next time," he said, "when I've had the chance to test some of my theories."

The next seven days were the busiest in all of his life. That very night he called a meeting of the best known statistical and marketing research experts in the country. They met in a private room at the University Club.

Howard Berck, the head and owner of Marketing Strategics, Inc., was already in the room. He greeted Arthur with a broad smile on his round face.

"Had to give up a date with a wild brunette, Art," Howard said, bowing slightly with his bulky body and shaking his bald head.

The two of them had been fellow students at the Graduate School of New York University and had kept in touch over the years. Arthur knew very well that Howard had not had a date with a wild brunette or anyone else. He was a compulsive worker, a typical workaholic, and the only date he might have had was with a computer.

"It must be important, old boy, and, I hope, exciting. Introducing a new toilet seat? Changing the form of your bidets?"

"Plenty of excitement, I guarantee you," Arthur said, greeting the newcomers. They were Professor Anthony Stolzer, a small man with horn-rimmed glasses and a tiny moustache, who looked as though he were in his late fifties and who smoked a pipe; and Archibald Cartoux, who appeared to be in his late thirties and was an expert in the field of public-opinion surveys.

"I have a challenging little job for you boys," Arthur said as they sat down around the table.

"Out with it, old boy," Howard said.

"Suppose that I want to sell—"

"I don't like it already," Professor Stolzer said. "The word *suppose* indicates a theoretical—"

"Okay, it won't be theoretical, Tony," Arthur said. "This is it: I want to market the Polish language. I want to begin the polonization of America."

"A good beginning for a new Polish joke," Howard said. "I don't know this one."

"Are you planning to sell language courses or textbooks?" Cartoux asked, opening his tweed jacket. He looked more like a professional tennis player than an expert in the psychology of opinion.

"No, not at all," Arthur said. "I want to market the idea that Americans would be better off if they spoke Polish instead of English."

The three guests, accustomed to the most unusual requests from their clients, did not evince any surprise whatsoever.

"What's your budget, Art?" Cartoux asked. "Are we talking about a feasibility study or a campaign?"

"I love it," Howard said. "I can see a billboard already: 'Laugh more, know Polish.' Or a television commercial: 'Learn Polish—put some fun in your life.' I love it!"

"Arthur, you'll need a good stratified probability sample," the professor said. "The standard variation will be high, and after we run the pilot study we'll determine the size. You wouldn't need the standard error to be less than five percent."

"Forget the feasibility study, Archie," Arthur said. "I'm ready for the campaign. I'll get the necessary dough. Tony, I want the sample with a double stratification for testing the best approach to a winning strategy."

An old gentleman looked sternly down at Arthur from a portrait on the wall. He certainly did not approve. The sound of traffic on Fifth Avenue below reached them through the closed windows. Arthur was sorry that Stasia was not at the meeting. She probably would not have been able to follow the technical language, but he missed her. The seven days before he would see her again seemed an eternity.

"It can be done, old boy," Howard said. "But it'll take time. Unfortunately, Polish or any other language can't be acquired by taking a pill. There have been some experiments in teaching languages by playing records to students while they sleep. I'll have to look into it."

Arthur was glad that no one had asked him why he wanted Americans to give up the English language for Polish. He would have to tell them the truth—that he had fallen in love with a woman who happened not to like hearing English spoken around her—only Polish.

"I trod these waters once before," Cartoux said. "Not much doing with the records for teaching people in their sleep."

"*Divide et impera,*" Tony said, puffing at his pipe. "We must wage a multi-stage campaign."

"That's what I had in mind, fellows," Howard said. "I see it in three stages: first we attack English where it is most vulnerable—its spelling. Would Polish spelling be a good substitute, my boy?"

"That was exactly what I would consider the first stage," Arthur said. "With a few exceptions you could reproduce the sounds of English with the Polish alphabet, and you would achieve, based on my sample with 11 percent standard error, 16.4 economy of letters. Shakespeare with eleven letters would be replaced by Szekspir, an eight-letter word; Seattle with seven letters, by Sjatl with five letters. However, some other words would not benefit from Polish spelling. Still, 16.4 is a significant saving."

"It would mean an annual saving of several millions of dollars in paper and ink," Tony said, sliding his glasses back up his nose. "Not to speak of the savings in labor, printers, secretaries, and, most important, eyesight."

"We would get significant support from printers," Arthur said. "They would benefit from the reprinting of millions of books. And we could bill the project as a significant inflation fighter."

The gentleman in the portrait looked even more sour than before. He appeared to Arthur to be focusing his gold-rimmed pince-nez on him.

"The second stage would not give us too much trouble," Howard said. "Through a set of manipulations, we could make Polish the required language in schools and universities in places where the majority of Poles, or Americans of Polish descent, are living now. Of course there would be a demand for similar treatment for other Americans of Italian, Spanish, and other origins. That would help us by weakening English. Stage three will be the most difficult: adopting Polish as the official language of the United States."

"Thank you, Howard," Arthur said. "I have some strategies in mind, but I don't want to talk about them right now." Arthur thought about Stasia. Would she press her body closer when he danced with her the next time and told her about this meeting? Would she desire him? Would she want him to take a room in a hotel for a purpose other than feeding him Polish cooking?

"I wish to recapitulate," Arthur said. "I need from you the outline for stages one and two of my strategy. You can keep the chaff for yourselves. Just give me the kernel. It is for my eyes only. Any questions?"

There were none.

"I'll tell my brunette that I wouldn't have missed this meeting even for her charms. And because of this meeting I'll have to skip seeing her for the next few weeks." Howard shook his bald head again as he was leaving.

"I ask you to promise me," Tony said, lighting his pipe again, "that you'll attend my first lecture in Polish."

"You are so determined with your project and have such enthusiasm," Cartoux said, "that I must conclude that there is a female behind it. No, no, I don't expect your comments on that conclusion."

When they had left, Arthur went to the window, opened it, and inhaled the November air. Stasia will be a little happier when she hears my report on this meeting, he thought, and he imagined her eyes lit with a special glow.

That same night, Arthur called his lawyer and arranged with him to form a Foundation for a New Spelling of English, and the next morning he called his broker and instructed him to buy, in the name of the new foundation, stock in all corporations involved in book printing. By noon the value of the stock the foundation owned doubled. He invited a group of publicity people for lunch, and, while they were sipping cocktails, told them about the new-spelling-of-English project. They all called their offices, and before lunch was over a messenger brought *The New York Post* with the headline, "New Spelling of English a Fact." The stock of the printing companies skyrocketed, and Arthur calculated the assets of the foundation to be worth twenty-seven million dollars. He expected to double that within the next few days and to sell the stock within a week, when the foundation papers were ready.

It would be nice to tell Stasia that he had managed to earn fifty million dollars for her cause. He was convinced that the printing companies would match this amount in contributions to his foundation; thus he would have some hundred million dollars for stage one.

He retained the three best public relations firms in the country to publicize the Polish way of spelling English as the most suitable replacement for the current system.

As he danced on the next Wednesday to the tune of "Jest Jedna Jedyna" (There Is Only One), a Polish hit of 1938, in the ballroom of the Hotel Pierre, decorated with thousands of white and red carnations, he told Stasia about his activities and about the hundred million dollars. She stopped in the middle of the ballroom and kissed him, this time opening her mouth. The tips of their tongues met for a fraction of a second, and Arthur felt victorious.

"It is a new experience," she whispered, as the orchestra played "That Last Sunday," a popular tango of 1939, and they continued to dance.

"Do you mean our campaign?" Arthur asked.

"No, no. The kissing with the open mouth and the tongues," she said, blushing.

"Everybody does it," he said.

"I never did," Stasia said.

"It was so wonderful for me," he said, "kissing you this way."

"I would not mind trying it again," she said.

He was ready to kiss her.

"But the orchestra," she whispered.

"All right," he said. "I'll get rid of them."

"But it would be nice, with the music playing. . ."

Arthur immediately summoned the hotel manager and requested that a curtain be put up to separate them from the orchestra. The request was granted without delay. And as they danced to the tune of "Golden Chrysanthemums," they stopped in the middle of the empty ballroom and kissed. For the first time, Stasia responded, and Arthur detected a slight quivering of her hands.

As they were cutting Polish sausage, smoked with cherry wood and served on cabbage, Stasia asked, "What do you propose to do about stage three?"

"I will need your help," Arthur replied, eating with relish potatoes with *prawdziwki* (*Aedulis edibilis* mushroom) sauce, especially flown in from Poland.

"My help?" Stasia asked.

"Yes, Stasia, I would like to arrange a meeting with the heads of all the Polish organizations we can contact here and abroad. You may know the people here better than I." He looked at her neck with its sprinkling of freckles.

"When would you like to have this meeting?" she asked.

"It wouldn't be possible before Christmas. Let's say January tenth."

"And where?"

"I have a hunting lodge, near Poughkeepsie, New York. We could meet there."

Later on, when Arthur took Stasia to the bus terminal, she allowed him only a kiss on her cheek, and he felt disappointed.

In the next weeks he continued to meet Stasia on Wednesdays, and he danced with her in the fanciest ballrooms in New York City. Each time the orchestra played behind curtains, and each time they kissed. In between, he was receiving and analyzing the reports of his marketing confreres.

Cartoux, the surveys expert, recommended the slogan, "Learn Polish, have fun!" and Arthur approved, despite the surveys indicating that 53.7 percent of Americans did not know that Polish was a language, 92.7 percent associated *Polish* with *polishing* (as in nails, cars, and shoes), and that 26.2 percent had never heard of Poland.

As Arthur continued to see Stasia, he grew to love and desire her more and more. Any time he thought about his short stay in bed with her and how he had kissed her breasts, he shook as if he had received an electric shock. And even the memory of contact with her pubic hair behind the screen of her silk slip set his hands trembling to such an extent that he was unable to hold anything in them.

The last Wednesday before Christmas, it was impossible to rent a ballroom, so they registered for a suite in the Prince Arthur Hotel, planning to dance to radio music. As Arthur finished the registration formalities and they were about to take the elevator to their room, he noticed a messenger from his office, who was looking for him. As they met, the messenger gave Arthur an envelope that he opened in the elevator. It was a letter from his secretary informing him that the stock shares of the printing companies had dropped. The afternoon papers would carry articles about the spelling of English "best as it is."

Arthur didn't need to read the rest of the message. He knew that all his hopes and plans had been in vain. He looked at Stasia, who had been watching him. He didn't have to tell her the contents of this letter. She knew.

They entered their room in silence, put their overcoats on the chairs, and moved to the window. Rain mixed with snow was falling outside. Arthur put his arm around Stasia. He felt like crying.

"Will you forgive me, Stasia?"

"There is nothing . . ."

It was dark in the room.

"Will you still love me?"

"Why are you asking?"

"I failed."

"It has nothing to do with love."

"What is love, Stasia?"

"Searching to know each other, to understand . . ."

He felt her hand taking his. It was delicate and warm.

He looked, and her eyes were as clear as the surface of a lake in the Tatra Mountains.

"Do you want to know me, Stasia?"

She nodded. She smiled, and a magic stream of light reflecting the hues of a rainbow filled the room.

3

After my return to Paris, I read my notes on Arthur's story many times. I concluded that Stasia did appear to have some of the physical characteristics of my lady lion tamer. This finding brought me as much joy as the discovery of a new cure for a dreaded disease would bring to a medical scientist. I decided to share my elation with Bernadette. As usual, I proposed a meeting in my apartment. To my disappointment, she didn't seem to share my enthusiasm and wasn't at all keen for a rendezvous in my place. But she consented to join me at lunch for *choux croûte à l'Alsacienne* at the Café Lipp on the Left Bank, the best restaurant in Paris for that dish.

I reserved a table, arrived on time, and while I waited smoked many Gauloises in the crowded, smoke-filled room where the smell of sausages, hams, and sauerkraut sharpened my appetite. I was feeling pangs of hunger and could hardly wait for Bernadette.

Finally she arrived, about half an hour late, and, to my chagrin, was wearing a mauve raincoat over a brown woolen dress—colors I abhor. As was our custom, we delayed conversation until after the meal. But as soon as the coffee had been served, I told her Arthur's story and my revelation about Stasia's similarity to my lion tamer.

Bernadette stirred the sugar in her coffee, watching the movement of her fingers with the concentration of an artist putting the last strokes of paint on his masterpiece.

"And you think this fact would help you to find her?"

"How could you doubt that? Of course."

"Dear Monsieur Majeski, you are dreaming, as usual."

"I learned some other interesting characteristics of that woman. Stasia cooked my friend Arthur a meal during their third encounter. Really, at the first opportunity she had . . ."

Bernadette's loud guffaw interrupted my exposition. It was so loud that even a sleepy headwaiter, who had seemed so uninterested in his customers that he would not have paid attention if they had begun to shoot each other, turned his head.

"Through the stomach etcetera is a well-known practice, applied successfully by a great majority of women in the world," she said, wiping the tears from her eyes.

"But she inspired him to accomplish a lot, Bernadette."

"That, too, is not so unique. You are extremely naive if you think that these so-called great discoveries of yours can be of any possible use in finding your lion tamer."

"Since I've discovered a physical similarity between Stasia and my lady, it's conceivable that the other women my friends had fallen in love with have common traits, too."

"Very farfetched," Bernadette said, frowning.

"In moments of love, one's personality is magnified, and so are one's characteristics; they stand out and are clearly discernible. I have formed a hypothesis: If I can learn about the love of each of my colleagues, about the one true love of each of their lives, I will discover in each of the women some outstanding trait. This will allow me to compose a profile of my lady lion tamer, and so give me a chance to find her. I tried to find her the obvious way, by publicizing her image. That didn't work."

"Judging by your results so far, I'm very doubtful about the outcome of your search with *this* method."

"My dear Bernadette, I'm sure my theory will work. I'll find her."

"A pity. Dear Jan, I think that it would be far better for you if you never found her."

"Why? Why do you say that?" Her statement shocked me as much as if she had said Paris was ugly or French cuisine was inferior to English.

"I said it as a friend who wishes you well."

"Why? Please explain!" This time I was the one who raised his voice. Three elderly ladies eating their *gateaux* stopped their conversation, but continued to devour their pastries, watching us as they ate.

"It would be better for you, Jan Majeski."

"You say that with the self-assurance and the benevolence of a grandmother telling her granddaughter that candy is bad for her without giving a reason for the pronouncement."

"Simple. You love that poster."

"I love the woman."

"Oh, no. You love that piece of paper more than you have ever loved any woman."

"I'll love the lady lion tamer. I'll adore her."

She put her gloves on. "I must return to my office. You know very well that your love for me was as deep as the ink on your picture. If you find her, your feelings for her might evaporate as quickly as drops of water in the Sahara sun."

"Wait, wait, Bernadette. What you are implying is that I am incapable of love."

She got up. "It depends on your definition. If you consider love to be like one's wish for a glass of water when one is thirsty, then yes."

"You mean I never loved you?"

Buttoning her coat she said, "Did you care enough for me to find out how I feel about my daughter, or my parents, or for that matter about you?"

All this conversation with Bernadette was for me as unexpected and unpleasant as an edict in France prohibiting the drinking of wine. Yet she was right. The only facts I knew about her were her tastes in food, because they concerned me. Nevertheless—we had had such an excellent arrangement and it had lasted so many years—I didn't want it broken this quickly.

"*Bonne chance,*" she said, walking away.

Since the waiter still hadn't presented me with the *addition,* I couldn't leave with Bernadette. 'May I see you again?"

"Perhaps, perhaps." But her words didn't sound convincing.

I wondered what had happened to her. Before my trip to London, she had been her usual self. I had to try to see her again if only to find out the cause of her sudden lack of sympathy for me.

To console myself I returned home and read Arthur's story once again. Another element in his behavior irked me. Arthur had noticed Stasia when she spoke Polish to her dog. He felt guilty for having changed his name and abandoning any tie to his native country. He had tried to assuage his guilt by his efforts on behalf of the Poles. It didn't matter that he had failed. He had tried.

I didn't share those feelings. I considered myself a Frenchman, and I was pleased about that. I had always felt that cutting my ties with my native country was an accomplishment. But now, after my meeting with Arthur, I began to feel less sure about it.

Suppose the lady lion tamer turned out to be Polish, like Stasia. What would I be able to tell her? Arthur had been a hero in the Polish resistance, while I had remained aloof from the danger, just an indifferent bystander. I didn't know. Yet the encounter with Arthur had given me new incentive to go on with my search. He had told me about one of our other childhood friends, Romek;

that when Romek had been taken prisoner by the Germans during the war, he had tried to escape through Munich. I might learn about what had happened to him there.

The next day I was on a train to Munich to begin my investigations. I was fortunate enough to locate a few former Polish and German officers who had known Romek. From many interviews—one in particular with a woman called Erica—and some documents, I was able to piece together his story.

Romek crawled through the narrow escape tunnel, working his squarish body between the rocks and hard clay. There were moments when he wanted to scream from pain and give up the flight, but he concentrated on the end of the tunnel and what it meant and forced himself to continue. It meant freedom, the end of his German captors, the end of standing in line for the tasteless meals and—this was vital—the opportunity to have what he had missed most in the prisoner of war camp where he had spent a grueling eighteen months of captivity. And that meant the sight, nearness, perfume, touch, and love of a woman.

He and five of his fellow captives slithered toward freedom. Six months earlier, they had selected Monday, February 21, 1941, for their escape. The date had been chosen because it was Rosenmontag (Rose Monday), the first day of Fasching (Carnival); it meant that many thousands of people in costumes and disguises of all kinds would be drinking and merrymaking all over Bavaria, and especially in Munich, an important point on their escape route. Nothing could be better for the prisoners than to get lost in crowds of people dancing and laughing, their identity hidden behind masks and disguises.

The prisoners expected to emerge from their tunnel at four-thirty in the afternoon, just as it was getting dark, the light of day being dimmed by the first shadows of the night. The powerful searchlights would not be on yet. At this time of year there was snow on the ground in this part of Bavaria near Murnau, and the six men were dressed in white carnival costumes, and all were masked. Romek had made his own costume, that of a Harlequin like the one in the painting of Watteau, out of his bed sheets. The others wore the costumes of a nurse, a doctor, death, a Roman soldier, and an angel, all easily fashioned from sheets, the one material at hand. They wore their prison clothes over the costumes to keep them from getting soiled.

"Here it is," the captain breathed.

"We made it," Romek repeated for the man behind him. They had anticipated the bad air in the tunnel and divided the party into two groups of three men each. The second trio would have better air once the hole at the end of the tunnel was opened.

Romek heard a crash, and cold, damp air bathed his face. Gray light filled the tunnel. He saw the captain's torso struggling through the opening, then disappearing into the world above the ground. They had arranged that if everything was all right, the captain would pull a string Romek held as a signal for him to climb on out. Romek waited, breathing in the fresh air. The pull came. Romek stretched his hands and pulled and squeezed his body through the narrow opening. The captain was lying stretched out on the ground a few meters away. It was dusk and the air was misty. Romek slithered toward the captain, who nodded, and Romek pulled the string signaling the third man to come up. Romek's face was close to the captain's.

"Do you know the one about the Pole, the Englishman, and the German?" he asked in a whisper. Romek loved to tell jokes and stories, and in moments of danger or excitement he had a compulsive need to turn narrator to relieve the tension.

But the captain was familiar with Romek's propensity, and he abruptly whispered, "Stop it!"

The third man was crawling out of the hole. Outlined behind him Romek could see the contours of the watch tower and the walls of the camp. In the misty light it looked like a medieval fortress.

The third man, a small, narrow-shouldered lieutenant, crawled out to lie panting next to Romek.

"You have joined us at just the right moment," he whispered. "An Englishman, a Pole, and a German meet in a neutral country and discuss what they would do after the war."

"Junior Lieutenant Kaganoff, I order you to keep quiet," Captain Silski said, pulling nervously at the long moustache on his round face below his bald crown.

"We will fall asleep here from boredom," Romek whispered. The snow began to melt under him from the warmth of his body. He could see the outline of a forest of fir trees only a hundred meters away.

"The Englishman says that he will make a trip around the world; the Pole—"

"Oh, no, not the Pole," the captain said.

Looking at him, lying on his side, Romek thought how he looked like an overturned snowman.

"They are taking a long time," the lieutenant whispered.

"The German says that he will buy himself a bicycle and travel around the beautiful *Heimat* [fatherland]."

"I hope, if they shoot," the captain said, "that they get you with the first bullet, so we won't have to hear the end of the story."

The hundred meters to the woods were snow-covered only in patches. Would the Germans spot the six fugitives in white disguises crawling on the dark ground? he asked himself.

"Then I would die laughing," Romek said.

"Not from your joke," the lieutenant said.

"No, no, but from seeing your tragic faces," Romek said, watching the first man of the second trio surfacing.

"The Englishman says, 'That will be fine for the morning. What will you do in the afternoon?' Do you get it?" he asked his unresponsive companions.

"Why only the morning?" the lieutenant asked.

"Because Germany will be so small, dummy," Romek said. All six of them were now lying on the snow awaiting the captain's orders. According to the plan, the first three of them were to crawl first, the others twenty meters behind them. The captain raised his right hand. It was the signal to proceed.

A feeling of joy overcame Romek as he crawled between the captain and the lieutenant. Every moment brought him closer to the woods, closer to freedom. When he had thought about the escape in the days of waiting he had always worried about this crawling, the most exposed and dangerous part of their flight, and he had been scared, frightened to death. Now he felt ready—ready to sing, laugh, dance. He thought about his father, who before the war had been a successful banker. Would he be proud of his son's fearlessness? What would his German nurse, Fraulein Hilde, have said, or his French nurse, Mademoiselle Chariot? His mother would have been sick with fear, he knew, just listening to the story.

The captain was breathing heavily and, despite the cold February wind, perspiration had broken out on his bald head. They reached the edge of the wood. The others joined them and they all kept moving, crawling now on the snow under the trees. The captain should give them the order to get up and cheer, he said to himself.

"Halt! Halt!" came the command in German. Romek looked in

the direction of the voices. Two German soldiers stood directly in front of them, covering them with their rifles. For a moment he did not believe his eyes and ears. This could not have happened to him. Not now, when he had reached the woods.

"*Hande hoch* [Hands up]! Don't move!" both of them said.

It's all over, Romek thought. All the many months of preparation wasted! For a moment he considered what would happen to him. According to the Geneva Convention, prisoners of war, he knew, were subject to punishment for escaping, but could not be executed unless they resisted arrest or killed their guards. Would these guards observe the rules? Both of them were young, possibly younger than Romek's twenty-three years. And they were more nervous than the prisoners on the ground. The rifles shook in their hands.

"*Meine Herren* [gentlemen], from Dunkirk there escaped on a boat some Polish, French, and English soldiers with some French girls," Romek said in German, a language he spoke fluently. He had been chosen as the member of the group to serve as translator. In the camp he had often translated, and since many of the guards were Bavarians, he had learned something of that language too. "After a long journey," he continued, "they arrived in England. The French girls complained, suggesting. . ."

The soldiers were stunned by his unexpected words and stood like two frozen statues. The captain, at Romek's right, moved, and it brought the soldiers to their senses.

"Shut up!" one of them shouted. It was dark and getting darker. But the soldiers still had not decided what to do next.

"To cut off the Englishman's fingers, the Frenchmen's tongues and—"

"Get them!" the captain shouted, jumping up toward the soldiers.

All of them jumped up. Shots rang out. Within seconds everything was over. Three of the Polish officers and the two German soldiers lay on the ground dead or wounded. In the distance there were shouts and additional shots. Voices were coming closer.

"Disperse and run!" shouted the captain. Romek ran into the woods, and after hours of running and walking he reached the railroad tracks and jumped on a cattle train. He leaped off it, leaving his prison clothes behind, as soon as the train reached the outskirts of the city he knew must be Munich.

In their escape plans, they had anticipated the possibility that they might become separated. Romek had an address in Regensburg, a town some hundred kilometers from Munich. He had been assured that the people at that address would be able to arrange for him to get out through France to Spain, then to Portugal and England. He had enough money to buy a ticket and to take care of traveling expenses.

There were many people on the streets, and Romek was pleased to see that many had costumes and masks on. As had been anticipated, no one seemed to notice him. He asked a man dressed as a samurai warrior for directions to the train station and was told to take the streetcar on the next corner. Twenty minutes later he was there.

Romek anticipated that boarding the train to Regensburg would be one of the most dangerous moments. The Wehrmacht would be watching everyone entering the station and boarding the trains. If he were caught, he would be executed on the spot.

As he was trying to make up his mind whether to buy a ticket or jump a train, a group of men walked by shouting, singing, and laughing. Further away in the darkness he saw five or six uniformed men. He moved on, passing the entrance to a hotel where he could hear an orchestra playing a tango. As the door opened, the light from inside brightened the blacked-out street and he was able to recognize the uniforms: SS men with the black swastikas on their armbands. His heart began to pound and, despite the cold wind, he felt drops of sweat gathering on his forehead. He was sure that the SS were there to catch him and arrest him. Like a trapped animal trying to escape from its hunters, Romek, not knowing where else to turn, ducked into the opened doors of the hotel.

The scene inside was dazzling. The light from the crystal chandeliers and sconces glittered off the jewelry in the deep décolletés and off the satin, silk, and chiffon of the women's evening dresses. No less splendid were the men in their parade uniforms, tuxedoes and tails. Some of the guests wore masks and others were in carnival costume.

For the moment, Romek faced the door, still fearing that it would open on SS men, come to capture him. The door swung open, but instead of soldiers, a group of people in carnival costume entered the lobby. All of them were masked. The leader of the group, marching in front of the others, wore a Viking outfit and carried a wooden shield with metal trim, singing as he marched, "*Warum is die Banana gelb und rot ist die Apfelsine* [Why is the banana yellow and the orange red]?" The others, a Roman soldier in a white toga, a Saxon Napoleonic officer in white coat and black gaiters with brass buttons, and two ladies looking like Boucher Pompadours joined in the singing: "*Warum schlaeft der Hans nicht zu Hause, sondern bei Christine* [Why is Hans not sleeping at home, but at Christine's]?"

Romek felt lost for a moment. He did not want to leave the hotel for fear of encountering the SS men. But it would be impossible for him to remain standing alone in the lobby. In desperation he simply followed the singing group.

They paraded up to the entrance to a ballroom. Through the open door, Romek could see couples dancing to a foxtrot played by an orchestra he could not see. In front of the door stood a broad-shouldered, square-faced colonel of the SS with a lady in a dirndl dress and white woolen socks. The Roman soldier raised his right hand and shouted, "Hail, Caesar!" The Viking handed the colonel a group of invitations or tickets. The two ladies in eighteenth-century French dresses spoke in unison, raising their right hands, "*Vive la France et le Roi Soleil* [Long live France and the Sun King]." In daily life these people might have been severely reprimanded for this mockery of the Nazi salute, but it was Fasching, thought Romek, and obviously many of the standard prohibitions did not apply. In this lighthearted atmosphere, everything that was normally *verboten* was now allowed. He raised his hand and, marching behind the ladies, spoke directly to the colonel, "*Vive la différence*!"

The colonel looked at them and smiled like a grandfather indulging a group of frolicking grandchildren at a Christmas party. Glancing at the tickets, but not bothering to count them, he mumbled "*Ach, der Fasching, der Fasching.*"

As they all entered the ballroom, the orchestra was playing "Komm Zurueck" (Come Back), a Schlager of the last year. Everyone inside the room wore a carnival costume and a mask. There were at least three men to every woman, and despite their disguises they all seemed to recognize one another. "*Frau Schilke sieht gut aus* [Mrs. Schilke looks good]," said a geisha, looking at one of the ladies in Romek's group. "Herr Sturmbannfuehrer is irresistible as a Viking," a South Seas beauty observed. Romek noticed that many of the people were studying him, apparently trying to identify him. The women were dancing now, and the men who did not find partners formed small groups and stood exchanging jokes and laughter. There were not more than a hundred people there, obviously all of them friends and acquaintances. For a moment it occurred to Romek, standing alone by a column, that the colonel would come and demand his documents.

What would be the reaction of all these happy people to learn that the Harlequin in their midst was an escaped prisoner of war and a criminal to boot? A chill moved up his spine. He glanced at the door. The colonel appeared to be looking his way. Romek was conspicuously alone among all these people.

He noticed that at a distance of some ten meters stood a blond woman with her hair combed back from a center part. In her long blue two-piece silk evening dress and dark blue mask, she stood studying her well-proportioned body in the mirror. She looked about thirty years old.

"*Danser, danser*?" Romek asked, approaching the lady. He saw now that she had a plush serpent draped over one arm and a fig leaf attached to her dress. He could not see the expression on her face behind the mask, but she stiffened as if he had proposed an indecent act.

"*Wrklichch? Se missn* [Really? You must] . . ." she said in Bavarian-accented German.

"*Amour, amour,*" he said in French. He wanted to avoid speaking German for fear that she would recognize his foreign accent. He knelt down. "*Harlequin, pleurer, pleurer* [Harlequin, cry, cry]." He noticed that a number of people were watching them. She nodded, but her mouth did not smile. The orchestra began to play the tango "Jalousie," a hit of a few years before.

"You have guts," she whispered as they began to dance. "You must be drunk to think yourself safe in this disguise. You are in danger."

Romek's legs turned to rubber. How had she known? But she couldn't, could she? A slight aroma of lavender emanated from her body. Her hands were warm.

"There is nothing courageous about choosing the most beautiful woman in the room for a partner," he said in German.

"Then you don't know me?" she asked.

"I know you are the most attractive woman in the Third Reich . . . in the world . . . a fact that I can establish even though you are masked."

"Have we met before?"

"I've loved you for ages, my Eva," Romek said, extemporizing on the fig leaf and the serpent. More and more people seemed to be watching them, and Romek tried to keep her talking. He feared that she would stop dancing with him and that he would be left alone again.

"Who are you?" she asked, looking at him and inspecting him from behind her mask. "I don't recognize you. I checked the guest list. All of the people here should be known to me. I repeat, you are in danger."

The lights dimmed and the orchestra began to play another tango. Some of the guests began throwing confetti and serpentines. She is curious, he thought. Maybe that will keep the conversation going.

A new group of about twenty people arrived and immediately joined in the dancing.

"With every minute," she said, "your situation is getting more hopeless."

"I know it," Romek said. He began to assume now that she must have heard about the escape of the Polish prisoners and the slaying of the German guards.

A waiter, the only person without a mask, was circulating with a tray of champagne glasses filled with bubbling wine. He stopped in front of them. The woman hesitated. Romek took two glasses and handed one to her.

"I don't usually drink," she said.

"I am drinking to my eternal love for you, my Eva . . . more beautiful than Boticelli's Primavera, more feminine than Cranach's Eve."

"That sounds very charming, but I drink to your escape."

This time her words pierced him to the core. What would happen to him in the next twenty minutes, the next hour or two? While all these Vikings, Roman soldiers, and Napoleonic officers slept with the ladies, he might be being tortured, he might even be dead. At the thought, he shuddered, and she noticed it.

"You must leave now. At least tell me your name!"

"My name would tell you nothing. I am an artist who loves you."

"Oh," she said. "I wonder . . . There is no one at the door. It would be a good moment to leave." She pressed his hand slightly. "Good luck."

For some reason he hesitated. He did not wish to leave this mysterious woman. He somehow felt secure in her presence. But Eva was right. The colonel was no longer at the door. He had been replaced by two other uniformed men who were so busy checking the tickets of two people dressed as medieval knights that they did not even bother to glance at the departing Harlequin.

The lobby was as crowded as before. The voices of the people seemed louder now. A loudspeaker was broadcasting the news of the day, but no one on this night of the Rosenmontag seemed to be interested, except for Romek, who was eager to hear the news announcing the escape and the killing of the guards.

The voice of the newscaster reported the standard German radio fare, emphasizing the most recent and inevitably successful Luftwaffe raids on English targets, the retreat of the British *Kolonnen* (detachments) in the Sudan; Dutch Prince Bernhard's training to fly the Spitfires and the Hurricanes; a Mussolini speech full of confidence about victory; the opening of the Leipzig Spring Fair with the outstanding Pavilion of the Soviet Union; new movies and sports events—but nothing about the escape of the Polish prisoners.

He took another quick look at the people in the lobby. At a distance he recognized the SS colonel talking to another officer. His squarish figure stood sideways, but his head was slightly turned toward Romek. He had the distinct impression that the colonel was keeping watch on him. Romek knew he had to get out of the hotel as quickly as possible. Would the colonel follow him? He would not need to do even that. Not many of the revellers were dressed as Harlequins. All the colonel had to do was to alert his troopers, standing in front of the hotel, to follow Romek.

With his head high, Romek strolled outside. Snow was falling. Large, wet flakes hit his face. Several uniformed men stood near the entrance. Romek began to move to the right, walking a bit unsteadily as if he were drunk. He stopped a few minutes later in front of a kiosk and, aided by the light from a poor blackout curtain, pretended to study the posters advertising the new movies: "Zu Neuem Ufer" (To the New Strand), with Zarah Leander, and another one, "Kampfgeschwader Luetzow" (The Luetzow Fighting Squadron), about the battle of the Luftwaffe in Poland. Hoping to detect whether he was being followed, he glanced back. No uniformed men in sight. The only silhouette he saw approaching him in the darkness was that of a woman: Eva, running toward him.

"I am glad . . . so glad . . . to have caught up . . . with you," she said, trying to recover her breath. She had come out without an overcoat.

"You'll catch cold," he said.

"No, it's all right. I am quite hard . . . physically."

A car passed, and in its headlights he could see that she was smiling.

"Why did you follow me, Eva? You might endanger yourself."

"I needed . . . I wanted to ask you . . . whether we had met when I worked for Hoffmann?"

"What difference would it make—" he began.

Two SS men passed them, talking aloud. Eva stepped back and averted her face, as if she wanted to avoid being recognized, but they did not seem to notice the two of them.

"You must tell me what you know about my being in danger."

"What danger do you mean?" she said.

He hoped that she would tell him where she had heard about his escape.

"You said I was in danger," he said.

"That was your own doing," she said, shivering now. "I wanted to find out whether you knew . . ."

A dozen people in a variety of costumes emerged from a café. They were holding hands and singing the Rosamunde song. One rotund female dressed as a witch approached Romek and began to kiss him on the mouth, while the rest of them were singing, "*Kuess mich, bitte, bitte kuess mich* [Kiss me, please, please kiss me]." A tall, broad-shouldered man in a clown costume picked up Eva and started to dance with her, holding her in the air off her feet.

"You are breaking up a couple of lovers," a female voice shouted.

"It's Fasching," the clown shouted. "A good time for a new love, a fresh love." He was still holding Eva in her arms.

A truck pulled up to the curb.

"Our transportation is here," the clown said, placing Eva on the truck's platform. The others began to scramble to join them. Romek was the last to pull himself up as the truck moved away. Soon it gained speed and was racing through the empty streets of Munich while the group sang, "*Denn wir fahren, denn wir fah-*

ren nach Schwa-a-a-bing [For we are going, going to Schwabing]" to the tune of the Luftwaffe song, substituting *Schwabing* for *England.*

Romek, standing on the back of the platform holding the round body of the witch, looked to see whether the truck was being followed and was reassured when it was clear that no car was speeding behind them. He was happy to be with this lively crowd that was unwittingly aiding him in his efforts to escape.

It was not long before the wheels screeched and the truck stopped with a jerk.

Romek jumped down and stood aside, trying to be as unobtrusive as possible. The clown carried Eva down and into the door of the *Bierstube.* The others followed him, Romek bringing up the rear. They walked down the steps into a basement restaurant. Hundreds of people were milling around in the small space where the air was thick with tobacco smoke and the odor of beer. It was so crowded that Romek lost sight of Eva. After a while she appeared at a distance, standing on a small stage with a five-man band dressed as Bavarian peasants. Romek expected the band to play some Bavarian folk tune, but instead it launched into "Boo-Hoo," and Eva began to sing. The tall clown who had led the expedition to the restaurant appeared on the stage with a tray bearing a liter-size glass. He stopped the music and began to sing, "*Trink, trink, Schwesterlein, trink* [Drink, drink, little sister, drink]," and some of the people joined in the singing. Eva picked up the glass and drank, to the applause of the crowd.

She seemed to be enjoying herself, radiant, a different person from the one he had met at the hotel. He could hear her vivacious laughter above the applause.

Romek pushed his way toward her and reached her just as she was jumping off the stage.

"Excuse me, please," he said, facing her.

"*O blaudiga Heenadregg* [Oh bloody chickenshit]!" she exclaimed in Bavarian. "*Wo kema Se her* [Where did you come from]?"

"I came . . . I came to ask you about the danger," Romek stuttered. He was stunned by her reaction to him.

"I thought you'd be in jail by now, accounting for yourself. Oh, damn it!"

"But why?" he asked. "Why did you—"

A man dressed in a cossack tunic and fur hat came up to them. He had difficulty in standing steadily and grabbed Romek's arm for support. Romek's legs turned to rubber again, and only with great difficulty did he keep his balance.

The cossack was holding a large mug which he put to Romek's mouth and turned up. Helpless, Romek drank the brew, which seemed to be a mixture of beer and wine as well as several other alcoholic beverages. Some of the drink spilled onto his costume. The alcohol did nothing to allay his fear. Eva had spoken of arrest. Obviously it was imminent. Was he being followed? Fortunately, the cossack decided to refill his mug and moved away.

"Why arrest me?" he asked Eva, following her as she tried to push her way toward the exit.

"Because I told them, you—"

"But you *warned* me of the danger! Whom did you tell?" He was trying to keep up with her. She had appeared so trustworthy, and yet she had denounced him. Despite the overheated air in the *Bierstube*, he began to shiver.

"General Mueller, the chief of counterintelligence forces here."

"What?" He was not sure whether he had heard her correctly because of the din of voices, music, and laughter.

"It's Fasching! My joke. Oh, hell, I lost."

"You lost what?"

"Stop playing stupid with me," she spun around and said. "I know who you are." She headed off again.

"Who, then?" he barked, chasing after her again.

They reached the exit door and started up the stairs.

"You are the spy for *him*, or perhaps for my watchdog Olsza." She laughed with abandon.

"Who is *him*? And who is Olsza?"

They were at the top of the stairs.

"You shouldn't think that I am so stupid. I know you, Herr Major Stechert." She grabbed his mask and tore it from his face.

"O blaudiga Heenadregg," she gasped, sinking to the stairs. "I am so sorry, so sorry."

A couple in Bavarian folk-costume entered, holding hands, and walked down the steps. They were both big and fat, and the woman's skirt exaggerated its wearer's large behind.

"Eva, that reminds me," he said, sitting down next to her, "of a story: a soldier from Bavaria—"

"What reminds you?" she asked. "This is all a mistake. It's crazy."

"You'll find out. I can't tell you now. It's the whole point of my story. So the soldier didn't speak French and the clerk didn't speak German. He wanted to buy a pair of silk panties for his wife. The clerk guessed what the article must be, but trying to find out what size she wore, he asked, '*Pour quelle age* [For how old a person]?' "

Eva looked away, her eyes focused on the distance.

"So the soldier heard the word *age* and said, '*O mei Oide . . . den Orsch habt ei grossen* [My wife has a large behind].' "

Eva did not laugh.

"You must think I'm an evil woman," she said, after a period of silence interrupted only by music and cheers from the *Bierstube* below.

"I'm not thinking anything now," he said. It was true. At that moment he had stopped caring what happened to him or what she did and why.

"But I want to tell you—"

Suddenly, the man dressed as a cossack appeared with a mug.

"Hey, Harle . . . here you are, hid . . . ing . . . my good drink . . . ing companion." He approached them.

This time Romek took his mug and drank from it.

"Share it with me," Eva said. She took the mug from him and drank a few gulps from it. "Hey! It's Fasching! To hell with the rest of the world."

She took both Romek and the cossack by the hand. "Let's dance and sing and love." The cossack whooped and bounded away as the orchestra started in with the aria from *Rigoletto,* and the two were left alone by the door.

"*I ben bsouffas* [I'm drunk]," Eva said, switching to Bavarian.

"I am sorry," he said, "but I feel very sober. I want to be drunk, too."

"And I want to dance, to dance, to dance!" Eva sang. She was trying to twirl around with him, but it was impossible to move for the crowd of drinkers. The smoke was thick, and it was difficult to see past two or three meters.

"Let's get out of here," Eva hissed. "Enough of these *Wogscheidl* [alcoholics]. I want fresh air, fresh air, fresh air." She took his hand and led him out. "I must dance on the streets, the streets . . . in the fresh air . . . airrr!"

As they reached the exit door, she stopped and began to laugh wildly. "It's so funny. Oh, it's absolutely ridiculous, crazy."

"What's so funny, Eva?"

"Funny, funny! To think of all the Harlequins being rounded up tonight in all of Munich, for identification."

"They will be angry," Romek said glumly.

"Let's go out and dance. I want to see how soon they will catch you," she said and laughed again. She opened the door. Romek hesitated, thinking her a witch, a sadist. She noticed his reluctance.

"Don't you worry," she said. "I will come with you. They will check your papers, but they'll release you. We'll have a lot of laughs, a lot of laughs!"

"No, they will not release me."

"Come on. Don't spoil my night. Don't spoil my fun. I guarantee you."

"They won't release me."

"Why won't they?"

"Because my papers aren't very good." He had the sudden urge to tell her everything. "They are not very good papers, since I am—it's hard to find the right words to tell you. I'm an escaped prisoner of war."

"It's not true," she said. "You're joking."

"It's true."

"A French prisoner of war!" Eva laughed uproariously. "*La Grande Illusion.* How romantic!"

"No, a Polish Army prisoner of war, but I am Russian and Jewish, born in Poland, also part Polish."

Eva laughed again. "How sexy, how sexy," she said. "And to think that you selected the ball for the SS Elite Corps, *his* Elite Corps." Eva was shaking with laughter now. Tears appeared in her eyes. "And to think that you chose me—*me*!—as your *Gschbusi* (girlfriend). That's so funny." And she laughed some more, then looked at him, inspecting his features with curiosity.

"Surprised, disappointed, shocked?" he asked.

"Amused, amused. I love it. What is your first name?"

"Romek," he said.

"I want to dance with you, Romek, in the fresh air, Romek."

Two musketeers, one devil, and two angels entered the establishment. The devil pinched Eva and kissed her, and one of the angels bit Romek's ear. All of them reeked of alcohol. Soon they rushed off to drink some more and left Eva and Romek alone.

"So you wish to dance in the streets and get rid of your Harlequin?"

"I did not say in the streets. I said in the fresh air!" she said, taking his hand. Despite the many comings and goings of the night, Eva's hair had stayed in place and she looked as if she had just come from her dressing room. Romek's white costume was badly stained from spilled drinks, the dirt of the stairs where they had sat, and the truck. "Come, come," she said.

They walked out of the café and went a few steps; then she led him through a door in the next building. The stairs were narrow and dark. She strode so rapidly that Romek had difficulty following her. Stopping to catch his breath, he heard her voice from a distance, high up, calling, "Come up, come up!"

He ran up several more stairs and overtook her.

"Harlequin could use some mountain climbing practice," she said as she threw open a narrow door. "We are going out on the roof."

At this point Romek did not care where he was going. Had she said Gestapo headquarters, he would have followed her.

The cold, fresh air hit him.

"The roof is very steep," she said. "But there is a small ladder. We'll climb to the top. There is a narrow ledge on top."

Eva went through the door and began climbing the ladder, coated in places with snow. With his bare hands he felt the icy iron of the ladder. Despite the cloudy night sky, he was able to see the outline of Eva's skirt above him. A few instants later, they were both on the roof of the building. Three or four stories below, Romek saw a car moving. He could also distinguish at a distance the contours of the neighboring buildings.

Eva stretched out her arms to the sky.

"Fresh air! Fresh air!" she cried triumphantly.

"How did you know this place?" he asked, sitting down carefully on the snowy surface. The wind was blowing hard and the ledge atop the steep sides of the roof was several meters long but less than a meter wide.

"I was born here, in Munich. One of my childhood pranks was to climb up here."

"Now I know that when you said I was in danger you meant danger!"

"No, no, no!" she said, spinning on one foot like a ballerina. "I thought you were someone else."

"Why would the spy you thought I was be in danger?"

"Because *he*—my lover—is very jealous. *He* never fails to destroy any man showing an interest in me. Once upon a time he even killed a suitor of mine."

Romek was sitting, holding onto the roof with both hands.

"Now he will want to destroy me, too."

"Of course. You have spent more time with me than any other man except for him. He will try." Romek could hear people shouting on the street and the sound of cars.

"Are you afraid?" Eva asked.

"What for? The counterintelligence, the *Wehrmachtpolizei*, are already after me. Does it matter if *he*, too, joins them?"

"It does matter. Believe me. But let's dance," she said, taking his hands and pulling him to his feet. Her touch felt warm and pleasant. She began to whistle a tune Romek could not recognize and they began to dance.

"What if we fall?" he asked.

"There would not be much for all your persecutors to pick up," she said, laughing and dancing. "And it would be a fall to make history, if I were found alongside you."

The wind seemed to intensify, but the dancing on the narrow ledge, his fear, and her nearness kept him warm. For a moment he forgot where he was, stepped off the ledge onto the slanting roof and lost his balance, but Eva stood firm and pulled him back.

"I thought I'd kill myself once by jumping from this place," she said as he was trying to recover his breath from the panic.

"Why did you want to do it?" he asked.

"But it seemed such an utterly unesthetic way to die."

"Why did you want to kill yourself?" he repeated.

"Because of him, but now . . . It's Fasching." She pushed her body against his. "Give me a *Bussal,* Romek."

He looked disoriented.

"*Ein Kuss* [A kiss]," she translated from Bavarian into German.

He kissed her quickly on the mouth.

"Let's dance some more," she said, and began to whistle a waltz as she took him firmly in her arms. A church clock struck midnight. He began to get annoyed. By this time he had hoped to be far away from Munich and the Fasching. Eva was just wasting his very valuable time. He began to wonder if he could possibly steal an overcoat to cover his Harlequin costume. Would she alert the police if he left now?

"Let's sit down," he said. She obeyed and put her arm around him. They sat on the edge of the ledge with their legs on the steep roof. His pants were soaked by the melting snow. Her skirt was now wet, too.

"You cannot see very well now," she said, "but on a clear day it's a beautiful sight from here. *Minga,* I mean München is marvelous." She kissed him on the cheek. "Don't you like it?"

"I don't know it," he said. Time was running out. He was feeling he should take control of the situation and leave.

Eva laughed. "It's so funny," she said. "Fasching, and you." She brought her face close to his. Their lips met. She leaned backwards, drawing him with her. They were lying across the ledge with their legs on one side of the roof, their heads in the air over the opposite side. He felt the wet snow on his back.

"I always thought," he said, "that one could tell a woman skier from a man skier . . . because she would have snow on her back and he on his knees."

She laughed briefly.

"How long were you held prisoner?" she asked.

"Five hundred fifty-seven days, eleven hours, and twenty-three minutes."

The wind blew hard in his face; their cheeks touched.

"And the last time . . . a woman?"

"Forty-one hours and seventeen minutes before my capture."

He remembered the moment well. He and a group of Polish soldiers had been sleeping in the field near a village. A young peasant woman had brought them milk and bread at dawn. She had blue eyes and blond hair with flowers in it, lion's paw, he remembered. Their eyes met and she nodded for him to follow. They made love in the bushes. She did not take off her clothing, not even the scarf that she wore around her head. And during the five hundred fifty-seven nights of prison, he had thought about that nameless woman and desired her.

"That's quite a lot of days and hours," Eva said.

"Considering the interest the Wehrmacht and the others have in capturing me, it might have been the last time forever," he said, feeling the cold dampness penetrating his underpants and undershirt.

"You can do something about it."

"About the cold? What?"

"No, no," she said, pressing her body close to his. "About that last time. It does not have to be your last time."

"I still don't understand," he said.

"Why don't you try to get some snow on your knees?" she asked, smiling and kissing him on his neck.

"Here?" he exclaimed, jumping up. He would have fallen down to the street if she had not held him.

"Yes, here," she said, pulling him down again. Lying on her back, she brought her skirt up and placed his hand between her thighs. She felt warm. He kissed her and began to caress her. She responded with passion, and undulated. He wanted to make love to her quickly, then leave, but he was finding he had no desire. He was peering over the roof when he suddenly noticed a military truck. He pulled his head back, frightened, not so much because it might have been a military police vehicle, but because he realized how high he was above the ground. He began to shake.

"I can't here, not here," he whispered.

"Too bad, too bad," she said, getting up and trying to shake the snow from her dress. "You're not used to heights."

Soaked and cold, they walked through the door to the stairway. The sound of the Rosamunde song wafted up to them.

"You cannot go out in the street like this, even if it is dark," she said. "Harlequins are being hunted tonight, remember."

"But what can I do?" he asked, looking at her now disheveled hair and wet dress.

"I will give you my skirt. There is another one underneath. That will do in the darkness."

She took off her skirt and gave it to him. Her taffeta slip clung to her legs. He put the skirt over his wet Harlequin pants.

"You look so pitiful like that," she said, putting her arms around him and kissing him on his forehead. "I do understand you. I'll help you. We'll go not far from here to the house of a friend of mine and change our costumes there."

As they passed the *Bierstube,* Romek noticed the man dressed as a cossack sitting with his head down, looking as though he were asleep.

People were on the street in groups, all of them drunk, singing, laughing, some dancing. From one such group two men in lederhosen detached themselves; one tried to kiss Romek, the other Eva, but Eva and Romek were able to escape the attack and reach her friend's house. It was a large building; her apartment was on the second floor. The door was open, and a recording of a Brandenburg concerto was playing, but no one seemed to be listening, and no one seemed to notice their arrival. A roomful of partiers engaged in loud discussion, gesticulating with their hands, their beer mugs, champagne glasses. It was warm. Bottles and empty glasses were arranged on a side table under a group of paintings that could have been Kandinski, Nolde, and Jawlenski, Romek thought. He poured cognac for Eva and himself, and they drank in silence. He drained his glass with one gulp and refilled it.

A man dressed as Napoleon, with black boots and fitted trousers, came forward.

"That's quite original: half man, half woman," he said. "Are you supposed to be a hermaphrodite?"

"He is half Harlequin, half Eve," Eva said, joining the conversation. "If you like his costume so much, you might persuade him to exchange with you," she said.

"I would be very much interested, if I could get you, too, as part of the deal," Napoleon said, looking at Eva. Romek hoped she would agree. The man was about Romek's height, and his uniform would fit him well. After his failure to make love to Eva on the roof, she should realize, Romek thought, that he was not interested in her. She was a very attractive woman, but she left him cold. Just make the exchange, he thought, and let me go.

Eva looked at Romek. She took his hand.

"I like my companion," she said, adjusting her mask. "Some other time."

The man moved away with a smile on his lips. Romek threw back another cognac.

"Why do you like me?" Romek asked, putting his arm around her.

"I have always liked people from your world," she said, and kissed his lips. "They have always fascinated me. That is why *he* hates you people."

"Because of you?"

"He is very jealous of anyone or any people who might be the subject of my interest. He can be very mean."

Someone changed the record to a Mozart quintet.

A woman without a mask, dressed like a character from a Wagnerian opera, approached them.

"It's you, Eva," she said. "You look as if you have been having a marvelous time. You're all wet from the snow."

"Oh, Erica," Eva exclaimed, "the night is just beginning! I want to go on having a good time."

"I'm afraid it will be difficult," Erica said, looking at Romek. "Someone's been looking for you, Eva."

"*O blaudiga*—that bloodhound Olsza!" Eva sighed. "What did you tell him?"

"Well, that you were not here and that I did not expect you. He told me to call him immediately if you showed up."

"I am still not here," Eva said. "My companion and I need a new disguise. Have you got anything we could use?"

"For you, Eva, it will be easy. I have a Spanish dancer costume I wore last Fasching. For him, it will be more difficult."

Erica was taller than Eva. She surveyed Romek with her smiling dark eyes. "I will be able to provide your Harlequin with a man's suit. It will be much too large for him, but it's Fasching. No one will notice."

An American Indian approached Erica. "Here you are, hostess," he said, taking her in his arms and lifting her up off the floor. "I want a beer."

"Is that all?" Erica said, laughing. "All this effort, and just a beer?" Then Erica and the Indian disappeared into the crowd.

Romek was concerned about the man Olsza who was looking for Eva. Perhaps he would want to investigate Romek as well.

"Why is this man after you?" Romek asked.

"Because I escaped from him. He was supposed to guard me, not let me out of his sight even for a split second, and I imagine if *he* finds out, Olsza's head will roll."

"And who is this *he*?" Romek asked, but she ignored the question and continued looking pleased with herself.

"As we were dancing, I noticed that Olsza moved away from the door; that's when I told you to leave. Then I myself slipped out by the side exit. I had arranged to make my escape with a big clown, but you were there. As a lark, I decided to run after you." She laughed with delight. "It's all so funny."

"Raphael's madonnas are too realistic, they stink," said a man with a pointed beard, wearing lederhosen and a Tyrolean hat. "The more real the less artistic art is."

"In my opinion, art, painting, must be representational," a man in a medieval knight's outfit stated. "I don't enjoy looking at a few dots and a couple of straight lines."

"Because you don't have any imagination," Romek said. "Art must be different, something more than reality."

"Take this landscape by Nolde," the knight said, pointing to one of the paintings on the wall. "For me those are a few blurred spots, nothing more."

"But they have harmony, poetry," Romek said. "There is music—"

Eva pulled at his sleeve. "Time to go and change," she said, starting toward Erica and the Indian.

"Where can we change?" she asked Erica, who was serving the Indian a glass of beer.

"In the bedroom," Erica said. "Come along."

Once in the bedroom, which was also decorated with modern paintings, Erica gave Eva her Spanish dancer's costume and Romek a man's dark brown suit. As Erica left, Eva locked the door with the key in the lock. It was warm, and the light from a lamp on the night table gave the room a cozy atmosphere.

The suit looked big to him. Would he look like a civilian? Wouldn't the police recognize him?

They began to undress, putting their wet clothing on a chair. Eva took off her dress, then her stockings and her panties. Her body was beautiful with firm, well-shaped breasts, although her legs were a little too muscular.

"Do you like my body?" she asked, seeing how he was looking at her.

"You are beautiful," he said, approaching her, his heart pounding. "More beautiful than I imagined."

They kissed and she pulled him down on the bed. He kissed her and caressed her body and she moaned, full of desire.

"I want you, I want you," she whispered, but again he was without desire. He tried to think about the peasant woman, looking at Eva's breasts, her legs. She caressed him, trying to encourage him, but it was no use.

They lay close to each other, and he saw tears gather in her eyes. Her eyes were the color of a lake in the mountains of Bavaria, reflecting the sky on a summer day.

"Why are you crying?" he asked.

"No one wants me. No one desires me," she said, weeping.

"But you have *him,*" he said.

"I haven't for a long time. *He* only likes to look at me taking a bath—to see the shape of my body."

"We have known each other for only a few hours—"

"Not even you, after a year and a half without a woman," she said, still crying. "I would have liked to tell *him* that on a Rosenmontag . . . to make him realize that I am desirable . . . *blaudiga* . . ."

He caressed her breasts, touched her between her legs, but he was totally void of any desire to make love to her. She knew that.

"No use, no use," she said, getting up.

"I'm sorry," he said, putting the borrowed pants on. "If we had more time—"

"Nothing would change," she said. "You don't want me; no one wants me."

Romek felt both frustrated and sad. Perhaps there was something wrong with him. In the camp, there had been talk that the Germans had been feeding them something to depress desire. It might be that his inability to make love to Eva was the result. He was sorry for Eva, the slave of an impotent, jealous monster; she had had an opportunity to make love and had been rejected. But he was sorrier for himself. Would his own impotency be permanent, he wondered, and shivered at the thought.

Eva put on the carmine red skirt and the black lace blouse, and wrapped the carmine scarf around her throat. Romek's suit was too big, but it would have to do. The outfit made him appear much older, and for that he was grateful.

There was a knock at the door. Eva rushed to open it. It was Erica.

"You look so charming and beautiful in this disguise," she said, inspecting Eva. "Although I must say you don't look Spanish. So blond and blue-eyed."

"I need a brooch to keep the scarf in place," Eva said.

"Here is one," Erica said, picking up a little gold brooch from a drawer and handing it to Eva. "It's not Spanish, but it will do." A lion's head was etched into the gold.

Eva looked in the mirror, fastening her scarf with the brooch.

"How do you like it?" she said, turning around.

The costume was tight, and the skirt was a little too short, but she looked beautiful.

"Irresistible," Romek said, realizing that she had a few freckles on her neck.

"I have good news for you," Erica said. "The Indian has a car and is willing to drive you."

"Oh, yes. We are ready. All we need is two overcoats. I'll return them to you later."

Erica handed them two coats. Again his was too big and Eva's was too short. Romek felt a great sadness coming over him. He looked at Eva and began to regret her being dressed. The image of her nude body came to him, her breasts pressing against him, the nearness of her mouth. At the thought of touching her legs, he began to quiver. The room, Eva, Erica, the paintings on the wall, the world began to whirl around him. Aware that he was going to faint, he sat down on the floor.

"Water, water," he said, leaning against the wall and closing his eyes. He heard voices, but was not sure who was talking or what was said. A while later he felt the cold rim of a glass. He opened his eyes and saw Eva's hand, then her face. She was concerned.

"It's all my fault," she said, pouring water into his mouth. "Forgive me. Everything was too much for you."

Erica was standing next to Eva. "Perhaps he could sleep here," Erica said. "He will feel better in the morning."

"No, no," Romek said. "I must go. I must move on." He looked into Eva's eyes. "I have to take a train."

"The Indian will drive you," Erica said.

"Poor boy," Eva said. "So tired and hungry."

"No, no," Romek said, getting up. "No, quite the contrary."

Erica was still there, and he did not want to tell Eva in Erica's presence that he had fainted because of his sudden lust for her. She came close to him and caressed his hair. Their eyes met. There was softness and sadness in Eva's eyes.

"Do you still want to leave?" Erica asked. Her eyes smiled at them.

"I must," Romek said, although he wanted nothing more now than to stay with Eva in this room forever.

"Both of us must," Eva said.

"Yes," he said, and the feeling of loss overcame him. The thought of being alone, without her, was too frightening.

"I will tell the Indian," Erica said, leaving.

"You should know," he said, putting his arms around her, "That what happened tonight—" He drew her face in and kissed her, and the kiss made him passionate. She felt his desire.

"I just fainted because I wanted you so much, I desired you. I desire you now."

There was a knock at the door and Erica stuck her head in. "The Indian is waiting."

"Such a pity," Eva said.

"For some reason," Erica said, "Fasching nights are always too short."

The Indian was waiting at the door. A small, round-faced brunette, dressed as a Gypsy in one of Lehar's operettas, accompanied him. The four of them walked down the stairs without exchanging a word. The Indian led them to a Volkswagen parked only a few steps from the door. Eva and Romek crammed themselves into the back seat of the car. The space was so narrow that their bodies were squeezed against each other.

"Railroad station?" the Indian asked.

"Yes," Romek answered. "Thank you."

"Three more days, then back to the barracks," sighed the driver, speaking to the Gypsy in the front seat beside him.

"We won the war! Now it's only fun," the Gypsy said, laughing.

"It's just the beginning, my dear," the driver said soberly.

Romek did not think about the war. Even the prospect of getting caught was far from his mind. Eva was so close! He reached up and touched her scarf. His fingers moved down to her breast. He slipped them under the fabric of her dress. The contact of his fingers with her bare nipple made him quiver again.

"That's not what our leaders say," the Gypsy retorted.

"I want you," he whispered into her ear. "I have never, never wanted anyone so much."

"I am not sure they know what they're saying," the driver said.

Romek brought Eva's hand below his stomach. The contact with him made her tremble too.

"I want to be inside you," he whispered.

"I hear that despite our repeated victories," the Gypsy said, "our rations will be cut."

"I want it too," Eva whispered, caressing him.

"That's only one of many such measures," the Indian said.

Eva and Romek turned to each other. The lack of space made it impossible for them to kiss, but by stretching their necks they were able to touch tongues.

The car was passing groups of people singing and laughing. Some marched in the middle of the street, forcing the car to slow down.

"Look at these people!" the Gypsy said. "Who would ever guess we are in the midst of a war—pardon me, at the *beginning* of a war."

Romek managed to raise Eva's skirt with his free hand and touch her knees. The image of her naked body, her muscular legs, her abdomen, came to him. He pictured how she had spread her legs, and began breathing with difficulty.

"You never know," the driver said. "It might be their last Fasching."

Romek worked his fingers higher, beyond the silk of her stocking. At the touch of the skin on the inside of her leg, he jerked as though he had received an electric shock. Several merrymakers tried to cross the street and the driver braked abruptly, throwing Eva and Romek forward, but since they were wedged into the small car so tightly they did not move far.

"Fool," the driver spat. "These men are trying to make sure this is their last Fasching."

"Always a pessimist," the Gypsy lady said.

"Speaking of pessimists," Romek said. "In our cam . . . I mean, I heard that in Po . . . General Government, they say, 'The pessimist learns German, the optimist, English, and the realist, Russian.' "

"Ha, ha," the driver laughed. "There might be some truth in that joke."

There were more people walking in the streets as they approached the station and came to a stop.

As soon as they got out and the Indian and his lady friend drove away, Eva turned to Romek. "Where will you go?"

"Regensburg."

"We had better put our masks back on," Eva said, taking them out of her pocketbook and handing one to him.

The central hall of the station was filled with people. Some were in uniform, others were in civilian clothing, but the majority wore costumes or folkloric outfits. Some were standing in long lines, others were in circles passing bottles and drinking, and still others were singing. A few couples were dancing. It was noisy, and the smell of tobacco smoke and wet clothing hung in the air.

Eva checked the departures. "Your train, the first to Regensburg, leaves at 5:13. We still have about two hours," she said, looking at the huge clock suspended high over the hall. "Let's go to the restaurant. You must be hungry."

The station restaurant was even more crowded than the hall. Many people were standing among the tables and drinking or eating. Romek and Eva milled around for a while, until there were two seats free at a large table. All the men and women at the table wore Bavarian folk costumes, the women colorful dirndls and aprons, the men lederhosen and bright shirts with black or brown vests stitched with gold or silver. As Romek and Eva sat down, the people at the table began singing, and Eva joined in. Everyone linked arms with his neighbors. Romek could not follow the words. At the end of the song everyone exchanged kisses, and Romek got a quick kiss on the cheek from Eva and a longer one on the mouth from the plump, middle-aged woman on his left. All the people at the table were eating white sausages and drinking beer, and Eva ordered the same. "This is the standard fare during the Munich Fasching," she told him.

Across the table from Romek sat a large man with a gray moustache and rather long, gray hair. He had a good-sized beer belly and was smoking a long Bavarian pipe of porcelain. Hearing Eva's explanation in German, he observed Romek for a while then asked with a smile, "*Beesh de a Saubreiss* [Are you a Prussian pig]?" When Romek did not reply, he waited a moment and continued, "*Vastanga de boarisch* [Do you understand Bavarian]?"

"He is not a Prussian," Eva interjected. "But he does understand Bavarian." The man nodded his head with satisfaction.

Eva leaned toward Romek and he put his arm around her as other men were doing. It was warm, and now the smell of sausages and beer was mixed with the tobacco smoke.

"I want you, Eva," he whispered into her ear. "I can't stand it."

The Bavarians began to sing again, and Romek had to take the plump hand of his neighbor on the one side and Eva's on the other. Perhaps they could escape together, he thought, maybe she would come with him. She would get away from her jealous monster, and he from the fear of captivity or death. He looked into Eva's eyes, and she returned his stare. They were still singing, moving their bodies to the left and to the right.

"Will you come with me, Eva?" he shouted.

"Where?"

"Wherever I go," he shouted. He was not sure that Eva had understood him. "For life, all your life with me." Eva got it, and pressed his hand harder.

"Where did you want to take me?" she asked in a whisper.

The singing stopped and the man across the table said, "It's a pity that because of the war instead of *Senna* we have now *Sennarin*."

Eva, noticing that Romek did not understand, translated, "Instead of *Almhirten* [male cowhands], we have *Almhirtinen* [female cowhands]."

"And as we all know," the Bavarian continued, "they are

Raadschkakkl [talkative female beings]. So one such *Raadschkakkl*, the old Gretl, meets the fat Trese."

"I'll take you far away from the war," Romek whispered. "We'll start a new life where we can be free."

". . . and Gretl continues, 'I had a dream last night.'

" 'What did you dream?' Trese asked.

" 'I dreamt that you had died, my dear Trese,' she said . . ."

Some people at the table made side jokes and frequently interrupted the story with laughter. Romek thought it was a pity Pieter Brueghel had been dead for centuries. He would have appreciated the scene.

" '. . . and they buried you,' Gretl continued, 'under the old oak tree, and in that place weeds grew, and my brown cow with the white spot on her tail came and ate the weeds.' Trese then asked, 'And what happened then?' and . . ."

Eva was one of the people who were laughing loudest. The old Bavarian was an excellent raconteur and imitated the voice and the facial expressions of the two women cleverly. Romek held onto Eva's hand and it felt warm. He could see her profile, and laughing happily as she was now, she was a stunning beauty.

"You are tempting me," she whispered.

" '. . . and my cow ran on the field, then stopped, waving her white spotted tail back and forth,' the old Gretl was saying. 'And what then?' Trese asked . . ."

"It will be spring, the sun will shine on an avenue lined with flowering trees," Romek whispered. "You, Eva, and I will be walking, holding hands."

" '. . . waved its tail, and then: boom! A big pie on the ground.' And Trese asked: 'And what did you see in your dream then?' And Gretl said . . ."

A fat waitress in a red dirndl dress served them. Eva gave her some ration coupons and money. The Bavarian stopped telling the story, not willing to lose listeners. The sausages tasted good. Romek ate them with horseradish.

Eva said, while eating with appetite, "I'm even ready to give up the white sausages, to be free."

". . . and I am looking, looking, looking at that brownish pie on the ground and wondering, wondering . . ."

People at the next table were singing and shouting so loud that it was difficult to hear the story, but Romek had heard the joke before, so it didn't matter. He wondered if Eva would really come with him.

"I wish for you everything that is beautiful," he said. "I will paint portraits of you, of your body, to make your beauty eternal."

She smiled at him, nodding her head.

" '. . . and what then?' Trese asked. 'I tell myself,' Gretl continued, 'My dear Trese, after your death you've changed so much.' "

Everybody roared with laughter.

"I love you, love you," Romek whispered in Eva's ear. He was moved, and he pressed his arm closer around her. He began to imagine carrying her in his arms in a park with old trees around them.

The raconteur, pleased with the laughter, drank a liter-size beer at a gulp.

"It's a good story," he said, wiping the foam off his moustache with the sleeve of his shirt.

"But it's not the end of the story," Romek said.

"How is that?" the Bavarian asked, waving for a waiter.

"Let's hear more," Romek's plump neighbor shouted.

"Trese tells Gretl that she has had a dream too. 'I dreamt that you had died, my dear old Gretl,' and Gretl asked, 'What then?' And Trese said, 'They buried you under the linden tree, the weeds grew on your grave. My black cow came along, ate the weeds, ran in the meadows, waved her tail and boom: a pie.' "

Romek was trying to speak Bavarian. The people at the table roared with laughter after each word. It was possible that it was his accent that amused them and not so much the story. Eva squeezed his hand again, a little harder, and laughed with the others. Her laughter brought tears to her eyes.

"You are such a wonderful man, Romek," she said.

He continued: "Then Trese said, 'I look at this thing and wonder and say to myself that poor old Gretl, even after her death she has not changed, not at all.' "

His last words were greeted by another burst of laughter and applause. Eva kissed him, whispering, "I love you." The old Bavarian stretched his arm over the table and shook Romek's hand.

"I will follow you to the end of the world," Eva said, getting up.

As they stood near the table he took her in his arms.

"Will you marry me, Eva?"

"I will, I will," she said, kissing him. She began to turn, and they danced among the tables, with people around them drinking, singing, shouting, and laughing. They danced to the exit of the restaurant, through the crowded corridors and into the main hall of the railroad station. They stopped dancing only when they reached a line in front of a ticket counter.

"We will go far away," he said, holding her hand. "To some neutral country, in Latin America, perhaps. I will work, do anything."

"I can work, too," Eva said.

"And we will be free, free of fear."

"And we will have Fasching every night," Eva said.

She looked serious now, but happy.

"Don't worry," Romek said, although Eva did not seem to be

worried at all. "The people who are to make arrangements for my escape will make them for both of us."

They reached the counter. A military policeman stood next to the railroad employee.

"*Zwoa Billaedd no Regschbaug* [Two tickets to Regensburg]," she said.

The employee handed her the tickets. The policeman looked at the two of them with indifference. They had about an hour before the departure of the train, but they decided to board it then. They ambled slowly toward the entrance to the platforms for the departing trains. A railroad employee was checking the tickets, and behind him stood two tall Wehrmacht officers observing all the passengers and asking some of the male passengers questions.

"Pretend to be drunk," Eva whispered. Romek started to waver on his feet. Eva showed the tickets. Romek's heart pounded. They were moving on. One of the officers looked at some papers. Eva and Romek were now at the entrance to the platform.

"Excuse me, please," Romek heard the curt voice behind him. He turned around and saw the officer who had been checking papers looking at him.

"*Ihren Ausweis, bitte* [Your passport, please]!" he snipped.

"He forgot his," Eva said. "Don't you know it's Fasching?"

"I know it's Fasching," the officer said. "I still must identify the Herr."

"What for?" Eva asked. "Just leave us alone."

"Will you please follow me?" the officer said. Curious people gathered around them. For a moment Romek felt the impulse to run, run anywhere, to get lost in the crowd. The other officer came to them. It's all over, Romek told himself. He looked at Eva. Her face was white. She did not need to go with him, he said to himself, and he regretted implicating her. They walked into a small office. There were other uniformed men, one in an SS uniform. The office smelled of cigarette smoke and ink. The officer who had stopped Romek sat down behind the desk. He took a cigarette case and offered a cigarette to Romek, who declined.

"Sit down, Herr Kaganoff," he said, motioning to an empty chair next to his. Romek felt as if he had been punched in the stomach. The beautiful dream was over. The thought occurred to him that they would torture him. He saw the officer's gun and played briefly with the idea of grabbing it and turning it on himself.

Eva, hearing the conversation, rushed over to the SS man. "I need to speak to you, privately," she said to him.

The SS man looked surprised, but nodded in agreement. They walked off to a corner and Eva began to speak. Romek could not hear what she was saying.

The officer sitting next to him handed him a slip of paper.

"Will you please sign your name," he said, inhaling the smoke of his cigarette. Romek hesitated. "It's just routine, for identification." He had a scar on his face. It was the typical scar of the former student. Once duelling had been an obligatory part of the German university experience and later, long after the custom had died, it remained improper to have graduated from a university without a scar on one's face.

"What will happen to me now?" Romek asked, returning the slip of paper to the officer.

"You will stand trial," the officer said, "in the military court of the Wehrmacht."

"What are my chances?" Romek asked.

"Your lawyer will tell you," he said, pushing the butt of his cigarette into an ashtray. "You might be able to prove that you separated from the others before . . ." he said, lowering his voice.

Romek noticed that the SS man was making a call. After hanging up the receiver he approached the officer. "*Obersturmbannfuehrer* Olsza is coming to take over this case."

"This is a Wehrmacht case," the officer protested, lighting another cigarette.

"It is no longer so," the SS man said.

"I will call my commanding officer."

"Do whatever you wish."

While the Wehrmacht officer was talking on the phone, the SS man approached Romek and led him to the next office, where there were no people. There were also no windows. A while later Eva entered.

"O my love," he said, taking her in his arms. "I am so sorry to have involved you."

"I am sorry too," she said, kissing him. "It was a beautiful dream, but now it's over."

"Will you suffer?"

"Of course I will, my darling. Life without you will be terrible, boring, hopeless." Tears sprang into her eyes.

"But will you be all right? Will you survive?"

"Yes, naturally," she said. "Don't worry about me."

He heard many people coming and going in the next room. Then there were screams and shouts.

"You will be able to leave, too," she said with sadness in her voice.

"My God," he said. "How did you manage that?"

"I told you that Colonel Olsza was supposed to watch over me without losing sight of me even for a split second. If I tell *him* that I managed to escape, Olsza will be finished. I told Olsza that if he let you escape I would tell *him* that Olsza had been with me all the time. Olsza gave me his assurance. He has offered to give you six hours. Is that long enough?"

"I'm sure it will be."

There was a knock at the door and Olsza appeared.

"I'll accompany you to the train," he growled.

"I'll come along too," Eva said. Olsza hesitated, but she insisted. "What are we waiting for? Let's go."

There were no Wehrmacht officers at the gate now. They walked to platform eight, where passengers were boarding the train for Regensburg. On the platform there were many uniformed SS men. It was snowing again.

Romek entered one of the cars, and Eva followed. The train was full of passengers still singing and laughing. Eva was standing with Romek in the narrow corridor. Through the window Romek could see Olsza standing on the platform and looking at the railroad car.

"So this is our goodbye," Eva said quietly.

They kissed. She opened her coat. Her breasts pressed against him. A picture of her lying next to him on the roof came to his mind. He pressed against her.

"Oh, why aren't we alone?" he said, stirring.

"I want you, too," Eva said. "And I will do something about it." She broke away and ran out of the car.

Romek looked out of the window and saw Eva go up to Olsza. They were arguing about something. Then he saw Olsza nod. Eva came back.

"I told Olsza to clear this railroad car for us," she said breathlessly, kissing him. Already he heard the stomping of boots and the command: "*Raus* [Out]!" People objected to being evicted, shouting insults, calling the SS men names. But all of them left, including an admiral, a Wehrmacht general, and several other dignitaries. Romek looked out the window. The SS men formed four rows standing at attention. In front of them stood Olsza and the Wehrmacht general, and behind them, the evicted passengers.

They were no longer singing, shouting, and laughing. All of them stood silently, staring angrily at the railroad car.

Romek and Eva entered the empty compartment and sat down on the bench.

"The full significance of love, its dimension and its force," Romek said, "can only be understood when it is impossible, when it has no future."

"I began to realize that I loved you," Eva said, "when you were dressing in Erica's bedroom. I realized then how tragic your situation was."

"That was the moment I knew that I loved you," he said, looking into her eyes. "I saw you then as another human being with your triumphs and defeats, in your strength and your weakness. I really wanted you."

He kissed her and she helped him to take off his tie. He unbuttoned her dress, took it off and threw it on the other bench. The world around them softened and faded away to the tune of a delicate adagio as he caressed her and loved her.

Later on the shadows began to take on a sharper outline. He saw her delicate profile, tears in his eyes. Closing them again, he tried to hear the soft melody; he wanted to lose the contours of the objects around him.

"You are crying, my love," he said, caressing her hair. The bench was narrow and Romek was lying on her. Fearing that his weight might be too much for her to bear, he knelt down on the floor, kissed her feet, her knees, her arms. It was cold in the compartment, and he covered her body with her overcoat and remained on his knees looking at her. Still she appeared to be cold. Eva shivered. He began to kiss her neck, her breasts.

"I love you, I want you again," she said.

"So do I," Romek said, feeling a new surge of desire. "It's too bad—the cold here and the narrow bench."

"I will see what I can do," Eva said, getting up and putting her coat over her naked body. Running barefoot, she rushed out of the railroad car. Romek opened the window and saw her approaching Olsza.

"We need blankets, it's cold inside," she said.

"But the train has to leave in seven minutes," Olsza told her, looking at his watch.

"The train will have to wait," she said. "Get me the blankets. You must warm one of the compartments on this train."

"But where would I find blankets and how would I heat the train? It would take an hour."

"If I may suggest," the Wehrmacht general stepped up and saluted Eva. "There is an old method of heating a room." He was tall, narrow-shouldered, and he wore a monocle in his left eye. "Frederick the Great used it often. Fill the room with soldiers, and in minutes the room will be warmed up. I would suggest ten men to a square meter, preferably in underwear only, and without shoes. Otherwise it would be difficult to fit them into that space."

"Do it," Eva told Olsza. "And order your men to requisition a mattress from the nearest hotel. And rush it!"

She herself rushed back to the passenger car in her bare feet, only the coat covering her nude body.

Olsza commanded, "The men in the first row, take off your shoes, coats, tunics, pants."

"*Jawohl, Herr Obersturmbannfuehrer,*" the men in the first row shouted, and started to undress. Olsza dispatched the men in the second row to pick up the mattress and blankets. Within moments, men clad only in their underwear were entering the compartment next door.

"I am so cold, my darling," Eva said, coming close to him. "Take me in your arms. In a few minutes we can move next door."

"Isn't *he* going to be angry about this and angry with you?" Romek asked, holding her in his arms.

"With me?" she said with surprise. "I am a girl from Munich and it's Fasching." She caressed his hair. "Of course, he will be mighty mad at you, crazy with anger, when he finds out. But then you will be far away. He will have to find others, perhaps many others."

Olsza's knock interrupted their conversation. "Ready," he reported. Romek glanced through the window and saw several men being carted away on stretchers.

They moved to the next compartment where a warm bed had been installed. They took their coats off in silence.

Later on, as they lay exhausted, still locked in each other's arms, she said, "You made me so happy. I feel like a woman again for the first time in many years." Romek wanted desperately to tell her a joke, but decided not to.

It seemed to him only moments later that the train, filled with passengers again, began to move. Eva stood on the platform, waving goodbye to him with her red Spanish scarf. He had an urge to cry.

4

Would the unknown lady lion tamer be as protective, concerned, and devoted to me as Eva had been to Romek? I asked myself. Would she love me as much as Eva loved Romek? While Romek became a prisoner of war and suffered all the humiliations of imprisonment by the enemy, I had led a student's life that, despite the war, remained relatively comfortable. Was I in love at that time? No, I concluded. I had had many affairs, but I had never been in love.

I recalled now that at the time Romek had escaped, my own good friend and fellow student, André, had been arrested by the Nazis for participation in the French resistance movement. André had had a fiancée whom he adored. After his arrest, I visited her many times. Although I didn't find her attractive, and didn't even like her, I courted her and succeeded in having an affair with her. André somehow learned about his best friend's betrayal. He never came back from his captivity. He was shot by a German guard in a concentration camp. After the war, some prisoners who had been in the camp with him told me he had purposely offended a German guard. It was André's way of committing suicide.

I wanted to discuss these matters with Bernadette, but despite my many attempts to talk to her, I couldn't reach her. Her daughter answered the phone, explaining that "*Maman est occupée*" but would call me as soon as possible. Bernadette never returned my calls.

I decided one morning to turn to the next best person, Bernadette's ex-husband Marcel.

When I arrived at his one room with kitchenette near the Gare du Nord, Marcel didn't seem surprised to see me. He was already up and in the process of preparing his breakfast.

"Still in search of your lion lady?" He poured both of us steaming coffee and then hot milk.

"I am achieving some progress."

While we continued our small talk he opened a can of sardines and made us two sandwiches. The rays of the morning sun tried hard to break through the unwashed window panes.

"Bernadette doesn't wish to meet me or even talk to me," I said.

"That's not very considerate of her." Marcel immersed his sardine sandwich in his coffee and ate the dripping mess with the appetite of a hungry Doberman.

"Yet I would like to discuss with her my search for the lion tamer."

A layer of olive oil floated in his coffee cup. Nevertheless, he added a lump of sugar and drank it.

"And you would like me to convince your *maitresse* to listen to you?" I nodded.

The kitchenette was unbelievably messy. There were unwashed dishes in the sink. The door to the bedroom was open, and I could see an unmade bed.

"That would be difficult." Some of the oil dripped onto his unshaven chin. "An ex-lover is as tasteless to a woman as last week's bouillabaisse. Particularly if her lover left her for a print."

I was disappointed. "What you are saying, then, is that you can't help me?"

"It would be very hard. Could you show me that poster?"

I was surprised. What did the poster have to do with him arranging a meeting for me with Bernadette? But I pulled the poster, which I carried always with me, out of my breast pocket.

He studied the poster with the concentration of an art connoisseur examining a newly discovered Renaissance painting.

"She would be quite good in bed," he said. "Taming her lions, she must have learned a lot of tricks. He, he, he." He returned the poster to me, but not without leaving an oil stain on the edge of the paper. "Would you let me *coucher* [make love] with her if I persuaded Bernadette to be nice to you?"

"Oh, no. I would never share her with anyone," I almost shouted. His proposal disgusted me.

"You shouldn't get so upset, dear Jan. You think she is remaining a virgin waiting for you? She doesn't even know you exist. I'll try to help you anyway, but you should abandon some of your idealistic hopes. Besides, there's another female we could share."

I didn't like that kind of talk. Still, he had aroused my curiosity. "Whom?"

"The little redhead, the sales clerk in the poster store. Remember? You gave me the address."

While I couldn't have cared less about Marcel's sex life, the idea that I might have been responsible for his new conquest of this person irked me. I could imagine now his oily chin against this girl's breasts, his eyes smiling. I hated that image.

"Not interested," I said, finishing my coffee.

There was no reason for me to stay with him any longer. I assumed that he would talk on my behalf with Bernadette, bade him good-bye, and left to return home to admire the image of my lady.

Looking at my poster again and again, it occurred to me that perhaps a psychiatrist might help me complete my lion tamer's profile. An expert looking at the poster might notice things that I had missed in my own search. Immediately I called several libraries, professional associations, and the Sorbonne. After a few days of enquiries, I decided to consult a Professor Augustus Stolzer, at that time retired from the University of Heidelberg, but then in Paris working as a guest lecturer for some international institute. Stolzer had published a textbook on physiognomy, and many specialists I had talked to recommended him. I called him and he agreed to see me a few days later. I would meet him after his lecture.

I called on Professor Stolzer at his institute, but there was no place to consult him there, and we went off together to a café on one of the sidestreets off the avenue de la Grande Armée. The professor was a tall man in his early seventies. His gray hair was cut short. He wore glasses. There was a scar on his right cheek that must have been a duelling souvenir of his university days in Germany.

The café was a small room. Several people were sitting at the bar bantering in loud, cheerful voices and laughing animatedly from time to time. Fortunately, the few tables were not occupied, and we sat down at one of them. The café was filled with cigarette and cigar smoke and the scent of expensive perfumes.

After both of us had ordered coffee from a young, attractive waitress in a black velvet dress with a deep décolleté, I handed the professor my poster, which he examined with the care of a philatelist studying one of the world's rarest stamps. He turned it several times, adjusting his glasses again and again. This procedure lasted several minutes. Then he folded the paper and sat back with his eyes closed, murmuring something to himself.

I waited for his verdict like a person afflicted with a hopeless disease. Someone at the bar turned on the radio in the middle of a Beatles' song, and the words *all my loving* were repeated again and again until they trailed away.

"There is, unfortunately, very little I can tell you," he said, unfolding the paper again. "This is a photograph of a very young person, and as such, by definition, her life experiences could have left hardly any imprint on her face."

"I hoped—"

"Don't interrupt!" He collected himself and then went on, "Whatever people do or feel in their lives is eventually reflected in their faces. For instance, to take a simple example, a person's profession marks him. A doctor working in a hospital looks *down* to the patients in their beds. A priest preaching to his congregation looks *up* to heaven. There are different muscles used in lowering or raising one's eyes. This results in facial characteristics recognizable by professionals."

"I won't be able to find her then?"

It was only four in the afternoon, but the people at the bar seemed to be drinking a lot. One couple started kissing, but no one seemed to notice.

"I haven't finished yet," he said. He drank his coffee in silence for a while; then, studying the poster again, continued. "One of the findings I can present is that the muscle called *risorius* has not been as fully developed as in the normal person of comparable age bracket."

For a moment, I began to imagine interviewing circus people, asking them, "Have you seen a lion tamer with an underdeveloped risorius muscle?" The professor doesn't seem to be of much help, I told myself. But I didn't dare interrupt him.

"The risorius, or laughing, muscle contracts to produce facial expressions or laughter, and in her case it appears that she hasn't had much opportunity to produce either—at least, up to the time that this photograph was taken."

The crowd at the bar was getting louder. A middle-aged man,

putting his arm around one of the waitresses and resting his hand on her breasts, walked her out of the establishment. The radio blasted a series of commercials.

"You have helped me more than you can imagine, Herr Professor. Your observations add to the profile of my lady."

Somehow he got me to tell him everything about my search—my first encounter with the poster, my futile efforts to find her by publicizing her image, my theory of her personality, my friends' stories. He was watching me with the same attentiveness he had shown while studying the poster. When I told him about some of the features I had discovered in the ladies my friends had loved, I expected an outburst of laughter or at least a smile, but he remained silent and didn't interrupt my story.

After I had finished, he looked at me as if I were sitting on a time bomb about to explode.

"You are very vulnerable, Herr Majeski. It is dangerous."

I was about to speak, but he motioned to me to keep quiet.

"People in love idealize their partners. One might well compare this process to objects left in salt mines, on which, in the course of time, salt crystals settle. Among individuals who know each other, a similar sobering process may occur. If it does, the consequences are controllable, but in your case you are placing your crystals around a void. Your structure could collapse, giving you a shock."

"Then you think she may not love me."

Other couples were leaving from time to time. The girls at the bar kept looking at us, wondering whether to approach us. I felt ill at ease. Talking about love in this place was like touching the delicate petals of water lilies in a sewer.

"I didn't say that. She may or may not care for you. All I said was that she could be quite a different person from the one you imagine."

"I won't be disappointed as long as she loves me. Will she love me as much as I love her, Herr Professor?"

"There is, of course, the theory," the professor said, finishing his coffee, "defining love as '*die Resonanz der Seelen*' [resonance of the souls]. The emotional depth of one partner's love tends to equal that of the other."

"Then she *would* love me as much as I love her, even if she had never met me."

The professor looked at me for a moment as if he hadn't understood my statement. Then he said, "But in all my studies, I've never encountered such a case." He carefully put his glasses away. "I suppose it is possible, though, Herr Majeski." He smiled as if he wished me good luck. "It is possible."

During the next few weeks I frequented libraries, reading all the articles and books I could find about the war in Poland, hoping that one of them might mention my boyhood friends. In one of the articles I came across the name of one of them, Kurt Eisner. He had apparently worked for the Gestapo and had taken part in the persecution of gypsies. The name *Eisner* was not unusual, and it could have been someone else with the same name, but I decided to track him down.

I arranged many meetings with gypsies in Paris. After various disappointing encounters, I was able to establish that Gestapo Eisner was the Eisner who had attended the same nursery school as I, a finding that upset me. Thereafter, from repeated interviews, I managed to piece together Kurt's story.

Kurt stopped his motorcycle a good distance away from the dilapidated shack where, according to his informers, the Gypsies were hiding. Brushing the dust off his black boots and breeches, the standard clothing of the Gestapo men operating in Poland, he checked his gun. The Gypsies were usually armed with knives and stilettos, and both the men and the women were experts in their use. He had been told to expect only a woman, two children, and an old man, but still he did not trust them; the gun in his hand, he went slowly across a potato field.

It was noon, and the hot August sun was blinding him. He put on his sunglasses to see better. The potato field stretched only a short distance, bordered by an expanse of yellowish oats ending in pine forests. This summer of 1944 was especially hot; his face was covered with sweat. Kurt stopped a few meters away from the shack and listened. There were no sounds. He approached the shack on tiptoe and knocked on the rotten wooden door, then jumped a few steps back, aiming his gun at the center of the door.

He heard a movement inside, the screech of rusted hinges, and a Gypsy woman stepped out. Blinded by the sun, she covered her eyes with her hand.

"How many of you are inside?" he demanded. She was barefoot, her feet covered with dust. She did not appear to understand him, and he repeated his question in Polish. She wore a long skirt, which had once been black but was now a rusty gray, and a white cotton blouse.

"Answer, you—" he shouted.

Recognizing his Gestapo uniform, she retreated toward the door, shouting, "What do you want?" Her hair was dark and oily, her eyes light-colored like those of a snake. "Leave me alone!"

"How many?" he shouted again, stepping forward and directing his gun at her. He knew that her heart was pounding.

"Only me. No one else. Leave me alone!"

"Step back!" he ordered, entering the doorway. There was no furniture in the small area bounded by crumbling wooden walls. On the mud floor lay a bunch of carrots, a loaf of bread, and three eggs. Kurt guessed that she must have bought them from some local peasant who left food for her at designated times, picking up money in exchange. Such an arrangement was necessary, since the penalty for feeding or sheltering Gypsies was immediate execution, and no one would risk dealing with a Gypsy personally.

Kurt stepped outside, putting his revolver in his pocket.

"Your *Kennkarte* [identity card]!" he demanded.

She pulled out the document from under her skirt and held it out. He took the gloves from his other pocket, put them on, and only then took the document. In the left upper corner a two-centimeter *Z* was printed.

"*Zigeunerin* [Gypsy]," he said, nodding as if he wanted to say, You see, you naughty girl, you have no right to be alive. What are you doing here, then?

He opened the document and read aloud: "Dzinka Gorshlie. Married. Religion: Rumanian-Orthodox. Born: August 5, 1912." About seven years older than I, thought Kurt.

He was disappointed to have found her alone. A Gypsy woman would not carry her fortune with her. All those gold coins the Gypsies usually own must be hidden wherever the rest of the family were hiding. Kurt also knew that no tortures would force her to reveal their hiding place.

The Nazi policy of exterminating the Gypsies was a convenient way of robbing them, and now that the war was not going too well for the Third Reich, there was not much time left to get rich. The Soviet armies were only a few hundred kilometers away from Czestochowa, the Poles had begun an uprising in Warsaw, and the war might end within a few weeks.

The chances of a Gestapo man surviving in any liberated territory were nil. He hoped he might escape to some neutral country, but he would need gold—a lot of it—to survive.

"How many gold pieces . . . in your *sumadzi* [family heirloom]?" he asked. He had arrested many Gypsies and in the process he had acquired a few expressions in their language.

"I don't have any," she said, shaking her head. He knew she was lying.

"Where is your *cumpania* [clan]?"

"There is none," she said, looking at him defiantly.

She looked slim in comparison to his square figure and thick neck. Her skin was dark, typically Gypsy, but her eyes were a pale green, not like his blue ones.

"Then where do you live?"

"Here and there. I move around."

"Escaping the authorities," he said, mopping sweat from his blond, cropped head and his round face with his handkerchief.

"No, no. It is easier to milk a standing cow than a running one."

"I'll arrest you."

"*Banter* [So may it be]."

"You belong in the ovens of a concentration camp, you and all your *Barackenvolk* [people of the barracks]."

"*Banter.*"

She seemed to be resigned to her fate. Kurt did not trust her, and he began to wonder whether there was any one hiding, possibly a group of men, who would come to her rescue. He looked around but could not see any signs of the presence of others.

"Listen, the war is coming to an end," she said. "I have not done anything to you. Enough of our blood has been spilled. You go your way and I'll go mine." She spoke Polish with an accent, but her speech was that of an educated person.

"Come along," he said, not sure what he would do with her. She did not appear to be frightened and walked ahead toward the place where his motorcycle was parked. He despised her for being inconveniently separated from her family. For a moment he had the urge to draw his revolver and shoot her, the bitch. But he changed his mind, deciding to come back and spy on her. Perhaps he could discover the rest of them and get the gold he knew they must have.

He got on his motorcycle and started the engine. She looked at him with disdain and hatred.

"Don't you worry, you stinking . . . I'll get you and your brood, and I'll cut their throats first," he said with a smile, making ready to drive off. She jumped forward toward him, her body shaking, and spat into his face, shouting, "Beast!"

Then, still on his motorcycle, he struck her in the face and she fell to the ground. He was angry, disgusted. With his handkerchief he wiped the saliva from his face, stopped the engine and took out his gun. I'll kill the bitch now, he said to himself. He aimed the revolver at her. She was lying on the ground, her hand on her cheek, her nose bleeding.

"You whore's son!" she shouted. "I hate you, you coward!"

He held his finger on the trigger. A little pressure of his finger and the bitch would be gone. For a moment he hesitated. That would be too easy for her. That is what she wants, he thought. But I'll get even with her. I'll kill her children in front of her. Then she'll suffer and writhe with pain, the whore. He spat at her, boarded his motorcycle, and drove off.

He took the same road back to Czestochowa, only 10 kilometers away. Feeling frustrated and bitter about his failure to get the money, and blaming the Gypsy for it, his hands shook with hatred and the desire for revenge.

More than anything else he wanted to get even with her for spitting in his face. No one had ever done that to him, and he would never forgive it.

As he sped over the limestone road he began to consider where she could be hiding her family. He knew the area well. As a child, he had played with his schoolmates around there. He remembered the stalactite caves in the pine woods. He and his friends would hide in the narrow enclosures and play games. That had to be where her family was. The pine woods were just behind the oatfields he had seen from her shack. Perhaps she already assumed that he had given her up. Carrying her carrots, eggs, and bread, she might be returning by now. Her people did have to eat.

He turned his motorcycle into a side road. There was a way to reach the edge of the woods from where he was without being seen. It was hot, and there was no wind. His face was covered with sweat, and his brown shirt was soaked with it. The road led between two fields of oats, where wild red poppies and cornflowers were in bloom. The road was uneven, sandy, and he had to drive slowly, but he had plenty of time. It would take her much longer to reach the caves walking than it would take him to make this detour on the motorcycle.

After he had reached the edge of the wood, he leaned his machine against a pine tree and entered the forest. The air here, filled with the aroma of pines, was cooler, and he stopped to wipe away the sweat. For a moment, he thought of the partisans who might be hiding here, and a cold current moved down his spine. He tried to laugh off the idea, but the feeling of impending danger remained with him. Despite this uneasiness, he moved on toward the caves. The sandy soil under the pine trees was covered with dry needles, and he was able to walk without making any noise. As he reached the area near the caves, he saw they were surrounded by thick bushes, and he crawled in among them to lie in wait.

If I am right, she should be passing not far from here, he said to himself. She will regret her act, the damn bitch.

It was not long before he spotted her. She was walking along in her faded skirt, carrying a basket and singing. Her confidence suggested to him that her family could not be far away. When she drew near, he stole out and jumped her with the gun in his hand. She started to run, and he chased her. Her long skirt got caught on a branch, and she stumbled and fell to the ground, scattering the carrots, the bread, and eggs. One egg hit a tree and broke.

She turned her head toward him, her eyes full of venom.

"Ha! I told you I would get you, you dirty whore," he said, laughing in triumph.

"Get away," she cried.

"Why should I? I want to make the acquaintance of your family first. Get all of your gold pieces together and then we'll talk." He was pleased with himself. She turned on the ground, and he saw a metal object in her hand—a stiletto.

"Drop it!" he shouted. "Or I'll kill you."

"Shoot, shoot!" she screeched. "Alert the men hiding here. They would be glad to get a whore's son like you, and especially your gun."

Rising, she began to gather her belongings. She collected even the broken egg, putting it with the pine needles and dirt in which it had broken on a rag in her basket.

He knew that he had lost again. She might be bluffing about the men, but she might also be telling the truth. Besides, killing her would not leave him any richer.

"Robbing helpless people," she said, standing up. "Get the hell out of here, you bastard!"

There was a cool breeze, but he was as wet with sweat as he would have been from a shower.

"Damn it," he said. "I'll get you."

"Or we'll get you," she said, turning her back.

He spun and ran toward the edge of the woods, then walked through the oats, kicking at the red poppies as if they were responsible for his defeat by a Gypsy woman with faded clothing and dirty feet. Later on, despite the bumpy roads, he gunned his motorcycle and drove recklessly forward, narrowly missing a group of peasants on the road. He calmed down only as he entered Czestochowa, overpopulated now with thousands of refugees from the Warsaw uprising. Despite the bloody battles in Poland's former capital, the Poles strolled about here with optimism in their faces, hoping that at last the end of the war was at hand.

Czestochowa at that time was a city close to the battlefront. Several buildings had been taken over and made into temporary offices for the Wehrmacht. The Gestapo, too, moved to a new location, taking over an apartment house at Forty-one Adolf Hitler Allee. The next few days Kurt had to work there doubly hard, since he had received orders to be ready for a possible "temporary" retreat by the German armies, and he was to have his files packed for such an eventuality. Despite his hatred for the Gypsy, he put the incident out of his mind. At any rate, the activities of the partisans had increased, and it would be risky to venture alone into the country. He did not expect to see her again.

In the meantime, the Russians stopped their offensive, and the front stabilized on the Vistula River. He was ordered to unpack his files and to continue his work as usual. Since he was in charge of the resettlement, as it was called, of Gypsies, his job was to search out the few surviving Gypsies in the area and to arrange their transport to the extermination camps in Auschwitz. Since the Gypsies had been accustomed to living in the country for centuries, they were very skillful at avoiding capture, changing their hiding places swiftly and easily. With the front only a few hundred kilometers away, most of them moved east, crossing to Russian-occupied territory.

It was six o'clock in the evening in the beginning of September when the sentry at the entrance to Gestapo headquarters announced that a woman wanted to see him urgently. Kurt was used to such unexpected visits, since his work required that he deal with informers.

As she entered, he was talking on the phone with his back to the door. When he turned around he dropped the telephone receiver at the sight of Dzinka in his own office. His first reaction was the thought that she had come to sell him information.

"You here?" he said. She wore a brown gabardine coat and her bare feet were thrust into wooden clogs. She had changed in the weeks since he had encountered her. She looked tired and seemed to have aged.

"You must come with me," she said. "My daughter is ill. Right away to the hospital, or my daughter will die." She trembled, and there were tears in her eyes. At a distance, he could hear the sound of typewriters and the loud weeping of a woman, who might have come to plead for mercy for her condemned son or husband.

"You are crazy," he said, lighting a cigar. "You know that I can arrest you and send a battalion tomorrow to round up your group."

"Please, no, no. I will give you all my money," she whispered. And with trembling hands, she took from her purse a few gold coins and placed them on his desk. He recognized the coins: they were all twenty-ruble pieces. There were five of them.

"Take them ba—" he said. Somebody might see them, he thought, hastily transferring the pieces to a desk drawer. He did not collect the gold pieces to support a lavish life style. On the contrary, he led a frugal life, saving as much money as he could from his salary. As a boy, he had never received any spending money from his parents. There were four boys in the family and his father was poor. He used to watch with envy as the other boys in the school bought candy or ice cream during breaks between classes. Whenever one of the boys offered to share his treats with him, he always refused, claiming that he did not like sweets. He decided then that his great objective in life would be to become rich.

"My daughter," she said more assertively, encouraged by the fact he had taken the money. "She must be transported to a hospital at once."

"Impossible," he said, looking at the chart hanging on the wall below the portraits of Adolf Hitler and Heinrich Himmler. It was the tally of the number of exterminated Gypsies. The number now stood at 443,751.

"I will pay you much more if you do it," she said. "I will triple it if you take her."

He hesitated. On the black market, each piece would equal his entire salary for two months. Fifteen coins would mean an income that would take him two and a half years to earn.

"What do I have to do?" he asked, thinking about the fifteen gold coins.

"Pick up my daughter right now and drive her with me on your motorcycle to the hospital on Saint Barbara Street. The Poles don't have motorcycles, and curfew will come soon." She began to tremble again.

"What if I told you I would do it for thirty pieces?" he asked. He knew that he was demanding a fortune, a fantastic sum.

"I will give you fourteen," she said, wiping her eyes with a handkerchief. "That's all I have now."

"When will I get the rest?"

"When you pick her up. Please hurry. She has appendicitis. She must be operated on tonight, the Polish doctor told us."

Nineteen pieces in all, not bad for an hour's work. He took the five coins out of the drawer, put them in his pocket, and got up. He knew that no one would be suspicious that he was driving away with a strange woman. He often followed leads without delay, driving off with his informers.

The sun was going down as they drove through the streets full of hurrying people trying to reach their homes before the seven o'clock curfew hour. As he had expected, the Gypsies had changed their hiding place and were now staying in the woods near the village of Turow. He realized suddenly that this might be a trap. He checked his gun.

"Where do I pick her up?" he asked.

"She will be with my father, an old man, waiting on an open road," she said. She must have anticipated his fear and consequent caution. It was getting dark. She told him to slow down ahead, and he saw at a distance the silhouette of an old man holding a child in his arms. He stopped his motorcycle twenty meters away from them.

"Get her and bring the money!"

She ran toward the man. She took the child from him and argued with him before he gave her something, shouting at her. Then she rushed back with the child and a bundle.

"Here are the coins," she said, handing him a small purse. "Hurry, hurry!" He began counting the coins. There were fourteen coins as she had said, but two of them were smaller than the original ones.

"That's not right," he said. "We agreed on fourteen coins of the same size—"

"I swear, I will give you the difference," she said. "Please rush." He hesitated. But she pressed him, "I don't have it now. We don't have it now. I'll get it in a few days. Rush, rush!"

He was so angry that he was ready to tell her there was no reason to rush, that both she and her child should rightfully be statistics on the chart in his office, but instead he spat on the road and started the drive back to town. The child, he judged, was about eight years old and did not seem to be conscious. She was either drugged or dying, he decided.

The roads were empty, as were the streets, since it was already well past curfew, and it was dark as he stopped his motorcycle in front of the surgical hospital.

"Would you help me?" she asked, carrying the child and pointing to the bundle. He wanted to tell her to go to hell, but obeyed with reluctance. They entered the hospital and stopped in front of the receptionist.

"My girl has appendicitis," Dzinka said. "Call the doctor, please. My Ksenya needs—"

The hospital was so crowded that there were beds in the corridors with patients, some of them moaning in pain. The place smelled of ether and iodine.

"It's impossible," the fat, gray-haired receptionist said, shaking her head. "There is only one surgeon here, and he already has two operations scheduled tonight. He is performing one now. It will take him several more hours just for the first operation." The receptionist looked up and noticed Kurt. Not bothering to hide her hatred and disgust, she told them, "Try upstairs in the German part of the hospital."

Dzinka ran upstairs, leaving her bundle. Kurt ran after her.

"It's no use," he said. "It's only for Germans." She continued to hurry upwards. On the second floor a young, blond receptionist in a white uniform asked what she could do for her, but Dzinka did not understand. She just kept saying in broken German, "*Kleine Kind, kaputt, kaputt* [The little child, finished, finished]." Kurt could hear the Polish woman from downstairs saying, "That Gypsy, whoring around with a Gestapo man, should go to hell, to the Germans."

"Have you your insurance card?" the receptionist asked.

"*Kaputt, kaputt,*" Dzinka repeated, her eyes filled with tears.

"Damn it," Kurt said to Dzinka in Polish. "You are making trouble for me. It's for Germans only."

Three doctors appeared in the corridor. He could see their German military uniforms under their long white coats. Dzinka ran toward them: *"Kleine Kind, Kind kaputt, kaputt."*

One of the doctors, a tall man with gray hair and moustache, turned to her. "What's the matter?" he asked with a smile.

"Rumanian, Polish, Russian, French," she said, "but not German."

"French," the doctor said.

She spoke French quickly. The doctor asked a few questions and looked at the child.

"Will you please make ready operating room number two? "It's an emergency," he said to one of the two younger men with him.

"But we did not get her insurance identification," the receptionist said.

"Don't worry," the doctor said quietly. "It's my patient, and I will be responsible for the hospital fees."

The doctor took Dzinka's daughter from her arms and carried her into the operating room. He returned alone and spoke again to Dzinka in French.

Kurt felt it was his duty to warn the doctor that the girl was not German and thus by the Nazi rules and regulations, she could not possibly be treated here. He approached the doctor, who was still talking to Dzinka.

"Excuse me, *Herr Doktor,* but this girl is not German," he said.

The doctor interrupted his explanations to Dzinka and looked straight into Kurt's eyes. His own eyes were a steel gray.

"My name is Doctor Colonel Schramer. I am the medical chief of this hospital, and I decide here who will be treated." He spoke matter-of-factly, as if he were making nothing more than a comment about last year's weather. "This is a hospital and not a prison." Kurt detected an Austrian accent in the doctor's speech. "My profession is to save lives. We seem to be working at cross purposes. Now, will you please leave this hospital at once?"

Kurt's first reaction was to slap the doctor in the face, and kick and beat Dzinka, who had created this unpleasant situation for him. He could not arrest her now that he had brought her here. And making a report on the surgeon would be useless. They were needed badly right now to treat the heavy war casualties, and his report would be filed without action. But he would get even with her. He would make her into a statistic on his chart. The doctor turned his back to him and was talking again to Dzinka, who was smiling even as the tears rolled down her cheeks. He saw the doctor taking her hand and kissing it. Kurt turned in disgust and rushed out of the hospital. Kissing the hand of a Gypsy woman, he thought, and spat out, "The old fool must be taking himself for a Gypsy baron, old idiot." He put his hand into his pocket and the touch of the cold metal quieted him down. It had not been so pleasant, but within an hour and a few minutes he had earned more than three years of his salary. And she owed him some adjustment; the bitch was about to cheat him.

As soon as he had locked the doors of his two-room apartment, he put the gold pieces on the table and inspected them. They were genuine. Then he took out of his desk a box where he kept the previous collection hidden and arranged the pieces in piles of five, then ten. He had a total of forty-seven gold coins. His eyes sparkled at the sight of all this fortune.

The telephone rang. It was Ingrid, the woman who had been his mistress for the past seven months.

"What's up?" he said, still looking at the gold on his table.

"Why don't you come over and find out?" She was a native of Leipzig and had come to Czestochowa to work as a secretary.

"Perhaps not tonight," he said. He had too much on his mind to see her. They were lovers, but they had never become really close. He would not dare to tell her about the events of that evening, and even if he had done so she would not have been interested.

"I managed to get a bottle of French cognac." Ingrid liked to drink, and after they had a few drinks, if he had the urge to make love to her, he would wink or touch her behind, and she would rush to undress. They made love on the floor, since for some reason he did not understand, she did not like to make love in bed. In the process, she would always sing the Lili Marlene song, even when the radio was playing some other music.

"I have work to finish," he lied. The image of the doctor kissing the Gypsy's hand came back to him. Probably the old cadger is screwing the bitch now, he thought.

"Are you getting lazy?" Ingrid asked, laughing.

"I don't like cognac," he said and, not wanting to continue the conversation, he hung up.

For another hour, he played with his coins, then put them away in the drawer, locked the desk, and went to sleep, deciding to call tomorrow at the hospital and demand more gold from the Gypsy.

But Kurt could not go to the hospital the next day. He was called to a meeting of selected Gestapo officers in Posen, a town a few hundred kilometers northwest of Czestochowa. He knew in advance the purpose of the meeting: to promote the idea of a victorious Germany at a time when the situation was worsening on all battlefields.

About fifty men showed up for the meeting. The speaker was one of the top SS leaders, General Olsza, a stocky, gray-haired man in his late fifties. The recent German retreats on both fronts he characterized as great strategic victories. By drawing the enemies closer to the Third Reich, he pointed out, the Wehrmacht could annihilate the enemy more quickly. His speech was interrupted by many bursts of applause. Finally he changed the subject to the work of those present: "In the name of our Fuehrer and the Third Reich, I thank you for the successful work you have been doing. The new Europe will be eternally grateful for your heroic accomplishments. We have already *ausradiert* [erased] millions of Jews and Poles; our Wehrmacht has also annihilated millions of Russian prisoners of war. There are still millions of Jews and Poles left and only a handful of Russian prisoners. We will show our friends in the Wehrmacht [laughter] that we will not be second to them." The speech continued in the familiar pattern about the need to wipe out quickly, as quickly as possible, the Polish intelligentsia, the Jews, the Soviets.

Kurt listened with disappointment. The general did not mention the Gypsies even once. At the end of his speech the general asked whether there were any questions. Usually there were none, but this time Kurt stood up and identified himself.

"*Unterscharfuehrer* Kurt Eisner. You mentioned the need to wipe out the Jews, the Poles, and the Russians, but you did not mention the Gypsies."

The general looked at Kurt and did not appear to understand. There was a moment of silence.

"*Unterscharfuehrer* Eisner, you mention Gypsies. Isn't that a new kind of soap?" Another moment of silence was followed by a roar of laughter.

Everyone in the audience knew what the general was referring to. In many camps the bodies of the dead were being used in the manufacture of soap.

The general's speech was followed by many others, but none of the speakers had anything new to add. Kurt, who had laughed at the general's joke louder than the others, was congratulating himself on his audacity in putting a question to the general and on the attention he had received from his colleagues. The idea that

Dzinka should be make into a cake of soap amused him. That would be an appropriate punishment for her hateful behavior, her gall.

During the reception after the speeches, the general came to him.

"I toast the young talent," he said, raising his glass. "We need more young and devoted men who enjoy their tasks."

"*Jawohl, Herr General,*" Kurt said, saluting.

"I spoke with your superiors," the general said. "They are proud of your zeal in discharging your duties for the Fuehrer and our Reich. Such information is never lost, and I will report to the Fuehrer what I heard here." He offered Kurt his gloved hand.

The idea that he might be promoted appealed to Kurt. He began to think about the power he would have, forgetting his own doubts about the German victory. The thought that the general or his supervisors might learn that he had saved the life of a Gypsy child frightened him. That would mean not only the end of his career, but court-martial and a certain verdict of death. He must rectify the matter immediately and get rid of the two of them.

The general had moved on and was talking to the General Government's Gestapo leaders.

"I am arranging for the transport of Jews, giving them priority over the Wehrmacht," he said, lighting a cigarette. "I have pushed very hard for the eradication of all these peoples." He lowered his voice to a whisper. "Even the Fuehrer hesitated, but I changed his mind." Here he laughed conspiratorially. "Then, after the Fasching of Forty-one, he too . . ."

Kurt stopped listening. He was preoccupied with his own problems—with wiping out the two Gypsies, both mother and daughter, whose very existences could have consequences for his career.

Only two days later, he was able to visit the hospital. There was a new receptionist at the desk, a middle-aged woman. He detected fear in her eyes, protected by thick lenses. Her plump hands quivered.

"There is a woman here," he said. Since he had forgotten her name, he had to refer to her that way. "Her child was operated on Tuesday; an eight-year-old girl, appendicitis."

The receptionist, shaking now, opened a register and studied the list of patients.

"I don't see any girl registered here," she said, not looking at him. "What is her name?"

"I want to talk to Schramer."

She did not appear to understand.

"Doctor Schramer, Doctor Colonel Schramer."

"*Ein Augenblick, bitte* [A moment, please]," she said and disappeared into one of the rooms off the corridor. She came back a few minutes later.

"*Herr Doktor* is performing an operation. He will not be available for a long time."

"When is he going to be free?"

"He has many other operations scheduled. I don't know."

Kurt knew that the doctor could stall him for a long time. He would have to locate the Gypsy woman through other channels. He returned to his office and began to check with his colleagues in charge of spying on the Germans. He also arranged for one of his own German informers to enter the hospital as a patient to find out anything he could about the Gypsy and her daughter. In the next few days, he learned that the girl had survived the operation and had checked out of the hospital on the day he had visited there. She and her mother were staying in the apartment of the young receptionist, only a short distance from his office. He rushed there immediately. It was Dzinka who answered the doorbell.

She must have expected someone else, since she was smiling as she opened the door. But when she saw him her smile turned into an expression of fear. He pushed her aside and entered, closing the door behind him with a bang. Through the doorway into the next room, he could see the girl asleep on the sofa, her black hair spread out on the white pillow. Another door led to the kitchenette, and Dzinka stepped inside. He followed her.

It was an early afternoon, and the September sun lit up the clean kitchen, furnished with a small wooden table and two chairs. A pot was on the stove, and the smell of beans and onions filled the little room. Dzinka wore a white, well-pressed summer dress with a tight bodice and low neckline. Her dark skin contrasted with the white linen.

"You here, here, you dark-skinned Gypsy."

"As our saying goes, the darker the fruit, the riper, the sweeter it is," she said, trying to smile, but not succeeding.

"You know why I am here," he said. A big, open box of black coal stood near the stove, and two landscapes hung above it.

"Of course, the gold coin. I will get it in a day or so," she said. She was facing him across the table. There were no other sounds to be heard in the apartment, and he guessed she must be alone with her daughter.

"I came to pick up you and your daughter. I will dispatch you where the two of you belong."

"You can't do that," she said, approaching him. He could practically hear her heart beat and feel her warmth. A delicate aroma of violets surrounded her.

"I can do whatever I want with you, Gypsy whore." He wondered what she would be like on the floor, responding to his lovemaking. She had a pair of good-sized breasts.

"I'll get more gold coins," she cried out.

"Get your kid! Let's go!"

"You can't do that to us." Tears filled her eyes. "You took my money to save my daughter. Leave us alone. I will pay you whatever you want." She quivered. Would she quiver under him when he screwed her? He could do anything with her, whatever he wanted.

"Keep going," he shouted, grabbing her arm. The contact with her skin felt good. She struggled to free herself, shouting as she had that first day, "Leave me alone! Leave me alone!"

His grip on her strengthened. She bit hard at his fingers. He let her go, but her ferocity only strengthened his desire to hurt her.

"I will screw you first," he shouted. The sun was shining on her neck, on her arms. He grabbed her and pushed her toward the coal box and, with all his strength, flung her down. Her fall on the sharp coal must have hurt.

"Oh, oh," she shouted in pain. He lowered his pants and fell on her.

From the other room he heard the child calling, "Mama . . ."

Their faces were close. Her teeth caught his lower lip and she bit. He screamed with pain, tearing her dress. His blood began to spatter her dress. He put his hand against his lip. She struggled and freed herself. He went after her, but she grabbed a large kitchen knife.

The child was crying in the next room, "Mama, come here . . ."

Her dress was torn and soiled with coal dust and stained with his blood. One of her breasts was exposed. Wielding her knife, she attacked him. There was madness in her eyes. She attacked to kill. There was no time for him to get to his revolver. He tried to take the knife from her but the blade cut deep into his hand. He let it go, grabbed a chair with the other hand and threw it toward her, but missed her. He ran to the door out of the apartment. The blood from his lip and his hand dripped onto his uniform. He needed first aid, but that would involve a report and an investigation, and he was not supposed to make arrests alone. He decided to change his uniform and bandage his hand himself. On the street people stopped to look in amazement at the Gestapo man, running like a wounded animal, dripping blood, but he did not pay any attention to them.

In his apartment he washed the wounds, bandaged his hand, covered it with a glove and ran back to his office. By dark he was gathering his troopers to make Dzinka's arrest.

He had a plan. As soon as he entered the apartment, he would shoot the child, so that Dzinka would suffer first, before he killed her.

He and his troopers took a car, and the four of them ran up the stairs. Kurt stopped to knock at the door, and it was opened by the young receptionist who had admitted Dzinka's daughter to the hospital.

"Where are they?" he shouted.

"Who?" asked the receptionist in a quiet voice.

"You know damn well who, the Gypsies."

"What Gypsies? I don't know any Gypsies."

"You admitted them. Don't lie to me."

"You brought them yourself." But Kurt did not listen. The four of them entered the apartment and searched for the Gypsies, but there was no one there except the receptionist.

With the partisans in the woods, it was impossible to search for them now. His chase would have to be postponed. Enraged and hurt, he did not want to give up. He and his men searched the building and the neighboring buildings, but could not find a trace of the woman and her child. They did locate someone who confessed that he had seen a woman and a child picked up by a car with a red cross on it.

The next morning, Kurt organized an expedition of fifty armed troopers. They searched the woods and the area around the spot where he had picked up Dzinka and her sick child. They found traces indicating that people had been living there, but everyone was gone. To give vent to his pent-up hatred, he ordered the arrest of several villagers and dispatched them to the concentration camps. In spite of it all, however, Kurt did not catch Dzinka.

As time passed, the situation on all the fronts continued to worsen for Germany. The Russians launched a new offensive on January 15 of 1945 and occupied Czestochowa a day later. The Germans, who had not expected such speedy progress, remained in Czestochowa with a few exceptions. Kurt was one who remained. When the Russian T-34 tanks were moving along the main street facing his office building, he was ordered to set fire to the files and the building. He executed the order and ran parallel to the tanks to his apartment, where he changed to a civilian suit, picked up his treasure, and tried to escape west. But it was too late to get out of the city. It was a cold, dark night and snow was falling. In the general confusion, he had avoided detection by passing himself off as the Pole he really was, and he managed to hide for the next few weeks in staircases and basements, making his way on foot, finally, the few hundred kilometers to Krakow, which had also been liberated by the Soviets.

He chose Krakow because a distant relative lived there, a widowed woman in her sixties who had once been married to a Pole. She accepted Kurt in her two-room flat, already crowded with six other refugees, and allowed him to sleep in the kitchen. She also helped him to acquire, with two of his coins, a new passport, after he had lied to her that his own had been taken from him by the Soviets.

He had been aware all this time that if he were discovered he would be executed. Never did he feel any guilt for all his activities. He said to himself that in life you are sometimes a winner and sometimes a loser. He had once been a winner. So what? He feared being captured, and at night he thought about the tortures he would face if he were. He was less afraid of the Poles and the Soviets than of the Gypsies, who, with their international network, could catch him anywhere in the world. He knew that in the end they would succeed in capturing him, and that torture and death were in store for him.

But when the war continued for the next few months and ended in early May, he became more hopeful about his chances of survival. He heard of many Nazis reaching South America, and he decided to join them there. His plan was not well formed, but at least he knew how to begin: move west. After the armistice, Poland obtained territories that had been Polish in the eleventh century but that since then had been settled by the Germans. Kurt learned that the Germans living in these areas were being evicted in favor of new Polish settlers coming from all over the country, particularly from eastern Poland. It would be a good place, he decided, for him to hide.

In the early part of June, Kurt reached Danzig. Drinking vodka in a local restaurant, he met a miller who had been looking for a truck driver. Kurt volunteered and got the job. The only problem was that there was no truck to drive. In the fields near all the roads, however, there were many partially destroyed vehicles. The miller, Bronek Chlapczak, who was about Kurt's age but twice his weight and at least a head taller, prided himself on being able to throw a hundred-kilo sack of flour a good distance. Applying his strength, together with Kurt's, they were able to piece together a small truck. It did not matter that the brakes did not function or that there were no lights. The truck moved, and that was all that counted. They drove west, and after a few days' search Bronek discovered an abandoned mill in a village near

Koszalin. There was a store of grain as well. Business began to bloom. Bronek produced the flour and Kurt, his blond hair long now and with an amber-colored moustache, sold and delivered the product on the black market.

The flour that was supposed to feed the growing number of new settlers brought a much better price when sold to the hungry Germans. Kurt derived special pleasure when he exchanged a small package of flour for some cherished family heirloom, primarily jewelry and precious stones. His eyes were well trained to spot the hungriest people standing in the market with their belongings, hoping to exchange them for food. Soon he discovered that the Germans were afraid, and often he would promise them flour, take their jewels, and not fulfill his part of the deal. When they followed him, begging him for the food, he would just shout, "You German murderers, shut up!" And the crowd would applaud.

Once there was a blond girl with dark circles under her eyes, who was holding a fox terrier as emaciated as herself. The girl wanted to exchange her animal for a handful of flour. It was a bright August morning, and in the sun the girl's skin appeared as white as the bark on the birch trees. The market of Szczecin was crowded with Soviet soldiers, German soldiers, Germans, and Poles.

"A handful of flour is too much for this miserable beast," he shouted, trying to take the howling dog.

"Be nice to the Herr," the girl said to the dog, kissing it again and again, weeping as she let it go.

Kurt took the dog, which kept struggling.

"Herr, will you be gentle and good to the dog, please, please? Don't give me the flour, but be good—"

"You aren't going to tell me what to do," he said, laughing at her. "The little pisser will tell me . . . I can do whatever I like," he said, squeezing the dog's neck tighter and tighter until the animal stopped struggling. Then he kicked the dog's dead body and, still laughing, moved on to make another deal on the market. The crowd, watching in silence, did not applaud this time. He looked up at their silent faces with disdain.

Soon the crowd dispersed. Only one person remained, a lone woman who stood looking straight at him. She wore a yellow, flowered dress, her dark hair glowing in the light of the August sun. Her eyes, filled with tears, focused on him. It was Dzinka.

His first reaction was to put his hands around her throat and to strangle her as he had strangled the dog. He moved toward her. He could tell the police that she had been a German spy. Then he remembered that the same police might be interested in a few details about himself, and that might be quite unpleasant.

"You, Dzinka? You survived the war?" he asked, approaching her.

"Does it surprise you?" she asked. "And despite your efforts."

He looked at his hand. In the sunlight he could see the pink scar of his wound.

"Physical wounds heal quickly." She wore high heels and a large-brimmed white hat with a yellow ribbon.

They began to walk away from the market.

"How did you come here?" he asked, thinking that he might manage to get her to one of the wrecked buildings and kill her there. Even if she had not come to kill him or to report him to the police, he would have wanted to kill her.

"Didn't you mean to ask me why, instead of how?" she said, looking at him.

He kept silent for a while, then he said, "I know why." It occurred to him that as a greedy Gypsy bitch she would want first to recover her money before reporting him to the police. That would give him at least a chance to finish her. "I do still have the money."

"I know, and much more," she said. Her statement made him uncomfortable. How could she know that he had survived with all his fortune? The Gypsies must have been following him for some time.

"I will give you the money, all your coins," he said. "And more."

She only shrugged her shoulders.

The bitch came to kill me, he thought. She's not even interested in her money.

"I want to tell you—" she began, but stopped, seeing Bronek waving to them from the truck.

"How many sacks of flour did you give to get that ass?" he shouted.

An idea occurred to Kurt: take her to the mill and drop a hundred-kilo sack on her. Accidents like that occurred often in a mill. That would do it.

"Come along!" he told Dzinka, and helped her to climb to the back of the platform. "I'll give you the money. It's in the place where I live."

Bronek came to get a good look at her.

"Ah, we've got ourselves a good piece of ass," he said. "Let's hurry."

"Good-looking whore," he said with approval as they got in the cab of the truck, Kurt behind the wheel and Bronek next to him.

"Yah," Kurt said, nodding. "Not so young, but a good lay."

The roads were crowded with Soviet military vehicles and long stretches remained in poor condition from the recent fighting. Soviet women soldiers directed traffic, stopping people frequently to check their permits.

"The damn whore's delaying us," Bronek said, "when I am so ready to stick my big one into her."

It was already getting dark as the truck stopped in front of their mill. It was a water mill. Downstairs there was a corridor and a loading area. The sacks of flour and the grain were stored upstairs. Their beds of hay and an iron stove were in the loading area.

"Let's start the party," Bronek shouted as they entered the mill. "Hey, my angel, make a fire and scramble some eggs for us. About twenty each for me and my partner."

Dzinka obeyed, beginning to light the fire. Bronek lit a candle and poured himself a large half-liter glass of pure ninety-seven-proof *spirytus* (alcohol).

"In our family," Bronek said, watching Dzinka making the fire, "there is a tradition." And he laughed. "We drink one gulp a day, never a drop more. You see."

He rose, holding the glass with the alcohol in one hand and another glass filled with water in the other. "Together the two glasses amount to a liter of vodka; look."

Kurt was familiar with this performance. Bronek emptied the alcohol into his mouth, then followed with the water. "Have you seen, my little angel, anything like this before?"

Dzinka shook her head.

"We'll be good friends," Bronek said, winking at her.

Kurt did not like the way things were developing. Bronek would be angry at him if he disposed of Dzinka before Bronek had a chance to make love to her. He could be mad and, giant that he was, he was likely to become dangerous.

"Bronek can drink better than anyone I have ever known," Kurt said.

The two men sat on their sacks of hay while Dzinka was preparing the eggs.

"Hey, my little angel," Bronek said, eyeing Dzinka, who was on her knees breaking the eggs. "You've got a good ass, a swinging ass." He laughed again.

"Yeh, yeh," Kurt said, nodding his head in approval and drinking vodka from a smaller glass. "Dzinka has fire."

He recalled his own attempt to screw Dzinka. The thought occurred to Kurt that it might be Bronek who would kill Dzinka if she refused his advances, and save Kurt the trouble of doing it.

The eggs were ready, and Dzinka put the large pot in front of them. They did not own any plates or silverware, only wooden spoons.

"You may sit with us, my little angel," Bronek said, getting up. He picked up from the corner a loose bundle of clothing the two of them had been *szabrowac* (collecting from the abandoned German houses and apartments). He brought this and placed it near his own bag of hay. There were women's dresses, scarves, underwear.

Dzinka pulled a dress out and sat on the floor between them. The three of them sat and ate in silence. Bronek put his away in big spoonfuls; Dzinka ate more slowly. After Bronek had finished and wiped off the last traces of the eggs from his mouth and chin, he gazed at Dzinka for a while.

"I wonder, I wonder," he said, turning his eyes around toward Kurt, "what color panties the little angel has on."

"I bet she isn't wearing any," Kurt said.

"That's none of your business," Dzinka said, jumping up.

"Not so fast, my little angel," Bronek said, pulling her back down. "The one who is right will be the first to—"

"Let me go," Dzinka shouted, struggling to get free. Kurt remembered his own struggle with her and was happy to let Bronek handle her. It would serve her right.

"Sure we want to find out, my little angel, what is on your

ass," Bronek said, laughing and putting his hand up her dress.

"Help! Help!" Dzinka shouted. She bit at Bronek's nose, and the blood streamed from it. It did not seem to disturb Bronek, who was trying to pull her white panties off. Dzinka managed to free one of her hands and scratched his eye, shouting "Kurt!" Help! Help!"

"It serves you right," Kurt said, laughing at her predicament.

"Kurt! Kurt!" she screamed. "Help! Help!"

Bronek grabbed a scarf from the pile of clothing and, holding her hands, tied it around her mouth and her neck. She kicked and flailed, but Bronek held her tight, and with a single deft movement he tore her dress down the front.

Kurt looked at her face. Unable to scream, she pleaded with her eyes for his help. In the light of the wax candle, her face above the scarf looked white. He saw there were a few freckles on her forehead. At the sight, a strange feeling came over Kurt, a feeling he did not remember having before.

"Stop it!" he shouted at Bronek, who was trying to spread Dzinka's legs. "She is my Gypsy."

"No, no. She is mine," Bronek shouted, succeeding in pulling her legs apart.

Kurt grabbed Bronek by his neck and pulled hard. Bronek clutched Kurt's hand and twisted it, while Dzinka pulled herself free. Kurt managed to free himself also, but Bronek straightened his body and slapped Kurt in the face. They exchanged blows, Bronek shouting, "I will kill you, you whore's son!"

Kurt was no match for Bronek, who was much heavier and stronger. In their struggle, one of them knocked the candle over, extinguishing it; the mill was lighted only by the fire from the stove and the moon shining through the glassless windows. One of Bronek's blows threw Kurt against the wall. Kurt hit the back of his head on a wooden plank, but was aware that Bronek fell on him, and he felt Bronek's sweaty hands on his throat. Kurt was unable to defend himself now. He could not breathe. Suddenly the pressure of the hands was released.

He felt Dzinka's small hand pulling his.

"You must get up," she said. "We must leave."

With her help, he managed to get on his feet. He could see in the moonlight Bronek lying on the floor with a stiletto in his back. Dzinka pulled the blade out, cleaned it on one of the rugs scattered on the floor, and hid it under her torn dress. Kurt was standing, unable to move, his knees shaking.

"We must go, Kurt. We must leave right away," Dzinka told him.

Supporting himself on her, he managed to struggle toward the door and to reach the truck. His shirt, hands, and trousers were wet with his own blood.

"We must drive away," she said, helping him to his seat behind the wheel. She sat down next to him.

He felt weak; his vision was blurred from Bronek's heavy blows. It would be so good to forget everything and to fall asleep.

"Go ahead!" she urged. "Start the truck!"

"Why do we need to go?" Kurt asked. "Bronek is dead. He can't harm you any more."

"The Polish *Bezpieka* [security police] is after you," she said. "I came to warn you."

"You did not come to kill me, not for your money?"

"I brought you one twenty-ruble gold coin. I owe it to you. I swore to give it to you."

"Oh, Dzinka, you did that." Tears filled his eyes and he choked. "Oh, Dzinka."

He started the truck and began to drive. The lights still did not function, but the moon lit the road he knew so well. At first he did not know where to go; then he decided to drive to Bytow.

He had hidden all his gold there in one of the towers of the medieval fortress. They were driving along among the woods and lakes of an area called Swiss Kaszuby. He felt no fear. He felt the warmth of Dzinka sitting next to him, her aroma, and he felt safe.

Seeing one of the lakes at the side of the road, he drove into a field and stopped. They undressed and swam naked in the cool water to wash off the blood. Water lilies grew on one side of the lake, and he made a bouquet of the yellow blooms and gave it to her. She took one of the lilies and wove it into her hair. Kurt looked at her naked body, covered by the drops of crystal-clear water glistening in the moonlight. They sat holding hands. He imagined he could hear the notes of a sonata. The feeling of warmth and beauty overcame him. He did not dare to spoil it with words, not even words of love.

Later the clouds covered the moon, and he had to drive so slowly he could make no more than a few kilometers per hour. They reached Bytow well after midnight. The fortress was near the road, and he parked the truck near the entrance. They walked in through the arched gate, and he locked the thick iron gates behind them. During the war that fortress had been used for food storage, but now only empty cans and a pile of German uniforms remained. They entered an alcove with a low ceiling, and he found a candle and lit it. In its light, Dzinka looked beautiful. He went out and brought a bundle of clothing and spread it on the floor.

"You may sleep here, while I go to sleep in the *Rittersaal* [the room of the knights]." She looked at him, but did not nod.

They stood looking at each other in silence.

"Open up! Open up!" A loud shouting and knocking broke the silence.

"Quick, quick," he said. "I will show you where I hid the gold. You can pick it up later."

"I don't care," she said. But he dragged her toward one of the towers and showed her the brick behind which he had hidden his treasure.

"We will break in," someone was shouting, beating on the gate with a heavy log. "Eisner the Gestapo killer, we know you are hiding there."

Dzinka and Kurt returned to the alcove and sat down on the clothing.

He took her hand, and it quivered. "Dzinka, you still have your stiletto?" he asked, looking in her eyes, the color of a Kaszubian lake reflecting the sun. She nodded.

"Will you kill me with it?"

She sat motionless.

"I don't want to be interrogated, tortured. Will you, please?"

She did not nod, nor did she shake her head.

"Thank you," he said.

"In the beginning of the war, there were four of us, four brothers. The oldest, a cavalry man in the Polish Army, was killed defending Warsaw. The second fell in Africa, the third, Guenther, in Stalingrad."

"Guenther was a poet. He read poetry to me, but then I did not understand. I think now I do! All of us, who lived through these times, will have to find explanations, all of our lives we will attempt to create order out of the chaos of this tragedy, Guenther said. Poor Guenther froze to death, but now I remember his words."

He looked at Dzinka, her head bowed. He thought about her.

"How is your daughter?" he said, putting his arm around her. He felt warm and secure in her nearness. A salvo of machine gun fire echoed through the empty rooms.

"She is fine. She is with the *cumpania.*"

"And you? Will you go back to the *cumpania*?"

"It wouldn't be possible."

"Why?" he asked, kissing her cheek.

"They wouldn't accept me. Never, never again."

"Why not?"

"A *Rom* woman who has made love with a *Gaje*, a non-Gypsy, brings bad luck to the *cumpania*," she said, kissing him.

"But you did not," he whispered.

"No, not yet," she whispered.

He did not hear the shots or shouts outside the castle, but only imagined music as he caressed her body and made love to her. Then everything disappeared. He felt warm and close to her. Slowly the shouts and shots reached his consciousness, but they did not matter. He felt happy and wanted the happiness to last a little longer, forever.

"Please, not yet, not yet . . ." he said, remembering his plea to her.

But it was too late.

"Please, not yet, please . . . I love you. It will take them some time to break down the gate," he said, caressing her hair with the yellow water lily in it.

5

Shaken by Kurt's story, I was reviewing what I could remember of him from childhood when the telephone rang in my room.

"Marcel told me of your wish to get together with me." Bernadette's voice sounded strange and indifferent, as if she had been talking to a creditor who had been bothering her with an invalid claim.

"Yes. I want to tell you what I discovered about one of my friends."

"Not interested, monsieur."

"But listen. It was a Gypsy woman, and there was no special reason, hardly any motive . . . yet she loved that Gestapo man."

"I am sure *that* fellow didn't fall in love with a poster."

"He was bad. He was awful with her, yet she tried to save him."

"Fine. That's as much as I ever want to learn about it."

"So you wouldn't like to see me?" It was obvious to me that she wouldn't, but I still hoped to persuade her.

"It's not a good idea. I am in the process of getting remarried, and my beau is very jealous."

"But I just want to talk, to discuss . . ."

"Why don't you talk to the woman clerk who sold you the print? Marcel told me that you made quite an impression on her."

At that moment I could have killed that gossipy Marcel.

"I haven't seen her since that one time, and I don't care if I ever see her again. But I want to tell you that in the process of studying Kurt's story, I discovered that there was a big contrast between him and his Gypsy."

"Believe me, that's not very original, special, or unique."

I began to realize that perhaps the lion tamer would have characteristics opposite to mine. Actually, it would be hard for me to define my own character. Bernadette, who had known me for so many years, would be the most qualified person to define me. This was possibly my last chance to ask Bernadette to do that, so I did.

After a moment of laughter she said, "It's so obvious: you are a dreamer who lives in a fantasy world, and you are totally undisciplined and disorganized."

I had a feeling that Bernadette was about to end this dialogue.

"So, according to you, assuming that my theory is the correct one, my lion tamer would be well-organized and a realist. In addition, she might be an eager cook, who would inspire me to superb achievements, perhaps in the arts or in literature." I tried to keep our conversation going. "Also, she could be protective, concerned, and, of course, she would have freckles."

"Then, *mon ami*, I could be the lion tamer you are trying to find. Didn't you just finish describing me?"

I hesitated. She was right, but she was not the lion tamer, my lion tamer, whose image I loved.

Feeling my hesitation over the wire she said, "Anyway, I can't help you. *Adieu*, Jan Majeski, and *bonne chance*."

Without giving me the opportunity to say anything else, she hung up. Her adieu sounded quite final, and I realized that I would not be able to see her again. I needed more than ever to find the lady lion tamer.

Since I couldn't pursue my search in Paris, I decided to travel to Poland in the hope of finding some trace of my two remaining friends, Michal and Bogdan.

One of my remaining relatives was Frania, a cousin only a few years younger than I. We had once corresponded regularly, and she had been of great assistance in locating friends with whom I had lost touch during the war.

And, although our correspondence in recent years had diminished to the annual exchange of Christmas cards, she answered my letter announcing my plans with a telegram saying she would meet me at the airport.

The gray-haired woman who met me in the busy terminal had nothing in common with the eight-year-old girl I remembered, except for a pair of deep, green eyes.

I was touched by her gift of a small bouquet of red and white carnations.

In the taxi into the city, Frania told me that she had been a widow for ten years now and was working as a bookkeeper, living in a one-bedroom apartment with her mother. Her only son was now a student of literature at the University of Krakow.

I chose to register at the Forum, one of the newest hotels in Warsaw, and after I had checked in, I invited Frania for lunch.

In the modern, spacious hotel dining room decorated with kilims and Polish folk art paintings, I ordered beef boiled with new dill and potatoes, the favorite dish of my childhood.

As we were served vodka with hors d'oeuvres called *zakaski,* I told Frania what had brought me back to Warsaw after so many years.

She did not seem to understand, and I had to repeat the story of my chance encounter in the poster shop several times.

"What makes you think the woman is in Poland?" Frania asked, whispering, although we were seated at a corner table, several meters away from the nearest diners.

"Oh, it is not likely that she is here," I said, raising my glass to toast her. "Your health, Frania."

"Then what made you decide to look for her in Poland?"

"For some reason I seem to associate her now with some of my childhood friends. I came here to try to find out why."

"Many of your friends," Frania began, then stopped in midsentence as a young, formally dressed waiter appeared with our meal.

"Many of your friends may not be around," she continued, once the waiter had left the table and disappeared into the kitchen.

"Writers—and I am one—have the ability to reconstruct reality from just a few facts," I told her. The pleasant smell of dill rose up from my plate.

"So you plan to write here," Frania said. "I would like to read your work."

"It would probably not interest you," I said, relishing my meal. "Do you know what variety of potatoes these are? They are far superior in taste to the ones I have become accustomed to in France."

"Are there varieties of potatoes?" Frania asked. "As a writer, why should you not look at our country instead of—" She broke off as another waiter passed our table to serve a group of Swedes across the room. They were drinking heavily and chanting songs in their native language, a pleasure that is very expensive in their country.

"I must find the lady lion tamer first. Will you help me to locate the boys?" I recited their names to Frania as I remembered them, and she wrote them on a small, thin piece of paper, then sprinkled tobacco onto it, rolled it up quickly, and put it into her purse.

"Why this strange precaution?" I asked. But Frania motioned to me to keep silent as the waiter approached to ask whether we wished anything else.

"I would like some *prawdziwki,*" I said, remembering the smell of these exquisite mushrooms hardly available in western Europe.

"We don't have them," the waiter said, picking up our plates.

"Isn't it the right season?" I asked, while Frania looked most unhappy with the conversation.

"It is the season, but they are not available in Warsaw. Perhaps you could order them in Zakopane, but not here."

"That is all, thank you," Frania told the waiter, who bowed and quickly disappeared.

"You mustn't trust these people working in the establishments for foreigners," Frania said, rising. Then, "What are your plans for the next few days?" she asked as I walked her to the door. The sound of the Swedish songs followed us.

"The waiter spoke of Zakopane. As a child I used to spend my vacations there. I'll see you in a week or two," I told Frania as she boarded her bus.

That night, after having returned to my room, I spread my poster on the table and began to study it. Through living and writing my friends' stories, I was finding that my lady lion tamer was acquiring a new dimension. Beyond her image, I now sensed a living person, one still surrounded by the mist of many unknowns, but slowly emerging in an increasingly discernible shape. I hoped that my friend Michal's story would add new traits to this image.

The next day I took the train to Zakopane. I had remembered that Michal used to vacation in that part of the country. Slowly and painstakingly, I reconstructed his tale.

Michal did not even blink when the doctor told his parents that unless a dramatic change occurred in his health there was no hope that he might live. The three of them were sitting in Doctor Zarek's office on Floryjanska Street in Kracow.

"Well, what can we do, Adam?" Michal's mother asked, calling the doctor by his first name, since he had been her husband's high-school classmate.

"As you know, I have tried everything, but no medicine seems to help," the doctor said. "You can see for yourself. He continues to lose weight, and that is dangerous. If he loses one more gram we'll have to hospitalize him.

"My advice to you is to take a vacation in the mountains. Fresh air, exercise, regular meals with a good, healthy diet will help—perhaps." The doctor shook his bald head and drew his bushy eyebrows together.

"Of course you are right," Michal's father said, "But where would you recommend that we go for such a vacation?" He was a tall, broad-shouldered man with thick blond hair. He was a successful photographer.

"I would suggest Zakopane, where I go myself," the doctor said. "You could stay there in one of the many *pensjonaty* where you could have spacious rooms overlooking the snowy peaks of the mountains, eat the best French cuisine supplemented by our own good dishes, and be entertained by the sparkling conversation of charming, well-educated and witty hosts."

Michal knew from his father's reports that the doctor had wanted to be a poet when he was young, and he still liked to talk as if he were one.

"I hate small provincial towns," Michal's mother had said.

"Even you, my dear Zofia, would benefit from the mountain air with its aroma of fir trees, roaming on mountain paths, gathering wild strawberries along bubbling mountain brooks, or hunting for mushrooms in the dark woods," the doctor declaimed.

"All that doesn't appeal to me," she declared. And Michal knew very well that his mother would prefer to stay in Krakow during the summer. She was an actress in the theater and liked to be where she could see her many friends. She was a beautiful woman of twenty-seven, much too young to be the mother of a nine-year-old boy.

"Poland's greatest artists, poets, and writers congregate there," the doctor said with a smile. "But you must not forget that you are dealing with acute anemia. Your son is a sick boy."

In 1929, there were not that many *pensjonaty* in Zakopane. Those that did exist had been rented far in advance. So Michal's parents had to content themselves with renting a small cottage, with only one bedroom and a kitchenette.

Michal's shyness, weakness, and poor health prevented him from joining the other boys in their games of soccer, handball, and netball. He did not like to wander with them on the mountain slopes or swim in the mountain brooks. Michal preferred to spend his time with the family occupying the neighboring cottage: Frania, ten; Nina, eight; and their mother, Pani Maria Olsza.

Michal's parents loved to stay up late, discussing with their actor, writer, and philosopher friends the new novels, art, and ideas, drinking many bottles of vodka as they talked through the long evenings. In the mornings, of course, they both slept late, but Michal always woke up early, inevitably with a headache from the smoke that lingered on inside the cottage. He dressed quietly and left the room, stumbling over the empty bottles and clutter from the night before to reach the outdoors and breathe the fresh mountain air.

He would wash his frail hands, his pale face, his head with its close-cropped hair in a large washbowl, and then open his brown eyes to see the sun rising over the mountain peaks.

Michal would hear Pani Maria already up and moving around her kitchen in the next cottage. He would walk over, enter, bow deeply, sit down at the wooden table with its white linen cloth, and follow Pani Maria's movements with his eyes. Her own children never got up until later, but he did not miss them during these mornings. He enjoyed the quietude of the place, the smell of the burning fir wood, the warmth from the stove, and Pani Maria's pleasant smile.

"Did you have your breakfast?" Pani Maria would ask him.

"*Tak, prosze* Pani [yes, madame]," he would lie, looking away from her and blushing. And she would put a hot glass of fresh milk in front of him, a double slice of rye bread covered with a thick layer of butter, and a bowl of wild strawberries sprinkled with powdered sugar.

"Young boys like you can always eat another breakfast," she would say, and Michal, because she watched him, ate the bread, pretending an appetite he did not have.

Sometimes Pani Maria would ask him to bring her some wood from the supply stored against the wall of their cottage. And Michal would rush outdoors, select a few heavy pieces and, pausing to catch his breath from this exertion, would re-enter the kitchen with a smile, looking at Pani Maria standing barefoot in her gabardine coat over her blue cotton nightgown.

"Michal, you are carrying as much wood as a real *goral* [mountaineer] would," she would say, then thank him.

"I shall be pleased to bring some more, Pani Maria," he would say, and bow.

"Oh, not now," she would say. "But thank you anyway. I don't know how we could manage without a man's help in our household."

And Michal would bow and blush again.

Later in the morning the girls would get up and, still sleepy, would eat everything their mother served them.

Later on in the morning all of them would walk the three kilometers to the nearest grocery store, holding hands and singing, and on the way back everyone would share the work of carrying the packages. Michal volunteered to take the heaviest one. The heavy load brought sweat to his forehead, but he strode along with a proud smile. He enjoyed doing it for Pani Maria. And after the brisk walk with the bundles, she would serve them hot tea with lemon, and cookies they all had helped to bake.

Michal always dreaded the moment when he heard the voice of one of his parents, "Michal, Michal, where are you?"

And Michal would bow to Pani Maria, saying, "Will you please excuse me, Pani Maria," and walk reluctantly to his own cottage. He never knew what he could expect from his parents. Sometimes his mother, seeing his muddy shoes, would say, "You are dirty again! Your shoes, your hands, your neck! I just don't know how to handle such a boy. Oh, what a fate!" Raising her hands to the sky, she would complain, "Oh, why is the god of vengeance so cruel to me? Instead of staying with your parents you have to run around, run away from your home, from your own mother!"

At other times she would notice his pale face and say, "My God! What kind of mother am I? The doctor said good, nourishing food. God will punish such a wretched mother."

After such self-reproaches, the three of them would go to one of the most fashionable restaurants in Zakopane, ordering the most expensive dinners, and Michal's mother, with tears in her eyes, would beg him to finish everything on his plate. But he did not like the food in the restaurants; the dishes with the fancy French names he could not pronounce did not taste good to him, and in those moments he missed Pani Maria's simple, tasty cooking. On the way home his mother would buy ice cream for him from the barefoot, moustached vendor who wore a white coat and pushed a cart.

Michal did not like these expeditions with his parents. He much preferred to stay in the neighboring cottage and watch Pani Maria make dough. She would roll it out, and then invite the children to cut out squares, triangles, and circles with cookie cutters. Michal used to let the girls do it first, but Pani Maria would ask him to do it, too, and then she would praise him, saying, "What a perfect circle," telling the girls, "Michal does it with the greatest care." Then Michal would blush, feeling warm all over his frail body, and try to be even more precise in placing the tin form over the thin layer of the cream-colored dough. Pani Maria would then thank the children for their help, shaking hands with each of them, and Michal would kiss her hand, feeling proud of his success and good about it in a way he did not quite understand.

In the evening, when it was getting dark, bedtime for the girls, Michal had to return home where there were often many people, or else no one at all. If there was no one at home, Michal would sit on his bed in the darkness and imagine how Pani Maria would light the kerosene lamp, wash the dishes in its light, put the girls to bed, and read a book.

When he came home and there were guests there, his arrival was often not even noticed, since his parents and their friends would be absorbed in heated conversation. On rare occasions his mother would take him into her arms, kiss him many times, and make a great fuss over him.

"This is my only son," she would say. "Isn't he a wonderful boy?"

The guests would nod in agreement, and after a few moments and a few smiles they would resume their conversation. Michal would put on his nightshirt and close his eyes, but he would still hear the voices. One night, as he tried unsuccessfully to fall asleep, he heard his father saying, "Of course, photography has a great deal to offer to the artist. It opens entirely new horizons for him."

"Nonsense," his mother's voice broke in. "That lousy photography was invented to kill the art of acting. Real acting does not exist in the cinema. It's not possible there."

"Don't interrupt, Zofia," his father said. "I want to stress my point that photography has a feature, let us say, which makes it a superior art. In photography we have the negative. I repeat, we can look at negatives—"

"So what is so special about negatives?" Michal recognized the thin voice as that of a small man with dark bushy hair.

"When you study the negative," his father explained, "you are looking at the reverse of light and shadow."

They were sitting at the table, drinking vodka. Michal could see their faces illumined by the kerosene lamp. All of them smoked cigarettes.

"The same, of course, the same ratio of light and shadow as in the positive," his father continued. "But when you see the same picture in reverse, in the negative, you notice new elements, things you could never see before. And you know why it is like that? Well, I will tell you, Stefan. It's because you are so used to seeing the positive that some things are hidden from you. They are there, but you don't see them."

"Let's forget about the wretched negatives," his mother said. "Let's drink to acting."

"No, I drink to photography," his father said.

"The negative," the voice of the guest said, "is not unique in photography as an avenue of introspection or inspection. An author, a novelist, could look and write . . ."

Michal was falling asleep when he heard the name of Pani Maria, and the mention of her name worked like magic, waking him up and making him attentive to the words spoken around him.

"Of course the likes of Pani Maria Olsza," his father said, "are necessary for society . . . simply for physiological function . . . to . . ." Michal could not understand the word. ". . . to raise children and cook for them."

"But it does not mean," Michal's mother said, "that we have to be exposed to them. How often and how long can you talk about the blueness of bluebells or the redness of red poppies growing wild in the fields? I understand her favorite pastime is to run naked in the woods. I bet you the poor thing has never heard of Shakespeare or Molière."

Michal could not follow the terms of the discussion, but he concluded that they were pitying Pani Maria because she was very poor. And he began to imagine climbing the highest peaks of the Tatra one day and, somewhere on the top, discovering a cache of gold and precious stones. On the way back he would fight Indians and wild beasts and be wounded, but he would make it to Pani Maria's home and offer her the treasures. Then he fell asleep.

It was raining the next morning, and Pani Maria did not take the three children out shopping after their breakfast. Instead they played with a jigsaw puzzle. As more and more pieces were joined, a picture with wild beasts began to emerge. This time Pani Maria did not put her raincoat over her nightgown, since it was still wet from the preceding day. She was sitting in nothing but her nightgown, and to keep warm, she wrapped a cotton scarf around her neck. Her arms were bare, and Michal noticed for the first time that they were covered with freckles.

After the puzzle was finished, Pani Maria began reading to them from a book of fairy tales, but Michal did not listen. The discovery of the freckles pleased and fascinated him. Pani Maria was sitting near the window, and against the daylight Michal could see the contours of her body through the semi-transparent fabric of her gown. He saw her breasts with their nipples outlined under the blue fabric. For a moment the gray clouds disappeared for him and the sky became a translucent blue, the small cottage was filled with all the colors of the rainbow, sparkling and changing in the manner of a kaleidoscope. In his mouth he tasted chocolate and sweets, and he could smell the aroma of lilies of the valley.

When he came the next day to visit Pani Maria, she was wearing her raincoat over her nightgown again. Michal was disappointed. He wanted to see all the colors of the rainbow again, smell the aroma of lilies of the valley, and taste chocolate in his mouth.

That evening his mother noticed his pale face and the dark circles under his eyes. They walked him to the nearest store and put him on the scales.

"My God!" his mother exclaimed. "You have lost two kilos."

"We should take him to the hospital," his father said.

"The first thing tomorrow morning," his mother agreed.

But the next day it was raining again, so both parents slept late, and in the afternoon a few of their friends dropped in. The visit to the hospital was postponed.

A few days later, Michal was strolling with his parents on the lawn surrounding the cottages. It was a sunny afternoon. Not a speck of a cloud could be seen in the sky. The farmers were taking advantage of the good weather to harvest their hay fields. The air was filled with the aroma of fresh hay. Michal saw Pani Maria standing with her daughters in front of their cottage. His mother saw them also and led the way to meet them.

"You look very beautiful today," Michal's mother said. "You have a classical beauty, Pani Maria. You could easily qualify to play the leading role in any of the Shakespearean plays."

"My father used to say the same thing to me," Pani Maria said, blushing. "He was the leading actor in our national theater before his death."

"Your father was right, of course," Michal's father said.

"You are a true beauty," his mother said. "I ought to know."

Michal was not quite sure what they were all talking about, but he gathered that their conversation was a friendly one, that his mother liked Pani Maria, and he felt pleased and proud to have made friends with such a beautiful woman.

Pani Maria was standing barefoot, and her tanned legs contrasted with his mother's silk stockings and high-heeled shoes. His mother also wore a hat and white gloves.

"Very, very beautiful," his mother said. "By the way, Pani Maria. Would it be too much trouble for you if Michal slept in your cottage tonight? We are planning a small party with dancing in ours."

"I would be glad to have him," Pani Maria said.

"Of course he practically lives with you already, dearest Pani Maria," his father said.

"Michal has a very—" and here his mother whispered the rest in Pani Maria's ear. "It may be hopeless," she said aloud.

"Oh, God!" Pani Maria said.

"Before the summer is over, I mustn't forget to give you my portrait, Pani Maria," his mother said. "I will autograph it for you."

That night Michal did not fall asleep for a long time. He could hear Pani Maria's regular breathing in the same room, and from the distance he could hear the laughter, the singing and the music in his parents' cottage. Michal wished to get up and sleep in Pani Maria's bed next to her, but he did not dare.

The next morning he woke early, but he pretended to be asleep, and when Pani Maria got up he watched her body silhouetted through the thin blue semi-transparent nightgown against the light of the dawn. And he imagined her body without the garment. He felt a strangeness he could not understand or define.

As soon as Pani Maria had disappeared into the kitchen, Michal got up and, on tiptoe, ran to her bed and jumped into it. It was still warm and had the aroma of her body, mixed with the perfume of lilies of the valley and the hay and wild flowers of the mattress. He felt good and safe, and something more. He wanted to stay there forever.

When Pani Maria suddenly returned from the kitchen, he jumped down from her bed, fighting to keep from crying, his face turning red.

"Oh, no, Michal," Pani Maria said. "You may stay in my bed. It's all right. I know that the cot can't be comfortable." And Michal obeyed.

His parents had another party the next night, and they asked Pani Maria to keep Michal a little longer. Later they did not even bother to ask her. Michal stayed on and all the next week he watched Pani Maria getting up, then jumped into her bed after she had left for the kitchen.

At the end of the first week, at night, when the girls were already asleep, Michal lay awake in his bed and listened to Pani Maria moving about in the kitchen, washing dishes and perhaps cooking food for the next day. Then he heard the splash of water. On his tiptoes, he approached the kitchen door and put his eye against the keyhole. Pani Maria was standing in the middle of the room and he could see suds covering her naked breasts, but a chair standing in front of the door blocked his view of the lower part of her body. Michal blushed; he quivered and could not catch his breath. She turned around and he could see her naked back. Another turn and her wet breasts, now without the suds, glistening in the candlelight, appeared to him. Trying to see them better, he pressed his face harder against the door, slipped, stumbled, and hit the door with his head. He could not move from fear. He remained at the door as though paralyzed. He could feel the sweat on his forehead and it seemed to him that his heart had stopped beating.

The door opened, and Pani Maria appeared there naked, her body glistening wet, remnants of soapsuds still clinging to her skin. The room with the two girls sleeping in their beds, the stars in the dark sky outside the window—all of it began to turn for Michal.

"Come inside the kitchen, Michal," Pani Maria whispered, putting her finger against her lips and pointing with the other hand to the sleeping girls.

Michal did not understand her at first.

"Come! Please," she repeated, smiling to reassure him.

He followed on legs that felt as though they were made of rubber, and he leaned against the wall for fear of falling down. Pani Maria closed the door and returned to a small wooden tub, only a few centimeters high.

"Michal," she asked, turning to him, "you were looking at the keyhole?" She did not sound angry with him.

He eyed her, trembling and unable to utter a sound. Finally he nodded.

"It's all right," she said, standing sideways now. "It is natural for boys of your age. There is no reason for me, or for you, to be upset."

Michal was still clinging to the wall and trembling.

"When I was as old as you are," she said, applying soap to her arms, "I did the same thing. I played games with the other girls and boys, trying to discover their bodies. We did that in the strictest secrecy for fear of being punished. Children all over the world do the same. It is so natural and beautiful. There is nothing wrong with it."

Michal, listening to the sound of her quiet voice, relaxed. The burning twigs of the fir logs crackled in the stove, giving off their characteristic aroma.

"You could help me," she said. "Will you please hand me the sponge? It's on the table. Yes, nearer to the windows."

Michal picked up the sponge and approached Pani Maria, who turned to face him. In the light of the lone flickering candle, standing now close to her, he noticed that she had dark hair on her lower abdomen. Still holding the sponge, he looked at it as though hypnotized.

"Have you never seen a grown-up woman naked?" she asked, noticing his eyes focused on her pubic hair. She took the sponge from him.

"No, no, nev . . . er, *prosze* Pani," he stuttered.

"As boys and girls grow up, nature provides them with hair in these areas," she said, pointing to her pubic hair.

The aroma of lilies of the valley emanated from her body.

"Did you play doctor with my girls?" she asked.

"No, not at all, *prosze* Pani," he said.

"If you did or do, it will be all right, quite all right. You don't have to feel guilty about it. You don't need to tell me about it."

The soap slipped from her fingers. She bent to pick it up, and her breasts appeared before his eyes like two huge mountains. Then she straightened her body, and again her abdomen with its hair appeared to his eyes.

"Hand me the towel, Michal, please." Michal picked it up and stood in front of her, holding it.

"You could dry me with it," she said.

Michal pressed it against her body and moved it up and down with the care he would have devoted to the holiest of holy tasks.

"You are so good to me," Pani Maria said. "Your fingers are so gentle."

As he moved the towel over her body, his fingers touched the hair below her abdomen, and the contact made him quiver and his face flush.

As soon as he had finished drying Pani Maria, she put her blue cotton gown on, and seeing her clothed made him sad. It was like watching an exciting drama that ends all too abruptly.

"It is time to go to bed," Pani Maria said. "It is late and tomorrow is Sunday. We want to catch the early mass."

The image of the hair between her legs and her naked breasts kept Michal awake for a long time. And the same image stayed with him the next morning, as he sat next to Pani Maria on the wooden bench in the small wooden chapel filled with the odor of the fir trees surrounding it.

Looking at the other women in the congregation sitting in their colorful folk dresses, he began to imagine them naked: to see their naked breasts and the hair between their legs. Also the large statue of the Madonna caught his eyes. She was a woman, a virgin, the priest said. But Michal did not know what it meant for a woman to be a virgin. He knew now that a woman must have breasts, big ones, and hair in the same place where Pani Maria had it. Michal was frightened for a moment at that thought. It must be a terrible sin to think that way about the holy Madonna, and he tried to ban that thought from his head, but the image of her standing naked, her wet breasts glistening in the sunshine, and the pubic hair dark against her white skin, still haunted him. He tried to frighten himself by telling himself that he would go to hell if he continued to imagine it and be boiled alive in a kettle with many other sinners, like those he remembered from one of the holy pictures in a church in his hometown. But despite all the saints looking down angrily at him from their pictures on the walls of the chapel, the harder he tried to ban that image of the naked Madonna, the more it looked like Pani Maria.

Only the end of the mass disrupted his thoughts. Going home, holding Pani Maria's hand, he felt something different in the contact of her skin with his. Perhaps it was because they shared together the secret of what had happened the night before. As they were passing a shady field on the edge of the woods, he saw a few lilies of the valley growing there. He picked them and offered the delicate little bouquet to Pani Maria, who blushed and thanked him, telling him, with her eyes the color of spearmint candy, that she understood his reason for giving her the flowers.

In the afternoon, Pani Maria was cooking preserves while Michal played dominoes with the girls. For a moment Pani Maria's words about playing doctor with them came to his mind, but their flat-chested bodies did not appeal to him. He wanted to play doctor only with Pani Maria.

That same night, when all the children were in bed, he could hear the girls' regular breathing and, behind the closed door, the sound of Pani Maria washing the dishes. As soon as Michal heard the splash of water he began to shake like a leaf during a storm. Pani Maria, still dressed, was pouring the bath water into the tub. He got up and quietly entered the room.

"There you are, Michal," she said, and she did not appear to be angry with him. "You look very scared, Michal. You think that you are doing something very wrong in looking at my naked body, but it is not wrong."

He was not scared of anything, except that she might ask him to return to his bed. He shook as he anticipated seeing Pani Maria in the tub without her clothes.

"The human body is God's most beautiful, most successful creation," she said, taking off her sweater. "At least for us humans it is." Michal sat down, his teeth chattering as if he had a high fever, as he watched Pani Maria taking off her slip.

"You may apply soap to my body, if you like," she said, getting into the tub.

The fir twigs crackled in the stove. His hands quivering, he approached her, and she gave him a cake of soap. Her eyes, glowing in the light of the candle, smiled at him. She knelt down and splashed water on her breasts.

"You see my breasts are bigger than a man's—women's breasts are," she said, and she put his hand with the soap in it on one of them. "How does it feel? How do they feel to you, Michal?" she asked as he, encouraged by her words, touched them with both his hands.

"They feel like a soccer ball, when it's wet," he said, remembering how last Christmas he got one as a present and how it felt. He looked at her, not sure whether he had said the right thing.

"That's very good. I like your comparison," she said, laughing and standing up. "Maybe it's just as well that you did not play doctor with the girls," she said, placing his hands on her stomach. "They might not be ready yet, but their time will come too."

Michal was busy applying the soap to her abdomen. Pani Maria's smiles and her words made him sure of himself, and his hands steadied.

"You should soap there, too," she said, pulling his hands down. The hair felt wiry and strong.

"It feels like a brush," Michal said, and looked again at her to see her reaction.

"You are very observant," she said.

"But it is more than a brush, because . . ." He could not finish his thought, not being able to find the right words to tell her that when he touched an ordinary brush, he had a scratching feeling on his fingertips and nowhere else, but when he touched Pani Maria's hair, down below her stomach, he felt something happening to him everywhere, and especially between his legs.

"You are a great assistant, Michal. You are doing it so carefully. I thank you for your help."

Michal, reassured, moved his hands further down between her legs. His fingers discovered a groove that was soft, warm, and moist, and the wetness was not that of the water. His reaction to this discovery was even stranger than when he had touched her hair. Something very unusual was happening there. It appeared to him that an object was growing on him and it froze.

"I am getting sick, Pani Maria," he said, beginning to shake again.

"What is happening?" she asked.

"Something very wrong, *prosze* Pani."

"Let me see," she said. "Where?"

He pointed out the area. She stepped out of the tub, picked up the candle, and took off his shirt.

"Please don't touch," he said, seeing her stretching out her hand. "You might catch it too, from me."

She lowered the candle and both of them looked at the spot he had been pointing to. Instead of the small earthwormlike object he used to make water, he had a short, hard pencil.

"Oh, God!" Pani Maria exclaimed.

"Oh, I am so sick!"

"No, no, Michal, you are not sick. It is normal, beautiful. A very beautiful thing it is." The candle lighted his pencil.

"And you cannot catch it, get sick from it?" he asked, trembling.

"No, no, no, it is not contagious." Then she laughed. "Perhaps it is, but one cannot get sick from it. I did not know that it could happen at your age," she said, standing up and putting the candle back on the table. "It happens to young and grown-up men. You can be proud of your little *oloweczek* [dear little pencil], to have it at your age. I guess, or rather I am sure, that you are a man, young, but a man."

"What can we do about it?" Michal asked, still frightened.

"Go ahead and wash off my soap," she said, re-entering the tub. "Make additional explorations and it will go away," she said, smiling and spreading her thighs a bit farther apart than before.

With his fingers he touched the same area and it was even wetter than before.

"Nobody else could wash me so nicely," Pani Maria said, sponging off the suds from her breasts, "and with such precision."

As Michal moved his fingers up and down her groove he felt new pressure between his own legs.

"And your *oloweczek* proves," Pani Maria continued, looking down at him and his little pencil, "that you are a real man, like your father . . . a very real man . . . and what you are doing is beautiful, so beautiful . . . here . . . it is . . . it is so natur—"

Pani Maria shivered suddenly as if someone had poured gallons of icy water on her, and where he was moving his fingers she quivered violently.

"Oh, oh, oh," she murmured, breathing deeply.

"Did I hurt you?"

"Oh, no, no . . . oh no, it was so beautiful . . . so natural. I did not expect it . . . So pure without bad thoughts." In the room, the aroma of her body mixed with that of the burning beeswax candle, flickering now from her breath.

For a moment Pani Maria acted strange. She took him in her arms, raised him high, kissed his cheeks, looked at his *oloweczek*, touched it, and took it in her hand.

"It is so wonderful, your *oloweczek*, but I am afraid to abuse it. I might harm it. It is so delicate." She pressed his body against her. "You don't know how happy you made me." She put her nightgown on and began to button it up. He put his on too.

Michal felt a surge of sadness as she was getting in her bed.

"May I come to your bed?" he whispered. She did not answer.

"Just for a tiny little moment?"

"Yes, you little liar," she whispered. "You are quickly acquiring the habits of grown-up men."

As he approached her bed, she took off his shirt, whispering in his ear. "We will not get cold sleeping together." And she opened all the buttons of her nightgown.

The contact with her breasts and her body felt good. Michal felt safe and secure and warm and soon fell asleep.

The next morning as he entered the kitchen, Pani Maria was ready with his breakfast. Their eyes met for a moment, and she blushed a little. This was the first breakfast he had eaten with appetite. He asked her for a second and a third slice of bread, and he drank three glasses of milk. Then he took a long walk by himself, passing by cottages that he had avoided before, fearing that the boys who lived there might beat him up. And when he saw the boys he looked at them with contempt, saying to himself, "I bet you that you don't have an *oloweczek* between your legs, and that you could not touch and be gentle with Pani Maria and make her shiver and be happy, make everything natural and beautiful for her."

And if the boys wanted to fight with him, he was ready. Should they say anything about Pani Maria, he would hit them and kick them. He would even fight with his father.

Around noon he stopped to visit with his parents. They were still in their beds, but not asleep.

"You are here?" his mother asked.

"Pani Maria finally chased you away," his father said, getting up in his pajamas.

"Do you want to eat something? You should, I guess," his mother said. "You must have lost some more weight."

"I'll eat there," he said. He did not say *at Pani Maria's*, just *there*.

"That's fine with me, of course," his father said.

"I would like to take some food there," Michal said.

"There is not much here, but you are welcome to it," his mother said. "We have some cans of sardines and some canned fruit."

"They would not touch anything in cans."

"I knew that she would ask for—" his mother started.

"Nobody asked me for anything," Michal shouted. "Nobody!"

"All right, all right. Take whatever you want," his father said. Michal put a large jar of honey, some sugar, salt, and dried peas in a brown bag, and he carried it with a smile of triumph to Pani Maria's cottage.

"Why did you bring these things?" Pani Maria asked. "I don't need them."

"It's a present from my mother," Michal said.

After lunch, Pani Maria served bread and honey, and Michal ate three slices. Since the girls decided to play with their dolls, Pani Maria suggested to Michal that he accompany her for a walk in the woods. After walking for half an hour, they reached a clearing where the grass was studded with bluebells in bloom. It was a warm, sunny afternoon.

Pani Maria took off her dress and helped Michal to take off his clothing as well. Her nude body looked different than it had in the light of the candle. Her skin looked whiter, her hair lighter, and her eyes looked like the water in the mountain brook reflecting the young fir trees. He loved to look at her body, but it was different for him than looking at her at night. He did not want to touch her now, only look and look at her. It was like looking at the Christmas tree in the public square, big and beautiful with thousands of candles that Michal could admire forever.

"Try to catch me," Pani Maria said, and she began to run. He followed her. At first she circled the little clearing, then chose the rocky bed of a dried-up mountain brook and ran uphill. He tried to catch her, but she managed to stay ahead of him. After a few minutes, she reached a large rock that barred her way and, as she hesitated, he caught up with her.

Both of them were breathing heavily, and they lay down on the flat rock. The rays of the sun cut into the deep shadow of the fir trees and lighted parts of their bodies. For a while they lay in silence listening to the wind agitating the tops of the trees and to the songs of unseen birds.

"In the early part of the summer, water flowed over this rock and I saw the brook trout in it," Pani Maria told him.

"Did you come here before?" Michal asked, touching her hand.

"Yes, I did come here alone, often," she said, and she took his hand.

"On the edges of this brook, there were gentians and daisies, and now there are ferns, maidenhair ferns. They are so delicate. I like them very much."

His hand in hers felt good. He looked at the ferns, and then at her legs, covered with freckles, and the hair between her legs.

"You are more beautiful than those ferns, Pani Maria," he said.

"You don't have to call me Pani Maria," she said. "Call me Marysia. My father used to call me Marysia, and I like it."

"Marysia, Marysia, I don't dare," he laughed. "But I will try to call you that." He moved closer to her and leaned against her. Her skin was moist and warm, and it felt good to be so close to her.

"Are you so nice to me, Pa—Marysia, because I am sick?"

"You are not sick any more, Michal," she said, turning her head and looking up at the tops of the trees and beyond, at the pale blue sky. "There might have been an element . . . of concern for you in the past. I mean, I acted as I did now and then because I felt compassion for you. But not any more. I don't want to think about or analyze my feelings for you, to draw any conclusion about them or put them in a category and attach a label to them. That would be tampering with what is most beautiful and dearest in the world. It could spoil the spontaneity and purity. I can tell you, my Michal, that when I used to come here I felt lonely, and I don't feel lonely now. And often I used to feel very lonely with many people around me."

"I wouldn't like—Marysia, for you to go away, ever," Michal said, raising his head to follow her gaze through the black tops of the fir trees to the blue sky above them.

6

In the crowded train back from Zakopane, I reflected on Michal's story. This was my fourth investigation into the loves of my old schoolmates and, by now, I should have been able to draw some conclusions about the object of my own desires.

It was a sunny autumn day. Some of the leaves were still on the trees. But it had snowed in the mountains and was cold. Would my lady lion tamer, like Pani Maria, run naked in such weather?

As the train moved slowly through valleys and hills into the plains, my thoughts turned less optimistic. Suppose that my lady indulged in such extravagant activities, but kept them to herself. No one would know of them. Besides, it might be that such behavior wasn't so unusual among circus people. How would it be for me to go around asking, "Did you ever encounter a young woman who likes to cook, is well-organized, devoted to her lovers, and likes to run naked?" Such an interview would certainly generate laughter in the respondents. I needed to find my last friend Bogdan and learn about his love. It was possible that his story would be the great breakthrough I had been hoping for. Of course, it could be that my hypothesis was entirely wrong and my lady lion tamer didn't possess any of the features I was trying to establish for her. I would be wasting my time and would never be able to find her. But despite such doubts, I was still quite positive.

Upon my arrival in Warsaw, I was surprised and pleased to see Frania waiting for me at the station. I had asked her to make my hotel reservations for that date, but didn't expect to see her there. After we exchanged greetings, she handed me a parcel. It was a book *Artisten und Zirkusplakate* (Performers and Circus Posters). Immediately I began turning the pages feverishly, looking for my lady lion tamer's poster.

"She is not in the book," Frania said as we sat in a taxi. "But I thought it might give you some ideas that would help you in the search."

It was a recent publication of an East German house. None of the reproduced posters were photographs. The only poster of a lady lion tamer was that of Margarita Nazarowa, a Soviet *dompteuse.* It carried the date of 1968. Could that be my lady? My heart began to beat hard, but my elation was short. Nazarowa's name appeared in the book among outstanding performers, and her birth date was 1926. That couldn't be my lion tamer.

"Disappointed?" Frania asked.

I nodded.

"You will also learn from the book that the first lion tamer, a Frenchman, was born in 1793 in Marseilles, that the first circus posters were developed by a Mr. Barnum in America, and that some great artists designed circus posters, including Toulouse-Lautrec—nothing very helpful to you. However, you will see, at the end of the book, a list of the collections from which the posters in this volume have been selected."

Frania was right. There were several institutions mentioned, like Circus and Varieté Museum in Leningrad, World Circus Museum, Baraboo, U.S., and Zirkus-Archiv Tierpark in Berlin. I was delighted with this information and was so grateful to my cousin that I put my arms around her and kissed her on her cheeks, saying, "I will write to them immediately, send them a Xerox copy of my poster, and inquire whether they have it in their collection."

"I don't think that you'll be successful, my dear. I bought you this book more as a souvenir of your temporary obsession, which I hope will pass . . ."

"Why do you say that? I'll find her."

"Perhaps. But while you were away, I made some enquiries of some circus people here I met through friends of friends. According to them, there are only a few wild-animal tamers around the world. They are a close fraternity. If your lady were one of them, it would not have been hard to identify her and then locate her."

"But she was photographed taming a lion," I said, looking at the sparsely lit streets, where there were still many people rushing about.

"She could have been a model," Frania said, indicating with her head that we were approaching my hotel. "None of the people I talked to had seen a poster with a green lion, and they would certainly know if one had been used."

We arrived, but I wanted to continue my conversation with Frania, so, after having checked in, I invited her to the same restaurant where we had eaten a few weeks before.

"I am still trying to find a trace of Bogdan," I said, as I sat down and picked up the large menu.

"I have some leads."

"Oh, Frania, thank you! How wonderful!" In my excitement I dropped the menu on the floor. "I'll be grateful to you for the rest of my days."

"Your joy may be premature."

"When can I see him?" I said, and called the waiter to order champagne. I told myself that finally, in addition to having her image on the poster, I had her psychological profile almost complete.

"I am eager to help you," Frania said, ignoring my question, "because I know that only finding her will cure you of your fantasy. Being of the same family, I understand you, and in a way I sympathize with your state of mind."

"Then you should know that I will love her forever." The waiter brought champagne and worked on opening it with as much ceremony as if we were about to consecrate the launching of a full-fledged Polish armada. Frania stopped talking.

"To my lady and to love, forever," I said, raising my glass.

"*Na zdrowie*—to your health and your future!" Frania said, joining the toast. "I hope that everything will be all right. I hope that one day you will meet some nice Polish girl, start a family, take your children for picnics, to the parks, the zoos."

For a moment, an image of strolling on some sunny street with a couple of little girls appealed to me. I saw myself buying them balloons and candy, the girls happy and smiling. But I quickly dismissed this picture from my mind. There was no lady lion tamer in it, and I grew frightened.

Frania went on extolling the benefits of family life. It was hard for me to concentrate. I had to devote myself to Bogdan now, and to what I could learn from his love story.

Frania told me that Bogdan had been in Pruzhany in 1939, a town that had been invaded by the Red Army in that very year. She learned the whereabouts of a few people who had lived there at the beginning of the war. The next morning, I began to meet with them and to eke out the most remarkable account.

Bogdan could not keep his eyes off the woman who was to teach them Russian, from the moment she printed her name—TATYANA LVOVNA—in large Cyrillic letters on the blackboard.

That task accomplished, she turned to the class and smiled, pulling nervously at her green woollen scarf.

His heart began to pound, and the poorly ventilated, drab classroom turned into a paradise.

Bogdan could not tell why this change occurred, whether it was because of Tatyana Lvovna's eyes, the color of an Arctic lake reflecting the Siberian tundra, her delicate silhouette, like that of a young willow tree vulnerable to the slightest breeze, or because of the sprinkling of freckles across her little nose. Nor did it matter to the seventeen-year-old youth that she was at least twice his age, or that she had come to this Polish high school from the Soviet Union, the enemy that just a few weeks ago had attacked Poland, occupying half of his fatherland even as it was fighting off the German invaders. It did not matter that she was a communist. He knew only that when her eyes smiled at him he could forget that he was a refugee, living with his mother in a small room, in a town where they had no friends or acquaintances; that they survived by selling their meager belongings little by little; that his father, an officer of the Polish army, had either died or been captured; and that his country had been raped by the two successive invaders.

All that mattered was that when she was in the classroom he felt safe and happy.

Tatyana Lvovna was not the typical Soviet woman, squarish and self-assured. On the contrary, it was easy to detect the fear and uncertainty in her manner beneath the disguise of her eager smile. And Bogdan was aware that she understood how unwelcome she was in this classroom.

The other Polish students expressed their animosity toward the stranger by constantly carrying on loud conversations, or stomping on the wooden planks of the floor with their boots, or by ignoring her to study the pattern of the rain drops on the window pane. Tatyana Lvovna tried hard to penetrate their indifference, and, knowing that most of the students did not understand Russian, she patiently translated into Polish many of the words she used, often provoking bursts of laughter at her heavy Russian accent.

"In Russian we often insert a vowel," she said, "that is missing in Polish. We say, for instance *korova* [cow], Polish *krova; moloko* [milk], Polish *mlyeko.*"

"*Mlyeko, mlyeko,*" a tall, muscular fellow with broad shoulders and close-cropped hair repeated in his deep voice, and everyone giggled maliciously at her difficulty in pronouncing the Polish word *mleko.*

"There are words that differ in origin: Russian *tchernilo* [ink], Polish *atramyent.*"

Again there was laughter at her inserting the same extra sound in the word *atrament.*

But Bogdan never laughed. He followed every movement of her slender hands, every curve of her lips when she smiled, every frown that creased her forehead. He was sorry when the class bell announced the end of her lecture, and Tatyana Lvovna erased the Russian words from the blackboard with her sponge, covered her blond hair with a white beret, donned her heavy overcoat, bowed lightly to the class like an actress in a provincial theater, and exited from the classroom, holding her bereted head high as if she had just received resounding applause.

During recess, Bogdan tried to get another look at her. He pushed his way through the narrow, crowded corridors and walked out of the school building, but he could not find her.

That night, lying awake on his narrow couch, too short for his long legs, Bogdan imagined that he was sitting with Tatyana Lvovna on a bench under an old oak tree looking down into her smiling eyes. In his mind it was an autumn afternoon, and the wind scattered the golden leaves around them. She was trying to tell him something but he could not understand what she was saying. It did not matter, though, because he stood, gathered her up in his arms, and carried her tenderly through the muddy streets of Pruzhany to a small villa with marble stairs, down which came the sound of someone playing a Chopin nocturne.

As Bogdan continued to attend Tatyana Lvovna's lectures, he slept less and less and his imaginary visits with her became more intimate. After the second lecture he imagined that the two of them were in a small boat on a Siberian lake full of white lilies, and she appeared to be frightened.

He moved closer to her, put his arms around her, and she kissed him. After the third lecture, he imagined, she allowed him to kiss her breasts, and after the fourth he imagined that she had invited him to her villa, which was like a Venetian palazzo, where, on a Persian silk rug, he kissed every inch of her body, and she agreed to be his. It was a little difficult for him to imagine this last scene, since in real life he had never made love before and his only knowledge of it had been gained secondhand from his school friends in his native Czestochowa, a town now occupied by the Germans.

As Tatyana Lvovna's lectures progressed, the student began to enjoy her way of teaching. Every word, every sentence she spoke with gestures in the intonations of an actress in a Chekhovian drama. When she said a simple sentence—"I like to drink tea with my good friends"—one could imagine her sitting at a table and flirting with some gloomy-looking squarish men with beards and moustaches, wearing czarist uniforms. Bogdan followed every tone and inflection of her voice, every expression of her face, every pose of her fragile body. And the more he listened and watched her, the deeper he fell in love with her. During her fifth appearance, Tatyana Lvovna began reciting Lermontov's short poem, "The Sail," and she spread her green scarf between her arms to demonstrate the impact of the wind on the sail. Seeing Tatyana Lvovna, her arms outstretched to spread the scarf, her bare neck covered with freckles, her eyes and face expressing the horror of the lonely sailing ship searching for the storms and the hurricanes, Bogdan had an almost uncontrollable desire to run up to her and kiss her. This desire was so strong that he had to hold on to his bench with all his strength to keep from doing so. The only way he was able to resist was to promise himself to see her later, to catch up with her after school. So as soon as Tatyana Lvovna had bowed to the class, a little deeper than usual, put the green scarf back around her neck, struggled with her heavy overcoat, and walked out with a smile of triumph, Bogdan skipped the next lecture to follow her.

Pruzhany, he had learned, was situated in the center of the largest swamp in the world, and this year, to anyone who had not lived there from birth, it appeared that the fourth week of rain would surely sink the town into the swamp itself. Since the streets were unpaved, the mud was knee-deep in places. The only way to avoid sinking into it was to proceed carefully along a narrow, poorly maintained, wooden sidewalk that was missing many boards; those that were left were so rotten that they would not support the weight of pedestrians. But Bogdan ignored the hazards of the rickety sidewalk as he hurried after Tatyana Lvovna. It was already dark, and he was afraid that he might lose her in the murky drizzle.

"Will you excuse me, please?" he asked, trying to catch his breath as he caught up with her.

She stopped, adjusted her beret over her wet hair, and looked at him inquiringly.

"I would like to carry your bag," he puffed, out of breath from the pursuit.

"But it isn't heavy. It is almost empty," she said. He looked forlorn, and for a moment they stood in silence, getting wetter by the minute. "However, since you seem so disappointed that my bag is empty, please go ahead," and she handed him the bag. "I am not used to such gallantry, my—in Polish—*rycerz* [knight]—in Russian—*rytsar,* almost the same word. Since our destiny and more specifically the narrowness of the wooden planks do not allow us to walk side by side, and since you do not know the location of my castle, I will have to go ahead."

He followed only a few steps behind her, discerning the contours of her white beret with difficulty. In a matter of minutes they reached her "castle," a small, one-story house with a dilapidated wooden porch.

"Much obliged," she said. "I always have admired Poles for their chivalric behavior—in their literature."

The drizzle began to turn into a rain as she raised her hand to bid him goodbye.

"Excuse me, please," Bogdan said. "But I have to tell you something very important, something vital." Bogdan tried to make out the expression on her face, but it was too dark. He stepped aside to see her from another angle and sank to his ankles into the mud.

"Maybe some other day, at school, or here," she said, "when my chambers—oh, I am sorry, you seem to be disappearing into the mud."

"Oh, please, Tatyana Lvovna, please, it is private, very private." He managed to extract himself from the mud and to reach the first wooden step on her porch. "I must see you now, Tatyana Lvovna."

"So let it be," she said, walking up the five steps. He followed, trying to shake the worst of the sticky mud from his shoes and trousers. She entered a long, narrow corridor lighted by a small kerosene lamp standing on a wooden bench. There must have been other people in the house, for, from a distance, Bogdan heard female voices and laughter.

Tatyana Lvovna opened the first door to the left, and he entered. For a moment she stood in the darkness, searching in the pockets of her overcoat for a match. When she found it, she lit a candle. It was a beeswax candle, and it spread its pleasant aroma around the tiny room furnished only with the bare necessities. Since there was no bookcase, books and papers were lying on the floor. In the middle of the room was a small iron stove, in which the wood must have been arranged in advance. Tatyana Lvovna lit it, and when it began to burn, it added its light to that of the candle. However, the room remained as cold and damp as a deep cellar.

"Take off your coat," she said, adding more wood to the fire. "You can hang it on the hook in that corner, but be careful where you step. You might ruin the literary work of your classmates. And of course tell me, tell me, please, this vital and private matter of which you spoke. I am dying to hear it."

Bogdan was standing in the middle of the room, dripping mud from his trousers and shoes and creating a brown puddle.

"Will you sit down, please, Tatyana Lvovna?"

"Oh, you are assuming that I, weak, ephemeral being that I am, will faint when I hear what you have to tell me," she said, moving her hands and body flirtatiously. "Just a few more twigs and I will be ready to listen to your secret."

Bogdan did not take his eyes off her. At this moment, she reminded him of someone he had known. He had the impression that he was with some very dear and familiar woman, and it made him feel strangely secure and happy. He wished that he could stay there forever.

There was only one wooden chair in the room, and she reserved it for him, sitting down herself on the edge of her bed and turning her face to him. The door was closed, and only a faint echo of the voices could be heard now in the room, but the monotonous sound of the raindrops beating against the glass of the window had intensified. Tatyana began to take off her overshoes.

"I am sitting now," she said, straightening her slim figure.

"That's good, thank you, Tatyana Lvovna. I . . . I . . ."

She smiled at him encouragingly, a smile he realized she must have used often to her students as she encouraged them to recite their assignments.

"Will you sit down, please?" she said, still smiling. "It might be easier for you if you were comfortable."

He obeyed.

He wanted to tell her that he had fallen in love with her from the first moment he had seen her smile, but he did not dare for fear that the words might offend her.

"I . . . I . . . want to marry you," he blurted out, surprised by his own statement.

For the moment, she appeared not to understand.

"Marry? Marry whom? I did not catch it."

"You, only you, Tatyana Lvovna," he said, and sighed with relief.

Now she understood him, and she was stunned. She opened her mouth to say something, but changed her mind, closed her mouth, and searched for the right words to say.

"But that's impossible! How did you get such an idea into your head? I could be your mother; I am your teacher, and I am married and the mother of two girls." She rose and began to pace back and forth, trying to avoid the books and papers scattered on the floor.

"Nevertheless, I will marry you, Tatyana Lvovna."

"But you are being quite irrational," she said, looking at him as if she wanted to ascertain whether he was drunk. "I don't even know your name." She opened the button at the collar of her khaki shirt, as if she needed air. Her cheeks turned red.

"My name is Bogdan Mrozowski."

"Oh, yes, you are in the seventh class, the boy—excuse me, the young man in the third row sitting next to the window. But why on earth do you want to marry me, Bogdan?"

"I love you, Tatyana Lvovna," he said.

"Love . . . love . . . But do you understand . . . well . . . these are the most beautiful words in any language. It is like hearing sweet music, walking at dawn through a field of wild red poppies and inhaling their aroma. Love. You hardly know me. I arrived here only two weeks ago. You have seen me only two or three times."

"Five times," he said. "Five times."

"And when did it occur to you that you loved me?"

"The first moment I saw you, of course."

Tatyana blushed again. The fire began to heat up the room, and Bogdan was not sure whether it was because she had mentioned the red poppies, but he began to smell the aroma of these flowers, and for a moment it appeared to him that beyond the wet glass of the window were not muddy streets, but a sunny field covered with red blossoms.

"Of course, love is the most beautiful feeling in the world, the only thing worth living for, and all that you are saying is quite . . . flattering to me, Bogdan."

Bogdan lowered his head. He could see her knees covered by poorly mended stockings.

"Then will you marry me, Tatyana Lvovna?"

"One day, one day I—never mind," she said. And, moved and excited by her own words, she stood up on the bed. "One day you will remember this as one of the most ridiculous episodes of your youth. I can see you now, holding in your arms a girl with large eyes the color of the cornflowers growing among the golden Polish wheat, and smelling of Parisian perfumes. You will whisper into her ear, 'I will throw at your feet these Polish *haberki* [cornflowers], Russian *vasilki,* a different word,' and you will tell her in an emotional voice, 'I love you; I've never said these words before . . . except to my poor old teacher, in a moment of youthful imbecility!' "

The tears came to her eyes, and standing on her bed she spoke the words as if she were addressing a large audience and not merely her student, a narrow-shouldered boy of seventeen with bushy hair, dressed in a suit that he had long outgrown.

"Go into the great, wide world, and any girl will be happy to go out with you, to follow you, and be your faithful companion."

"I don't want any other girl. I don't want to tell any other woman I love her, because I will love you and only you, forever, Tatyana Lvovna."

"You will find a girl pure of bitter and painful experiences," she said, wiping her tears away with the sleeve of her shirt. "And, holding hands, you will march together down the road of life strewn with the petals of white roses and drinking the heavenly wine from the glass (*ryumka* in Russian, *kieliszek* in Polish, two different words, both from the Germanic, *kieliszek* from *Kelch, ryumka* from *Roemer,* a large wine glass), yes, from the glass of eternity." She stopped and giggled. "*Kieliszek* sounds funny to me," she explained, giggling again.

At that moment there was a knock, the door opened, and a plump young woman with a broad face and slanting eyes appeared. Seeing Tatyana standing on the bed and laughing, she stopped on the threshold and her mouth dropped open, showing two rows of perfectly white teeth.

"*Batyuskhi* [fathers], what is going on here?" she stuttered.

Tatyana blushed again, jumped down, and said, "I will allow you three guesses, no more, just three. And I give you only ten seconds to make them. Then even if you torture me and put my hands in the fire I will not tell you the truth, Olya, never, never, not even in a hundred years!"

"You were teaching this young man—reciting poetry, perhaps?"

"No, no, quite wrong. This young man came here to tell me that he loves me and that he wants to marry me." She laughed gaily. "You would never have guessed that, would you? And what do you say to that? Go ahead, make a comment! I want to hear what you think."

"I am ready to celebrate your wedding, Tanya. Or anything else," Olya said. "In the meantime you and . . . this young man are cordially invited to have tea with Vera and me."

"Of course, Olya," Tatyana said. "Lead the way. I will follow you to the end of the earth for a cup of hot tea." And, turning to Bogdan, she added, "Of course, my young friend, you are free to go, if you wish to abandon your frail, aging teacher and go out into the world of youthful frivolity and merriment."

"I would like to go with you, Tatyana Lvovna, wherever you go."

"It is only a few meters," Olya observed. "So this time, it should not be too difficult for the young man to fulfill such a promise."

Olya's room was a little bigger than Tatyana's. There were two beds and a large table covered with a white linen cloth. The water was boiling in a cast iron pot. A heavy, middle-aged woman with graying hair stood at the table slicing a pickle.

"I don't know what I would have done without the two of you," Tatyana said. "I am like a butterfly fluttering in the morning breeze, unconcerned with the realities of daily life, while you two busy bees provide me with everything."

In comparison with the other two Russian ladies, Bogdan could see, Tatyana looked very frail. Her narrow face, her shoulders, and her hands were half the size of the others. Bogdan was touched by the comparison. He involuntarily flexed his muscles and felt suddenly strong, very strong. He wanted to use his strength to protect and defend Tatyana, even though she did not seem at the moment to be in any need of such service.

"Do you know, Vera, what just happened to me?" Tatyana asked. "Bogdan declared his love for me. And his declaration was accompanied by a proposal of marriage. Of course I am in seventh heaven, or whatever the number of the best heaven might be. I am floating on a silvery cloud of happiness." Tatyana stood, raising her arms toward the imaginary cloud high in the skies, opening and closing her eyes.

"Tanya, Tanitshka, sit down," Vera said, "and tell us what you plan to do about this proposal."

Tanya did as she was told, and, lowering her head until her forehead almost touched the edge of the table, she said, "All happiness is destined to be brief, to break up like a soap bubble in the midst of its flight. When the rays of the morning sun strike the mist over Pruzhany, our happiness will be over."

"It is still a good many hours until dawn," Vera said. "In the meantime drink to your happiness with a cup of hot tea."

Vera must have been about fifty years old. She had pleasant features, a pair of blue eyes, and a high forehead. She appeared to Bogdan to be a reliable and trustworthy person.

"Oh, yes, one must pluck happiness," Tanya said, raising her head and spreading her arms, "like a bunch of fresh cherries. One day the frost will come and kill the bliss."

"Will you help me, please, Vera—" Bogdan asked. "I am sorry. I don't know your second name."

"Vera Petrovna. Help you?"

"Yes, Vera Petrovna," Bogdan said. "Help me to persuade Tatyana Lvovna to marry me."

"Oh, you want to make me your marriage broker," Vera said, laughing. "It is a little old-fashioned, a relic of the czarist time, a profession banned in the Soviet Union, but one could revive it."

"Do it, Vera. Do it, please," Olya said, pouring the tea. "Maybe you could convince Bogdan that I am a better prospect for him, since I am single."

"But I love only Tatyana Lvovna," Bogdan said.

Tanya glanced briefly at him, and he got the impression that she was pleased with his decisive answer.

"Love is inviolable," Vera said. "One cannot tamper with it." She put a well-buttered piece of bread on Bogdan's plate. "It is not like a potato that one can throw out of the window."

Bogdan was pleased to hear those words, with their indication that he had an ally.

"You could arrange a divorce," Bogdan said. "And later on our marriage."

"There are minor matters to discuss," Olya said. "Tanya is old enough to be your mother. Have you thought about that?"

"There is nothing to think about," Bogdan said, biting into the bread. "I am not asking for Tatyana Lvovna as an object for resale, like *krova, korova,* where it would have been important to know how much *mleko, moloko* she would produce in her life time."

"I like my suitor's simile," Tanya said. "It is practical, down to earth." She sighed. "Notice that he did not compare me with a bouquet of roses, mere flowers that will *zvyednoch* [wilt], Polish, *zavianut,* Russian, two words of the same origin."

"There are some practical matters to discuss," Vera said, laughing. "Like, how are you going to feed your future wife, Bogdan? One does not feed even a nightingale with fables."

"He is lucky on that score," Olya said. "Tanya eats so little."

"Did you consider, Bogdan," Tanya said, "that I might be like one of the heroines in Dostoyevski's novels: you will love me and I will torture you, devour you, and then in guilt for my behavior, I will give you my soul, heart, and especially my body?"

"As soon as we are liberated by the French and the English, we will move to my home town," Bogdan said. "I will work there."

Bogdan looked at Tanya and noticed how her eyes in the light of the kerosene lamp looked darker, like the surface of one of the many ponds around Pruzhany, reflecting the trees with their autumn foliage.

"The prospect of a capitalist life should appeal to you, Tanya," Olya said. "Maids, chauffeured limousines, five, or even more, dresses; maybe even another coat."

"I can see it all," Tanya said, laughing. "On sparkling parquet floors, groups of servants are milling around me, the frail being, executing with a smile my most outrageous and capricious wishes."

"You are not a Catholic?" Bogdan asked.

"She is not," Olya said.

"That's excellent," Bogdan said. "Were Tatyana Lvovna a Catholic, she could not get a divorce and marry me."

"Of course you will insist that the marriage be in the Catholic church," Olya said.

"Of course," Bogdan said. "Tatyana Lvovna will be converted to Catholicism."

"Couldn't she remain Russian Orthodox, atheist, or whatever she is?" Vera asked. "True love is supposed to be blind, and one should disregard such matters as political and religious convictions."

"We'll be living in Poland, a Catholic country," Bogdan said. "I am Catholic so Tatyana Lvovna will be Catholic too."

The tea was weak, but it tasted good, and Vera put out a plate of black currant preserves.

"Why should she become a Catholic," Olya asked, "if she does not believe in God?"

"She must become a Catholic in order to go to Heaven," Bogdan said. "Our priest in Czestochowa told us that the best way to reach Heaven is as a Catholic. Why shouldn't Tatyana Lvovna take the best path?" Bogdan remembered that particular lecture quite well. Father Stronski had made it very clear to them, even putting it on the blackboard: for Catholics the road to Heaven was a thick chalk line, for orthodox Christians it was a thinner line, for Lutherans a dotted line, and for other denominations there was no way to reach Heaven at all.

"You are making it very tough on your marriage broker," Vera said. "I don't know whether I would be able to make bread from this flour."

"At least he is sincere," Olya said. "Any other requirements?"

Bogdan looked at Tanya again. She seemed sad.

"You are taking all this conversation so seriously, Bogdan," Tanya said. "And all of us old women are only making fun. I feel terribly guilty. It is irresponsible on my part, as a mature woman and a teacher. Instead of discussing this matter seriously with you, I am acting like a clown, and not a good one at that. Please forgive me, Bogdan." Tears appeared in her eyes. "Forgive all of us for making fun. I am fond of you. I like you, and I think I understand you. There is nothing personal in it, but you must realize that our marriage is impossible. Your feeling for me . . . is a fleeting one. It does happen that students become enamored of their teachers. I myself worshipped one of my professors during my university studies. I wrote secret letters to him that I never had the courage to send. My feeling for this man left a dear memory, and I would not want our encounter to leave a bad taste in your mouth." A few tears rolled down Tanya's cheeks. Vera and Olya drank their tea in silence, keeping their eyes on the glasses.

"I would like to help you. I wish I knew how," Tanya said, looking at Bogdan through eyes filled with tears. "I think it would be best for us not to see each other, except in the classroom."

"That is impossible, Tatyana Lvovna," Bogdan said. "I want to be near you. I love you, not just because you are my teacher. I will love you forever."

The fire in the stove had burned out, and it grew cold and damp in the room. Tanya rose, thanked her hostesses for the reception, and led the way out. At the door to her room she and Bogdan shook hands.

"I wish you happiness, Bogdan," she said, and smiled.

As he walked out, the rain struck his face, and he turned slowly toward his home. But it hurt him to leave Tanya, and after he had gone only a few steps, he turned back to her house and stood in front of it, water dripping from his hair. He wanted to be with her, to look at her eyes, to touch her hands, inhale the air around her, feel the warmth of her body and her nearness. He kept looking at the faintly lit window of her room as if hypnotized. A huge truck passed by, splashing mud on him, but it did not matter to him. He sat down on the steps and waited, he knew not what for. In his mind he heard Tanya's words. He knew that he could not have expected that she would accept his proposal right away, but he was sure that one day she would say yes.

Some hours later, he heard noises inside her house. After a while Vera, dressed in her overcoat, appeared. She stumbled over him.

"What are you . . ." she began. "Oh, it's you! Why did you return here?" She was buttoning her overcoat.

"I never left," he said. "I could not move away from Tanya."

"You'll catch cold. You're all wet; your clothes are soaked!"

"I don't care."

"Here, get up. Your mother must be worried. I'll walk you home."

Bogdan did not move. Vera took his hands and pulled him up.

"Come along," she said. "We'll talk about Tanya."

They began to walk, she on the wooden planks of the sidewalk and he at her side marching in the mud. He was so soaked that it did not matter.

"Tanya is a beautiful woman, and not only physically," Vera said, putting up the collar of her coat. "She has suffered a lot. Her husband is a drunkard who deserted her and their small children. Her mother cares for them while she works thousands of kilometers away in this miserable place. I know that love, your love, is a powerful feeling. But you should think about her."

"I think about Tatyana Lvovna all the time."

"I meant you should think about her situation. She is your teacher, much older than you. Which way do we go?"

It was pouring, and Vera tightened a babushka on her head.

"We must turn here," Bogdan said.

"Your hanging around her house is not good for her reputation. She likes you, but you must see the problem you are creating for her. You do understand?"

As they reached his house, Vera kissed him on his cheek. "Go to sleep now, and try to forget everything. The morning is more clever than the night."

His mother was in bed, but not asleep.

"Let me help you out of your clothing," she said, getting up. "I could warm up a glass of milk for you."

"No, thank you, *Maman*. I am sorry. You must have worried."

"I wasn't worried, Bogdan," she said, hanging his soaking jacket near the stove. "Nothing bad ever happens to people in love."

Bogdan blushed. His mother's words surprised him. But soon he was thinking of Vera's advice to him to forget Tanya. Yet he could not. He kept imagining her sad eyes as he went to bed, the next morning, and during the whole day. In the evening he followed Tanya at a distance, and after she had disappeared into the house, he sat down on the lowest step and kept looking at her lighted window.

Olya, who was entering the house, stopped.

"Oh, we have a night watchman at our residence." She laughed at her poor joke. "What an honor. You are lucky that it is not raining the way it was last night."

She went inside, and ten minutes later she returned with a glass of hot tea and a piece of buttered bread.

"Drink this," she said, pressing the glass into his hand.

"I don't want to drink or eat anything."

"You must. The tea is sweetened with raspberry preserves, Tanya's preserves. It will warm you up."

He obeyed.

"Why don't you fall in love with Vera? She has a much better job than Tanya. Being a waitress in the canteen, she gets an allocation of more food than the two of us together. And she is fifty—she could be your grandmother. Why not go all the way, instead of falling in love with someone who could be your mother?" She laughed again. "You're a funny one."

"I love Tatyana Lvovna," Bogdan said forcefully, returning the empty glass.

"I will get you another one," Olya said. And before he could say anything, she had disappeared into the house.

"Tanya would like you to go home," Olya said as she handed

him the second glass. "She is very upset about your sitting here."

"I cannot leave, I cannot."

"Then take this," Olya said, showing Bogdan Tanya's green scarf. She put it around his neck.

"Did Tatyana Lvovna give it to you for me?" he asked.

"No, I stole it from her," Olya said, laughing. She left.

The aroma of Tanya's body and her perfume still lingered on the scarf. Bogdan began to imagine sitting somewhere in a park on a sunny afternoon with Tanya, holding her hands. He wanted to pour out his love and tell her how pitifully unhappy his life was. It would be especially good to tell her an unhappy love story of his past, but even making a special effort of the imagination he could not recall one. He had gone out with a few girls, kissed them at their doorsteps or, during summer vacations, in the woods. The girls responded and one, Halina, taught him to use his tongue when kissing. She had even allowed him to touch her breasts, but that was the limit of his sexual experience. It would be hard for Bogdan to call those experiences tragic, since the girl had been eager to see him again. It had been Bogdan, who, ashamed of his lust for her, had avoided any future meetings. Yet he liked to remember these experiences in the most gloomy light and with self-pity.

He did not love Halina. He did love Tatyana Lvovna. Bogdan would not be satisfied to touch Tatyana's breasts and stop at that. There would be no limit to his lovemaking with her. This thought kept Bogdan warm and his cheeks glowing. Even the gusts of cold wind could not cool them.

The door opened, and to his surprise Tatyana Lvovna appeared on the porch in her nightgown, her unbuttoned coat thrown around her shoulders. She carried a kerosene lamp, its light flickering in the wind. The porch was so narrow, she had to stand close to him, and he could feel the warmth of her body.

"I came here to tell you," she said, raising the lamp above her head, "that Heaven bestowed on me, in its infinite wisdom and charity, a suitor whose devotion and readiness to sacrifice himself has no limit. And I am eternally grateful for that honor. The only thing wrong with this drama is that it does not have the proper setting." Bogdan could smell her perfume, and the light of the kerosene lamp was strong enough to reveal the freckles on her bare neck.

"Pruzhany, a backward town, a town that was backward in the middle of the nineteenth century, that the events of history missed because it is situated among the worst swamps in the world, now occupied by our Red Army, is hardly the right background." She raised the lamp even higher. "For this kind of courtship, you need a castle, a *zamek*, identical word in Polish and Russian—anyway, almost identical—a marble balcony for me and an Italian garden for you."

As Tanya spoke, she gestured with her hands to emphasize her words, and as she did so she moved the lamp about. Anyone watching them from a distance could have interpreted the movements of the lamp as a series of secret signals.

"Instead of the castle," Tatyana Lvovna went on, "I live in a dilapidated shack, and you are not in an Italian garden but on the dirt walk in front of my shack, ankle deep in mud." With that she sat down on one of the steps, placing the lamp on the porch. "It would be possible for us to imagine such surroundings," she continued, as Bogdan sat down next to her, conscious that their arms were touching. "But then the scenario would go like this: the chevalier plays a love song on the mandolin, the lady comes out on her balcony, waves no, locks her window tightly, and the chevalier departs to play his song in front of another castle."

"I don't want to play in front of other balconies. I want to stay with you forever."

"I want to make an important point, Bogdan. We can imagine the castle and the balcony and forget for the moment this shack and the mud, but it would not change the reality. We must play our roles on the stage given to us. If our stage is a rope between two poles, we cannot run in circles on that rope. If our stage is a square meter in area, we cannot hold races on it."

"We could go to another stage," Bogdan said, looking at her profile.

"That would have been a valid argument, had it been possible, but I am afraid that both of us are chained to our stages—we just have this one stage."

Bogdan took Tanya's hand, and she did not pull it away from him. But she said, "The trouble with this play is that the actress is no longer suited for the role of romantic ingenue, Bogdan; and you are not seasoned enough to appear on the stage."

"You think, Tatyana Lvovna, that the only valid love is a conventional one: the boy-meets-the-girl-next-door variety?"

"No, not at all. But love must have a future to give it some dimension. If not, it would be very flat, and very brief, and it could hurt deep down to the core of the soul." Tanya's profile was reflected in an enlarged shadow. Her hand felt good in his.

"You must understand, Bogdan, that my life is not a stroll down a path strewn with white rose petals. It is as monotonous as the sound of the trains striking the rails on the Russian steppes under the gray sky with more grayness on the horizon. And while it is not the most exciting journey, I know where I am. I don't want to be ejected from my train to find myself nowhere, with a deep wound that would make my suffering unbearable."

He could see tears in Tanya's eyes as she moved to get up, but Bogdan held onto her hand.

"Please don't leave me, not yet," he said. "I want to be near you. There is no suffering in the world that I would not want to share with you. I want to look in your eyes both when you smile and when you have tears in them. And when the day is over, the last thing I wish to remember of that day is your warmth, and the first thing I want to see in the morning is your profile. A moment without you is time lost; life is only when I am near you. Caressing you would be ultimate bliss. I would want to stretch it out for hours, forever." Bogdan felt Tanya's hand quiver for an instant. Then she pulled her hand away and rose. "I would want," Bogdan continued, "to throw the rainbow of joy, studded with rubies and sapphires, at your feet and envelop you in a cloud of happiness, Tatyana Lvovna."

"You talk conventions, Bogdan," Tatyana said, gesturing again with the lamp. "I don't want to be a victim of convention: an old woman once loved by a young man, betrayed and abandoned. No, no, I don't wish to be the subject of a public whipping." As she said "whipping," she swept her arms wide and hit the window sill with the lamp, breaking it. "*Kitchortoo* [the devil]", she said. "Sorry, I should not curse. Incidentally, the devil is *tchort* in Russian, *cart* in Serbian, but *diabel* in Polish, from Italian *diavolo*. The Russian *tchort* comes from *tchornoy*, black, and I would wish that it were not so black and dark now."

"I will tell you I love you when the sun takes leave of the darkening sky, when—"

"In Pruzhany it is impossible to see the sky," she laughed. "You are still acting on the wrong stage. Here, the sky at noon is so dark that it cannot get any darker. Instead of saying 'forever,' you could say, 'When the sun greets the clear sky in Pruzhany, I will still love you, my Tanya,' but that would not be true. Oh, I really must face reality again, return to my senses. Bogdan, leave me, I pray you, I beg of you. Don't torture me, please don't. I want you to leave and never return. I don't want you to camp on the steps of my house. I forbid it." And, holding the broken, useless lamp, weeping aloud, Tanya disappeared into the house.

For a moment, Bogdan wanted to follow her. He had felt happiness so close, only to elude him so quickly. But, respecting Tanya's wish that he not stay on the steps, he crossed the road. On the other side there was no house, only a rotted wooden fence. Nor was there a sidewalk, only mud. For a while he stood, his back against the fence; later, tired and not caring what happened to him, he sat down in the mud, sinking into it, but not more than ten centimeters deep. And he remained sitting in that position until dawn. The next evening he resumed his vigil, sitting against the fence, and Olya, who brought him hot tea again, advised him to procure a gravestone. "One day you will sink below the surface, and with a stone at least we will know where to place the flowers." The next night it was drizzling, and he sank a little deeper into the mud. Olya fed him hot soup and came out a second time to see whether he was still alive. At the end of the first week, Olya told him that Tanya had applied for a transfer back to the Soviet Union; but after ten days, she told him that Tanya had not yet mailed the letter. As the rains intensified, the mud became softer and softer, and Bogdan was sitting further submerged in it every night.

It was the middle of November; it had been pouring since the preceding morning, and Bogdan's head was barely clear of the mud, when he heard Tanya's voice: "Come here, Bogdan." Except for seeing her in school, he had not communicated with her for a month now, and he hoped suddenly that she had decided to accept his marriage proposal. Pulling hard at the fence, he was able to extricate himself from the mud, and sinking up to his knees in it as he went, he crossed the road to the porch. The downpour helped wash some of the mud from his face, head and ears.

"You are carrying this too far," Tanya said, not looking at him.

She appeared to have lost weight, but Bogdan thought she was even more beautiful than when he had last seen her. "I am going to visit your mother because I am worried about your health. Lead me to your house!"

The wind-driven rain buffeted them. It was so dark that they had to proceed carefully to find the right planks in order not to sink to their knees in the mud. Bogdan went ahead and Tanya followed. As they reached his house, Bogdan saw that the light was still on in the window of his mother's room.

"You must understand," Tanya said, running to match Bogdan's quick stride, "I want to see your mother, not to complain about you, but to help you to solve your problem. Did you tell her where you were spending your nights . . . all alone?"

"She knows that I am in love," Bogdan said, knocking at the door.

"Does she know that you are in love with your teacher and that you have found a method of torturing her?"

"No, she does not know that," Bogdan answered. He had never told his mother anything about Tanya. Now he was afraid that his mother might start a political conversation, blaming the Soviets for Poland's defeat, a view that he shared; or that she might bring up the recent wave of deportations to Siberia, or the arrests by the Russian police, who came knocking at doors at night, picking up innocent Poles and their families, and carting them away in unheated cattle cars.

"Your poor mother. She is about to get quite a shock. I am so sorry for her."

The door opened, and Bogdan's mother greeted them in her navy blue dress. In the room on her chair lay a half-finished sweater she must have been knitting in the hope that she might sell it.

"I am Tatyana Lvovna Zverkova, and you are Bogdan's mother.

My job is to teach the Russian language in the high school here." Tanya looked as shy and frightened as she had during her first class. "I am very sorry to intrude here, and so late at that." She stretched out her hand, and Bogdan's mother shook it and smiled. "I came here to ask for your help. Your son has decided to marry me."

The room was cold and drafty. There was no fire in the stove, no pictures on the wall, no rug on the bare, rotting wood of the unpainted floor.

"I am pleased to welcome you, Tatyana Lvovna," Bogdan's mother said, not showing any surprise or emotion, but looking at Tanya with curiosity. "I must congratulate myself on having a son with such exquisite taste."

Tanya was a few centimeters shorter than his mother, who was a tall woman, just a couple of years older than their visitor. "I did not expect to see such a beauty here in Pruzhany, and I am proud of my son."

Bogdan helped Tanya to take off her coat.

"I am not such a beauty, not beautiful after all. My body is covered with *Vyznookhy* [freckles], that's the Russian word, *piegi* in Polish. Two diff— Look here," she said, pulling up her sleeve as if she were in a doctor's office getting ready for an injection. "I am covered with these *piegi*, ugly things."

"Believe me, Madame, prosze Pani [if you please], what you consider an imperfection actually underscores the important element of your beauty, your fragility. It is like crazing on one of the costliest porcelains, giving it distinction."

Bogdan was pleased at how well his mother expressed what he would have wanted to tell Tanya, who, exhausted now from her nervousness, sat down.

"May I offer you a glass of tea?" his mother asked. "Bogdan has never been in love before, and I am so happy for him."

"I must go soon," Tanya said. "It is kind of you to offer me tea." There was no mirror in the room, but the dark glass of the window reflecting the light of the lamp served the same purpose. Tanya approached it and looked at her bare arm.

"Bogdan was never in love before, and I am so happy for him," his mother repeated. Tanya turned her head toward her. "I think that first love is like the opening tune in a concerto that is repeated with growing force and added instruments as the work develops."

"My husband called me a spotted monkey. He claimed these freckles drove him to drink. And the drinking made him wild, brutal." Tanya took out her handkerchief and wiped at her tears. "I am such a lightning rod for disaster."

"We have had our problems, too, my dear Tatyana Lvovna," Bogdan's mother said. "My husband left me when Bogdan was a little baby. I had to take a job as a pianist in an orchestra, leaving Bogdan in the care of different relatives. He is in need of being loved more than anyone else I can imagine."

"But please, please. I am his teacher. The whole situation is absolutely hopeless. It is impossible."

"When love appears to be hopeless and impossible," Bogdan's mother said, "it deepens and fortifies itself; it reaches heights that it could not have achieved otherwise."

"Please, please, Pani Mrozowski," Tanya said. "We are dealing here with broken happiness, Bogdan's, mine, my mother's, yours, my children's. It is unreasonable."

"Was it not one of your Russian writers, Chekhov, I believe, who said at the end of his story 'On Love'—you must know the passage better than I do, and I may not be able to quote it precisely—'In matters of love, one should reason beyond what is reasonable and beyond what concerns happiness, or one should not reason at all.' "

"I remember the passage quite well," Tanya said. "But you know what suffering, what deep pain—"

"Pain and suffering in love are necessary, like the adagios in music that give the allegros their force. It is like the dark paints that give the lighter shades their gaiety. Otherwise we would have monotony in music and gray panels instead of paintings."

Tanya came forward, put her arms around Bogdan's mother, kissed her cheeks and began to cry. "Forgive . . . me . . . please. I am unworthy . . . of anything . . . I am a spotted monkey." Then she embraced her again, put on her coat and the white beret and, keeping her head down, left the room like an actress leaving the stage after being booed by the public. Bogdan followed her.

"I want to marry you, Tanya," Bogdan said, walking swiftly behind her. "My mother considers you a beauty. She is proud of me, Tanya."

"Please, please leave me in peace. Leave me alone!"

The heavy rain let up and turned into a drizzle, but it was windy and getting cold. It felt as if snow would fall soon.

Tanya stumbled along the sidewalk until she reached her shack and, without turning her head or even saying goodnight, disappeared into the house. In a few minutes the light came on in her window. Bogdan, standing there, began to imagine her undressing, putting on her nightgown, her breasts outlined under the tight fabric. He felt he could smell the aroma of the beeswax candle burning and the scent of poppies that must have filled the room. He did not have enough strength to go back across the road to his station. He was so tired and wet that he just sat down on the porch where he was.

Suddenly the beam of a flashlight blinded him.

"What in hell are you up to?" a bass voice demanded in Russian.

In the darkness and the drizzle Bogdan could make out the outlines of two men in uniform.

"*Vor* (thief)," the hoarse voice of the other policeman said. "He is waiting until people sleep and then he will steal."

The first policeman was huge, like a tank, the other smaller.

"I am not a thief," Bogdan said, standing up.

"You son of a bitch! You are a liar," the bass voice said. And its owner focused the beam of his flashlight on Bogdan's face. "It's a *maltshishka* (kid). Getting an early start."

"Let's get that *vorishka* (little thief) into the Komendatura," the hoarse voice said. "We'll teach him a lesson there."

A strong hand seized Bogdan's arm. "Ten years in the labor camp will teach you, you———"

At that moment the door opened and Tanya appeared. "What is going on here?" she demanded. She was buttoning her coat over her nightgown.

"This fu—this son of a bitch wants—" the big man started.

"You don't have to use abusive language," Tanya said. "I am a Soviet citizen, a teacher here, and I won't allow it."

"This is a thief," the other fellow said. "We are here to protect you."

"You can protect me without using foul language. It is prohibited." Tanya came down a few steps to approach them. "You must apologize. I demand it."

The big policeman turned his flashlight on her. She appeared pale and tired. "Oh, you are Tatyana Lvovna. I recognize you. You are a teacher. Sorry, sorry. But this fellow here, under your window, at this time of the night. What was he doing here?"

"Never mind, tovarich. Apologize," she said.

"We did. I said I was sorry," the man said.

"An *apology* to him," Tanya said, pounding the porch railing with her fist.

"I don't know what you want from us, Tatyana Lvovna," the smaller policeman said. "We use these words all the time. We don't mean any harm by it. Look at him. He didn't mind it. If you like, he can call each of us the same thing and we'll be even."

"I know what he minds or does not mind, better than he does. He is my student. Apologize."

Never in their lives had the two men been asked to apologize for cursing. They hesitated, but Tanya hit the porch railing with her fist again, and both of them said, "Sorry, sorry."

"Now I want you to conduct this young man to his mother," Tanya said.

The two men hesitated.

"He must be drunk," the smaller man said. "That's all right. We'll conduct the son of . . . well, to his mother."

"I will not go," Bogdan said as the big fellow grabbed his arm.

"Ugh, he must be crazy or something. He is as wet as a *khlyooshtsh* [wet hen] and still sitting here. Come on!"

"I will not," Bogdan said, trying to free himself. But the big fingers tightened their grip on him.

"Why in hell . . . sorry . . . don't you want to come?" the smaller policeman asked. "It's to your mother."

"I am in love. I want to stay here. I love, *love* Tatyana Lvovna."

The big man let go of Bogdan as if he had heard a command from Tovarich Stalin, and he turned off his flashlight. Then he stepped up on the porch, out of the mud, and began to make a cigarette by rolling a piece of newspaper and filling it with tobacco.

"Be so kind as to accompany the young man to his mother," Tatyana Lvovna repeated.

The big policeman finished making his cigarette and tried to light it with a match, but in the drizzle it got wet and the light was lost. He stepped inside the house and, after trying three more matches, he succeeded. Then, covering his lit cigarette with his hand to protect it from the drizzle, he began to smoke it, inhaling the smoke deeply.

"*Lyoobov, Lyoobov* [love, love]," he said, exhaling a cloud of dark smoke. "That's none of our business."

"We don't want to interfere," the other man said.

"But please, listen, I beg you!" Tanya said. "You'll be doing a good deed for him and for me."

"Interfering would bring us bad luck in our own love matters," the big man said, and began moving away.

Bogdan, accustomed now to the darkness, was able to make out Tanya's silhouette. She was trembling.

"The kid is so pitiful," the smaller policeman said. "I was—" They were on the road now.

"Not pitiful," the bass voice came from the distance. "I bet love makes him see cherries in bloom against a blue sky. The son of a bitch doesn't even know that it is raining and . . ." The voices began to fade behind the screen of fog and mist.

Tatyana stood still on the threshold and shivered. "She is suffering because of me," Bogdan thought. "I torture her so much. What have I done?"

He stepped up and took her hand. It was wet and cold. She did not take it away. He realized that the encounter with the policeman could ruin her reputation.

"Will you forgive me, Tatyana Lvovna?" he asked, kneeling. "I will go away," and he began kissing her hand. "I promise, I prom . . . ise." His voice broke and he began to cry. "I will never bother you again. I will never see you again, not here, not even in school."

Tanya pulled him up and kissed his cheeks. Their warm tears mixed, intermingled with the cold moisture of the drizzle.

"I want to tell you, Bogdan, Bogdanek, Bogdanotshik, during

the night when it's misty, and the sky is covered with heavy clouds, I will be thinking of you, missing you, and I hope one day you will think of me."

"I will think of you always, forever."

"I want you to have something," she said, and walked into her room. He followed her there. "Here is a scarf," she said, picking it up from the chair and giving it to him. "I hope it will keep you warm."

The beeswax candle flickered. The bed was made up, and there was an open book lying on the table. Her wet clothing, smelling of soap, was hanging near the stove.

Bogdan came close to her. The drizzle had turned into rain and was pounding on the window, producing a monotonous sound like the echo of train wheels beating on iron rails, somewhere in the vast spaces of Russia.

He put his arms around her. "I don't want to leave you, Tanya, Tanitshka, Tanyoosya, Tanyoosyenka." Their lips met. The aroma of red poppies mixed with the scent of the burning beeswax candle. He kissed her cheeks, her forehead, her eyes. When he kissed her mouth again, she put her arms around him and pressed her body against him. He felt her warmth and the quivering of her body.

"Will you forgive me, Bogdan, Bogdanotshik? Will you?" she asked, stepping back.

"There is nothing I should forgive you for, Tanya. I want your forgiveness." Through the open doors, voices could be heard. "I beg your forgiveness."

"Yes, there is quite a lot I need to be forgiven," Tanya said.

She went to the door and closed it, looking at Bogdan. He was not sure what was happening when Tanya took off her overcoat and hung it on a hook. "You could put your clothing on the chair, and move it by the stove, but not too near. It might catch fire."

She passed a mirror, and stopped in front of it, looking at her reflection. "So you don't think that I am—" she began. "Anyway, it is too late to think about it." She lay down under the blanket and turned her body toward the wall.

Bogdan's hands shook, and only with great effort was he able to unbutton his jacket.

"When you are finished undressing, Bogdan, blow out the candle. And is it true that you will be kind, gentle to me, for hours?"

The wind howled outside and beat hard against the window, as if it wanted to enter the room, intrude and separate the two of them. Bogdan struggled to take off his wet shoes.

"I miss you, Bogdan, Bogdanek. I feel very tender toward you. I tried to suppress my feelings, my love for you, but it was like trying to fight fire by throwing dry hay on it. What is taking you so long? I can't wait any longer. *Pospies sie* [hurry up], Polish, *pospyeshy*, Russian, two almost identical words." She turned toward him. "Oh, you are still all dressed." She jumped out of the bed. "*Predzey* [faster], Polish, *skerey*, Russian, two different words. I'll help you," she said, beginning to unbutton his shirt. Bogdan took her in his arms, and he did not have time to undress any further, even to put out the beeswax candle.

7

After completing Bogdan's story, I returned to Paris, my favorite city, the only place in the world where I could live permanently. Nothing had happened there during my absence, except that the uniforms worn by the meter maids had changed to the color of the periwinkle, and thus they had become known as *pervenches*.

I was not sure how much I had learned from Bogdan's story. Perhaps my lady would also speak several languages like Tanya, I told myself. However, reliving Bogdan's love gave me new incentive and added gusto to my search for my lady. While I continued a frantic correspondence with all the circus museums and galleries, I also worked on writing up a profile of my lady lion tamer. I was ready to start my interviews with the circus people, but I decided still to call Professor Stolzer in order to get his opinion on the strategy of my search.

On the phone Stolzer was friendly, and he asked about my progress before I brought up the matter. When I told him what had happened since my last meeting with him and about my plans to call on circus performers, both working and retired, he commented, "Circus people are too preoccupied with themselves. Your best bet would be to interview a scientist, an observant—"

"Where would I find a man like that?"

"Don't interrupt, Herr Majeski. You have this habit of interrupting when I have something important to communicate to you.

One of my colleagues, a Frenchman, now practicing in Brussels, has written a dissertation on the laughter of circus clowns, and he has kept good records."

I was so grateful to the professor and so elated at his good news that if I had been closer to him, I certainly would have embraced him. The professor told me that the name of his confrere was Pierre Andieux, and he suggested that I call him later that evening.

When I called Dr. Andieux, he had already heard from Professor Stolzer, and he agreed to receive me in his office the very next afternoon. In the morning I took the train, and I arrived in Brussels a few hours before my appointment. I spent the time walking around the city, oblivious to the rain and cold, warm with the expectation of finding my love at long last.

Pierre Andieux turned out to be a small, slim man of about forty, with a receding hairline and a pair of lively dark eyes. He took me into his study, a large room with an oversized oak desk covered with a stack of bluish folders. He noticed that I was looking at them, and he said, "I prepared these folders for our meeting. Only among these papers would I be likely to find any information pertaining to your case."

The number of the folders reassured me that this might be the right place for getting what I wanted so much.

He took my poster with his manicured fingers, glanced at it briefly, and put it aside, saying that he didn't recognize her, but that he agreed with Stolzer's observations about her risorius muscle. Although the professor must have told Andieux my story, he wanted to hear it again, and as I proceeded to tell it, he made careful notes on a pad.

After I finished, he kept on writing for a while. Then, looking at the folders, he said, "I couldn't have met this person. However, during a few years of my research work I met several clowns and interviewed them in depth."

"This study took you years?"

He didn't comment. "I have indexed all the interviews according to the reasons for the laughter of clowns." He began to shuffle a number of yellow index cards.

"Number fifteen: here is a girl of seven who made my clown laugh by kicking an old dog. The description doesn't fit your case: no mention of freckles, the girl had a messy house, etc."

In this way, we went through some twenty-five cards, but we didn't find what we were looking for. I began to despair.

Andieux put the cards away. "No luck with these," he said, pulling out another set. The sight of these gave me renewed hope.

"These are cards representing cases that made the clowns *stop* laughing. Here: clown number six stopped laughing because the girl, his daughter, lost her doll. No—not this one. The age doesn't fit your description. Your lion tamer must have been born in the last years of the war, 1942 to 1945. However, this one would fit your case. Clown number twenty-two. Girl, eleven years old in 1953. Let me see."

He opened a folder and searched for the right page. My heart, as it seemed to me, stopped beating.

"A girl of eleven, not related. Hm . . . She tried to teach the clown *how* to laugh, it seems. And he didn't take it too well. Other descriptions fit: freckles, clean, very neat. That's all I have. No name for the girl."

I wanted to cry with disappointment, and must have made a whimper of some kind.

"No, no, wait! Don't interrupt! I know the clown's whereabouts. He lives in Antwerp. He would certainly know her if she is still alive."

"Where is he?" I asked, but Andieux was already on the telephone. After a short conversation, he told me that the clown was named Gromko, was away on a tour, but was supposed to return in a few weeks. Gromko, a Russian émigré, had been a university teacher, but because of his drinking had lost that job and become a clown.

In order to be in Antwerp when the clown returned, I decided to take a room there and wait.

Weeks later, the telephone rang in my room. It was Dr. Andieux, calling to tell me that the clown had returned and that he had talked with him the night before. In thirty minutes, I was dressed and waiting for Andieux in front of the hotel.

We crossed many streets and got lost several times before we were able to find Gromko's place near the harbor, in a narrow street smelling of fresh fish and French-fried potatoes. As Andieux stopped the car in front of Gromko's house, a tall, heavyset man with a balding head greeted us with a deep bow. He was dressed in black baggy pants with patches—the pants showed traces of several meals—a loose charcoal-colored smock, and sabots over his bare feet.

"Here comes the lover-hunter," the man said in heavily accented French as he stretched out his big hand. "So why all this search for the lion tamer?"

I was surprised by the clown's attire. Anticipating this meeting, I had imagined Gromko in a colorful costume and not in this somber outfit, a kind of Brueghelian caricature of a peasant funeral director.

"I love her; it's natural I would want to find her," I said, trembling with excitement.

"The love of one unseen occurs in legends and literature," the clown said in a tone of voice that sounded more like an expression of condolence than an observation. "I have read about men who fall in love with portraits, dreams, lockets of hair; there was even one Indonesian hero who fell in love with a woman when he saw the marks of her teeth in a half-eaten fruit. But that poster is a new one on me."

"Did these men find the women they loved?" Andieux asked.

"They did, but many of their stories have tragic endings."

"I am sure," I said, "that she will love me."

The clown made a face as if he had swallowed a dozen unripe lemons.

"I live in the small room above here," he said. "And there is no place to sit down."

He had deep-set brown eyes and a big nose the color of a ripe tomato. As far as I could tell, that was the natural color.

"I know of a little café in the neighborhood. I will lead you to it," the clown said, striking out.

Since the sidewalks were so narrow that they allowed the passage of one person only, Dr. Andieux followed immediately behind the clown, and I brought up the rear. After only a few blocks, the clown halted in front of a small café, where a fiftyish woman in a lilac dress, wearing heavy makeup, very much *en bon point,* greeted the clown in Flemish.

"This is Dorotje, *my* girl," he said, and winked his left eye. "And I am Joris Gromko." Then, turning to the woman, he said, "This monsieur wants to find Edna."

When I heard the first name of my beloved for the first time, there was some activity in the region of my heart in response, a mixture of joy and fear.

"The lion tamer," I said. "You worked with her in the circus?"

"Edna, the lion tamer. Ha, ha, ha," the clown said, laughing so that the bottle behind the bar shook and the glass in the window rattled.

"I think she is a lion tamer," I said. "The poster . . ."

"Ha, ha, ha, ha," the clown kept laughing.

Even a passerby stopped, wondering what was going on.

"Monsieur Gromko has a severe case of professional deformation," Dr. Andieux remarked.

"Let's drink to it," Gromko shouted. "For me, the usual quadruple Bols, and give these good people a double of the same. My new friend is Polish. And you know, Dorotje, as they say, '*Saoul comme un polonais* [drunk as a Pole].' "

Of all possible cliches, I hated this one the most.

"I am French. I came to France in 1939 as a teenager," I protested, looking at Gromko finishing his drink, a full tumbler of Bols, at one gulp. "I feel very French."

"Ha, ha, ha. That's the worst kind. The French have enough bad characteristics," Gromko said. "But a Pole who has become a super Frenchman, gee wee! *Plus catholique que le pape* [more Catholic than the pope]! That's awful."

"You are drunk, Joris," Dorotje said. "You must see the gentleman is a fine man."

I was angry to the point of leaving, but the thought of losing the opportunity of finding Edna made me control my temper.

"Monsieur Gromko," Andieux said. "You just mentioned that Mademoiselle Edna is not a lion tamer. What is she then?"

"For all I know she might be a lion tamer," Gromko said, waving to the bar woman to serve another round. "But at that time—it was in Dijon, I think—she was not. As a matter of fact, she worked at the time as an usher. She was the daughter of one of the women magicians and an unknown papa. Well, it happens. Hey, give me that drink."

Dorotje did not move.

"This fellow will pay the bill, don't you worry," the clown said, and I nodded. "He will, he will. He's got the itch. After making love all over Paris to all kinds of Parisiennes—hey, what was I saying? Oh, yes, the *itch*—for a lion tamer he hasn't even had in bed yet!"

"But I love her," I said. "I want to find her, I want to discover the secret of why I love her, and—even more—I want to wrest from the gods the real secret of love."

"The gods may punish you for your curiosity. What was I saying? Oh, yes. The circus was going bust. Our woman lion tamer looked like a scarecrow. So they photographed Edna. They never used the damn poster. The circus went out of business."

"And what happened to Edna?" I asked impatiently.

The clown looked at the full glass for a few moments, drank it, and made a gesture of disgust with his large hands.

"No one wanted her. There was no place for her in the circus. She left and got married."

I began to shake. My hands trembled, and drops of sweat sprang out on my forehead. The idea that she might be married had never occurred to me. Was her husband another circus clown who touched her neck, her breasts with his big hands?

"Who is her husband?" I asked.

"A good man," Gromko said. "And they have two children."

"Madame Dorotje," Dr. Andieux said, turning to the bar lady. "Do you use thyme or marjoram in your *carbonades flamandes*? I have a recipe that specifies marjoram, but I don't like the result."

"But my love for her is a true love. No husband, no children can stop it," I said.

"If I were you, I would forget Edna," said Gromko, who was drunk now. He sat back and roared with laughter.

"But why?"

"She will not tame you," the clown managed to say between gales of laughter. "She will eat you, devour you, without your even knowing it."

"Thyme, of course," Dorotje said. "But the secret of good *carbonades* is the quality of the beer you use."

"I don't even know who you are," Gromko said.

"I use Alsatian beer," Andieux said.

Gromko waved his hands again, and Dorotje refilled his glass.

"I am a writer," I said. "Of course Alsatian beer is not good for *carbonades flamandes*. I want to meet her to write about her, to write the greatest love story of the century." Turning to Andieux, I said, "You should always use Belgian beer."

"An author!" exclaimed Gromko. "Of cookbooks, of course."

"No, not cookbooks," I said. "Case studies, tracts, novels, essays, biographies, panegyrics."

"Hey, then you are my cousin clown," Gromko said. "We both chose our jobs because we wanted to be noticed, we wanted to amuse and entertain. The only difference is that I do it from an arena and you from the pages of your books."

"Take our export beer, monsieur," Dorotje said.

The clown, having discovered in his new acquaintance a man in a related profession, drained my glass.

"You would be a better author if you could read your stuff to circus crowds," the clown said. "Then you would see quickly whether they laughed, cried, or yawned."

"I don't care about the crowds and masses. They are numbers, statistics. A person is an individual with feelings, sensibilities. That is what counts. Besides, I want to write for Edna, a long love letter in the form of a book."

"But you don't know her?"

"So much the better. I can be more objective, come closer to the truth. How can I meet Edna?"

The small room was filled with smoke, the odor of unwashed bodies, and the smell of alcohol. The clown dropped his head.

"I am not sure."

The clown's hesitation enraged me. Is he stalling because he wishes to derive some benefit for this arrangement? I asked myself.

"Don't you want me to meet Edna? Don't you want me to bring love into her life? You must know something about joy—after all, you are a clown."

I expected him to react with his standard, loud "ha, ha, ha," but instead Joris closed his eyes, and lowered his head.

After a moment of silence, he said, "The original clowns made up the wild horde of the dead."

Hearing these words, I felt a chill through my spine. I could imagine Gromko marching in a medieval parade, shouting his "ha, ha, ha" and inviting me to join the horde.

"That is how our profession began," the clown continued. "I'll call her, and I'll find out whether she will see you. I'll call her from the post office; give me some money and wait for me here."

After the clown had left, and while Andieux and Dorotje went over the various Flemish specialities—*choux rouge à la flamande* (red cabbage Flemish style), *waterzoi* (chicken in the pot), *lapin aux pruneaux* (rabbit with prunes), and others, I paced from one corner of the room to the other, with all the anxiety of a student awaiting the results of a crucial exam.

Two hours later Gromko reappeared. I stopped my pacing. The clown looked drunk, his nose appearing even redder than before. He stumbled as he approached the bar, grabbed the bottle of Bols, and took a swig.

"She will see you, she will," the clown said. "Take the plane from Brussels to London, then switch to a train for Norwich. It arrives in Norwich at 11:15, Edna said, 11:15, she said. Thursday in a week, in a week, Thursday, Thursday. She will wait . . . station . . . you, you should recognize her, ha, ha, ha."

He collapsed on the floor.

Later, as Dr. Andieux and I began our dinner with braised endive, I thought of Edna and our meeting on the platform of the railroad station in Norwich. If Gromko was to be believed, she had been all too willing to see me.

On Thursday, following Edna's instructions, I took the plane to London and changed for a train north.

The train was already slowing down and I noticed the sign—Norwich. Only minutes separated me from my beloved Edna. With my two bags, I rushed toward the exit doors and opened them before the train halted, jumping down from the moving car. As the cloud of smoke from the oncoming locomotive cleared, I recognized her. She was standing alone on the platform, near the stairs. Her hair was even shorter than she had worn it in the poster, but it had the same reddish glow. She wore a colorful dress, with a preponderance of green, and a loosely buttoned matching sweater. Her legs were covered with knee-high socks of bright design.

As I approached her, she looked at me. Her eyes, the color of a mountain lake softened by the morning haze, smiled at me.

During many sleepless nights, I had visualized the encounter with Edna, how I would take her in my arms, raise her high into the sky, cover her hands, cheeks, hair, mouth with kisses and shout, "I love you, Edna. I love you." But now I stood in front of her trembling, my face flushed, unable to utter a word.

"You are Monsieur Majeski?" she asked. And when I nodded, still speechless, she shook my hand. "I am Madame Carol." She spoke fluent, but accented, French. "Do you prefer to speak French?"

I nodded again. Edna had a honey-colored amber necklace around her neck, and when she noticed that I was looking at it, she said, "It is from Poland, your native land."

"Let me carry your bag," she said, picking up the larger valise. I tried to take it from her, but she refused to let me.

"Your train was six minutes late," she said. "But we will make the hotel in time. Our apartment is too small for house guests, so I reserved a room for you at the inn. They charge ten pounds a night. Considering the usual prices for hotel rooms, it is good value for the money."

We left the station and walked down a road in the October sunshine.

"When I saw your picture on that poster," I said, marching along beside Edna, "I knew right away that I must see you."

"You are so romantic, Monsieur Majeski. It's so rare nowadays. Norwich does not offer many places with comfortable accommodations, but I think you will like your room with its view of the cathedral. They have only three rooms with that view, and the clerk promised me he would keep one for you until 11:45. That's why I am trying to hurry."

We reached her car, a Volkswagen, and she opened the luggage compartment. I was ready to lift my bag into it.

"I'll do it. I know the right way," she said. "I want to place the bags so the weight will be distributed properly."

She wore very little makeup, a little face powder and lipstick. The white skin on her neck was sprinkled with a few freckles. Her energy and vivacity were contagious. After she had opened the car door, she took out a hanger and, putting her sweater on it, hung it on a hook inside the car. Then Edna invited me to sit down. In the seat was a faded red scarf and, on top, a small, stuffed, green plush lion.

Seeing these things and Edna smiling as she watched for my reaction to this display, I could no longer control myself. I drew closer, put my arms around her, and looked into her eyes.

"You may kiss me here," she said, pointing with her finger to her cheek. "I knew you would enjoy my surprise. The scarf is the one that I had when Randolf took that picture for the poster. We were not married then."

The mention of her husband's name and the news that he had taken the photograph was like the harsh sound of a whistle interrupting a beautiful dream. I dropped my arms.

"Oh, I didn't know it was your husband—"

"Will you fasten your seat belt, please?" she said, as soon as we were seated in the car.

"Are you going that far, on a highway?"

"Not too far. Only two miles. Still, it is safer."

I obeyed, and after struggling with the belt for a few moments, I was sitting well strapped in. She started the motor and we drove for a while in silence. I admired her profile, so familiar to me by now.

"You are more beautiful in person than in the poster," I said, and she smiled.

"I am not used to such compliments, being a provincial matron, as I am. When Gromko called, I could not understand him too well. He was obviously quite drunk, and the purpose of your visit was not clear to me, although I called and spoke to him a day later. I must confess that I agreed to see you because I was curious about this project of yours, writing about circus life. Is that what you are planning?"

Edna was reminding me of someone I knew. I scoured my memory for a clue.

"Partly, yes," I said.

"Anyway, I prepared a notebook, pencils, and ballpoint pens in blue, black, and red. Also, I managed to rent a tape recorder, for which I did not have to pay, since my husband makes photographs for the electric appliance store at a twenty percent discount. I have checked the recorder out, and it works."

She wore a perfume with a faint and delicate aroma that reminded me of flowering acacias, not in full bloom, but when their blossoms first opened, not at night but in the mist of dawn.

"Why did you select me as your subject for a book about the circus and the lion tamers? Gromko must have told you that I never was one," she said as we crossed a bridge.

"I want to find out why your image on the poster had such magic for me."

She stopped her car in front of the hotel.

"It is 11:40," she said, looking at her watch. "You'll get the room with the good view. I will pick you up in an hour. That will give you time to bathe and shave. Then I'll drive you home and we'll have lunch."

The idea of eating at her home appealed to me. There is nothing in life that gives more pleasure to a man than a meal prepared by the woman he loves, I thought. As I was checking in, I began to wonder what wine she would serve me. I had heard of English wines, but I had never had the opportunity to taste them. Would Edna serve me a bottle of rosé from Beaulieu Abbey or some wines from the Isle of Wight? There might be a good combination of these wines with mountain brook trout, for instance. But Edna might surprise me, perhaps, by serving some unknown variety of local fish that would taste well with Pfalz wine. The possibilities of Edna's forthcoming meal preoccupied me until her arrival.

When she appeared in front of the hotel, I told her, "You must have been very busy preparing lunch," hoping that she would indicate the kind of food she had planned to serve.

"Oh, no, Monsieur Majeski. I had to deliver some photographs. I prepared today's meal two days ago."

It could not be fish then, I thought. The only food that could have been prepared two days in advance and taste good would be either tripe or bigos, a combination of sauerkraut and various meats. Knowing I was of Polish origin, she might have tried to fix the tripe *à la polonaise,* with mushrooms called *Aedulis edibilis* here, *prawdziwki* in Poland. I began to wonder whether she had used mushrooms imported from Poland; that would be much better, since they had a more delicate aroma than the South American imports.

Of course, if she had decided on sauerkraut, she could have used venison as the main meat and English pork, which would not be too bad. I had decided to ask her, but she stopped the car in front of a two-story building, painted white. Next to the entrance there was a store with a large sign: "Edna and Randolf Carol, Photographers."

Edna quickly climbed the white-painted stairway and opened the doors. Immediately I began to sniff the air, hoping to catch the aroma of mushrooms and anticipate the menu. I liked to know in advance what kind of a meal I was going to eat. Such anticipation always gave me enormous pleasure. But the apartment smelled of fresh paint and detergent, and the only aroma of food I was able to detect was the slightest scent of chives.

As we entered the dining room, I saw that the table was set with white china on a white linen cloth. There were large soup plates, but no wine glasses, only water glasses filled with a reddish liquid. In the middle of the table stood a silver candle holder with yellow candles. The window was open, and I could hear footsteps on the pavement below, the sound of voices, laughter. The sun lit the beige walls, which were covered with framed photographs.

"Here are my girls," I heard Edna say.

I turned around and saw two neatly dressed girls, one about

ten and the other perhaps two years younger. Both had short blond hair and wore shiny black shoes.

"This is Jane," said Edna, as the older girl stretched out her hand. "And here is Magdalene."

I was just about to say something to the girls when I heard footsteps, and a tall man with broad shoulders, dressed in a dark business suit, appeared.

"I have looked forward to your visit with great pleasure, Mr. Majeski," Randolf said, squeezing my hand in his much larger one.

"So have I," I lied. "You have a beautiful home."

"That is all my wife's achievement," Randolf said without a smile. "She framed all these photographs, and she cleans the glass in all these pictures daily, sometimes twice a day."

When Edna lives with me, I decided, there would be no pictures hung behind glass.

"Randy is right about my cleaning the place," Edna said. "With all this dust, it does require a lot of work to keep it in somewhat decent shape. But all the photographs are his. I will show them to you one day, Monsieur Majeski. You will agree with me then that Randy is a very talented artist. I am proud of him."

"You will have discovered before that that the real talent is my darling's," Randy said, sitting down at the table and motioning to me to join him. "How wonderfully well she can cook!"

If a husband praises his wife's cuisine so highly, she must indeed be good, I reasoned. One can prepare a lot of excellent dishes with chives.

Edna left, reappeared carrying a tureen, set it down in front of her, and began to serve.

"Today is Thursday," she said, "a day on which we always eat stew, my speciality. That is why, I must confess, I asked you to arrive on Thursday."

I looked at the plate before me with fear. I had heard the horror stories about English stews, but I had never quite believed them. Now I, Jan Majeski, was poised on the brink of experience myself. With a shaking hand, I picked up my spoon and filled it half-full of the thick, yellow-green liquid and lifted it to my mouth. For a moment I could not down the gluey substance for fear of swallowing all the fillings in my teeth along with it.

The girls ate quietly, staring at their plates.

"Isn't it excellent?" Edna asked, smiling proudly.

I tried to swallow the concoction and in the process moved my head. Edna interpreted it as a nod.

"I knew you would love it," Monsieur Majeski," she said.

"It is too good," Randy said, finishing off three-fourths of his plate.

The idea occurred to me that maybe a few freshly ground berries of the highly aromatic pepper from the island of Guadeloupe would make the substance swallowable.

"Do you happen to have any Guadeloupe pepper?" I ventured.

Edna looked at me with surprise, as if she wanted to ask me how I dared tamper with her masterpiece.

"I have already seasoned this stew," she said, serving her husband another generous portion. "Besides, last Monday we had goulash, and since the girls giggled at the table they were not allowed a second helping. The goulash had a lot of pepper in it and I included it in this stew."

I could taste the pepper in the stew, but it was Indonesian pepper, good for some dishes in which its flavor should not dominate, as in omelets seasoned with herbs; but only the Guadeloupe pepper could have saved this unfortunate concoction. Besides, Edna did not move to get me pepper of any kind. All tampering with her cooking was strictly prohibited.

I made another effort, but the stew stuck in my mouth. I struggled to swallow it, and tears filled my eyes.

"It tastes fantastic," Randy said, making substantial progress on his second helping.

"With all this conversation," Edna said, rising, "I forgot to light the candles."

The room was filled with sunshine, and the candles could hardly contribute any light or atmosphere. But she lit them, and the aroma of burning beeswax reached my nose. As she reached over the table, I noticed the freckles on her neck again, and a feeling of security enveloped me. The anxiety over swallowing was gone, and I began to eat the stew, tasting the yellow peas, the lima beans, the goulash, the chives. I drank the reddish liquid, which turned out to be beet juice, with the gusto of a desert wanderer reaching an oasis.

After lunch, the girls cleared the table and Randy excused himself. He had to return to his shop. Edna suggested that I walk with her in the park next to the cathedral.

The leaves on the old trees were bright with color and chrysanthemums bloomed along the old city walls. Somewhere in the distance girls were singing.

"I must tell you, Edna, why I came—the real reason. The moment I saw your image on the poster, I fell in love with you."

She took my hand, and I felt the light pressure of her fingers.

"I knew it," she said. "From the instant our eyes met for the first time, I knew it."

"Your poster changed my life. Nothing else has mattered except you and my love for you."

Edna leaned in toward me, and her closeness felt good. We came to a bench and sat down.

"But you don't know anything about me or my life, Jan."

"I want to know you. I want to know everything you want to tell me. But you should realize nothing will change my love for you."

The wind shook the branches of an old horse-chestnut tree nearby.

I took out an envelope from my breast pocket and handed it to her. "Writing day and night about the meaning of love, I hoped to learn why I undertook this search for you. Read these pages, Edna," I said, and kissed her. Her lips were moist and delicate.

Later, we met in front of an eleventh-century tower that lent mystery to that starlit, but cool and moonless night. We wandered through the park and found a small clearing. As I kissed her, she began to tremble. She opened the buttons of her blouse, freed her brassiere and lifted my hand to her breasts.

We made love on the soft blanket of moss and when our pleasure subsided, I looked up at the stars, feeling the warmth of her body still beneath me. A faint aroma of acacia blooms was in my nostrils.

"Until I met you," she whispered, "I thought all that was beautiful and exciting was finished for me. Everything was settled, arranged. How wonderful to be wrong."

I kissed her again, and she responded with passion. We made love again and lay in silence until the medieval church clock sounded twelve times.

As we got up, Edna brushed her skirt, and later on the knees of my trousers.

"It will take time," Edna said, brushing her shoes. "It will be hard."

"What will be hard, my Edna?" I asked.

"To open a branch of our business."

"Why, what do you mean?"

"You will live in Ipswich, some thirty miles from here. I'll visit you often. There is a need for a photography shop there, and I'll open one." She produced a flashlight and inspected my clothing.

"There is a little spot on your elbow," she said, rubbing it with a handkerchief.

"But why in Ipswich, a small town, even smaller than Norwich?" I asked, presenting the other elbow for her inspection. "We could live in Paris, Florence, or even Rio. And then why open a new business? I can support you. I will write and I have an independent income anyway."

"A man without a steady job is a menace," she said, cleaning my other elbow. "You will work only part time in the shop, mainly in the mornings, while I clean the house or work in Norwich. In the afternoon, you will teach French in the adult education program. You'll be able to write on Sundays. There is not that much going on in Ipswich."

She finished the cleaning job and carefully put all her utensils in the proper place in her bag. She pecked me on the mouth and took my arm. We walked back in darkness, since the stars were now covered by clouds. The cool wind felt pleasant against my burning cheeks. I loved the nearness of her body, her perfume and her warmth. Wouldn't I have followed her anywhere? Australia, New Zealand, Alaska? Maybe Ipswich would not be such a bad choice after all.

"I want to make you happy, Jan," Edna whispered as we reached a street. She inspected my clothing once more under the streetlight with as much thoroughness as if she were about to send me home to a jealous wife. "I will keep a clean house. I will cook for you—"

The stew insinuated itself into memory.

"I'll be glad to help you with the cooking," I said with a spark of hope.

"A man in the kitchen is a nuisance. Besides, your time in the kitchen would not be as productive as elsewhere."

"But I am an experienced cook, and I could use some of my creative talents in the kitchen, my darling."

She squeezed my hand. "I would welcome those creative talents in another room of the house! Why should you waste all your creativity in the kitchen?"

I knew that her verdict in the matter of my cooking was final, and that it would not be possible to appeal it.

We strolled toward my hotel and finally parted.

A light aroma of acacia lingered with me for hours while I thought of Edna, the photography shop in Ipswich, Jane and Magdalene, my teaching the *petits bourgeois* the delights of French, eating stew every Thursday and only she knew what the rest of the week. But nothing mattered. I knew that I could not live without her, that I wanted to be with her, that I desired her.

The next day, Edna came in the afternoon and proposed a visit to Norwich Castle, a red-brick, ancient structure.

"Last night, into the early morning," she said as we walked up the narrow path into the castle, "I read your confessions."

"What do you mean, confessions?"

"Your—how do you call it—autobiography."

"What makes you think that that writing is my autobiography, my dearest Edna?"

"It has to be you. Only you can mess up your clothing in the mud, the snow, everywhere."

It was a sunny, windy day. A few white clouds appeared in the light-blue sky.

"I am so sorry for you, Jan. All those terrible women you've met . . . in the past."

"They were not so terrible. I think they were exceptional."

"Come on, Jan. A little kid getting a bit horny, so that dame, whatever her name is, exposes herself. She should have spanked the kid and let him play doctor with other kids. Or that teacher . . . letting the boy ruin his only suit."

"But they loved me."

The sun's rays hit the brick walls and the yellowing leaves of the oaks, and shone back at me from Edna's eyes.

"Did you have an affair with Hitler's mistress?"

"No, I did not even know he had one until after the war."

"So you were putting me on," Edna said with a smile. "You did not tell the truth in your autobiography."

"But I did tell the truth. Love is a composite of fact and fantasy."

"For me, only the facts count," Edna said.

"But facts are like the rhythm in a musical composition. And fantasy is like the melody. You cannot have music without melody. You would hear nothing but monotonous noise. The same is true of life."

"So you did not work for the Gestapo? Would you have liked to?"

"One also has fears and nightmares," I said, putting my arm around Edna. We had reached the shady side of the castle. The wind blew harder, and it was cold.

"Anyway, Jan, you had a tough life, and you have a right to have nightmares about it. All that money wasted on that Polish dame. All of it for nothing. You tried as a kid to discover a woman's body; as a teenager, you were full of pity for yourself; as a grown-up, you had fantasies of famous women. As an older man, you bestowed your riches on a woman you thought you loved. But all that time you missed the real thing."

"What do you mean, my love? What did I miss?" I asked, stumbling on the protruding root of a linden tree.

"Belonging to a woman you love, a woman who will domesticate you."

"You are so dear, my Edna, so wonderful."

We walked for a while in silence. Then all discussion about the past was finished. We never broached the subject again.

Life proceeded according to the plan Edna had outlined that first night. We made love in the shadow of the Norwich Cathedral. She opened a photography shop in Ipswich, a small town with narrow streets, old one-story houses painted white, and an old cathedral in the center.

I lived in a small room above the shop, and Edna came there twice a week to work afternoons while I taught French to seven retired women.

As we made love in the evenings, Edna took the opportunity to discuss the problems that had arisen with the business in her absence.

In the evenings when Edna was not in Ipswich, I found that I was too tired to write, and I fell into the habit of frequenting the local pubs. Sundays were equally unproductive.

In Ipswich, the problem of menus selected for our home cooking was solved for us by a doctor. Soon after Edna established me in the little town, she took me to a doctor, a tall man in his early sixties with short-cropped hair and the faintest hint of a scar on his cheek. He examined me very thoroughly, most of it in Edna's presence. At the end of the visit, while both of us sat facing him, he spoke only to Edna.

"Mrs. Carol," he said, "he is to have no alcohol whatsoever, no salt, no sugar, none at all; no butter, no coffee, no fats, no spices. From now on, three times a day, he will eat vegetable soup made of fresh vegetables without any seasoning. You could use some herbs. You can serve him rice, manna, and buckwheat."

I made an attempt to ask the doctor a question, but Edna waved her hand, signaling me to keep quiet.

The doctor did not waste his time discussing the nature of my problems or the results of his test. He was giving an *ukaz*, and it did not matter that I never felt better in all my life or that the twenty-one servings per week of vegetable soup might not agree with me.

"I will see *you* in six months," the doctor said. "Now I will see Mrs. Carol alone. Wait outside."

In a few days, I began the new regime and got used to it, and, despite my fears, the diet agreed with me. I felt stronger, slept better, wrote more pages than I ever had before, and had more energy for other creative activities.

Life with Edna was very happy. I loved her, it seemed to me, more every day, every hour, every minute. She beautified my life in every possible way. I told her how much I liked the aroma of burning beeswax, and she also learned that her perfume reminded me of acacia blossoms. She searched far and wide until she found a farmer who sold acacia honey, and she made candles out of beeswax for me herself. She knitted a sweater for me, incorporating the design of her silhouette with a green lion; and for my birthday she gave me a nude photograph of herself with a red scarf, facing a green lion, all of which had been shot through the petal of an acacia flower magnified several hundred times. She also sewed two shirts for me, with green lions embroidered on the collars.

In the beginning of November, Edna decided that we should take a long weekend somewhere away from home without the children. She selected Plymouth, where one of her girlfriends was managing a bed-and-breakfast place and could allow us a special discount. I would have preferred a weekend on the Riviera or in Paris, but since it was Edna's invitation and she insisted on paying for it herself, I could not argue her choice.

Our weekend Shangri-La turned out to be a small, white house on a narrow, steep street. All the floors, even in the bathroom, were covered by machine-made carpets in a wild pattern, woven with threads in all colors of the rainbow. We arrived by car late Friday night, but the smell of bacon from breakfast still permeated the air.

Next morning, Edna suggested an excursion to Dartmoor, only miles away. The day was sunny but windy, good weather for an outing, especially at this time of year. At first we drove through a hilly landscape, the fields separated by low granite fences. Edna drove, I navigated, and together we discussed the countryside, comparing it with French landscapes.

Eventually, on the horizon, we could make out a building of dark granite stones, Dartmoor prison. I knew that in that prison, built in the beginning of the nineteenth century, thousands of dragoons and grenadiers of Napoleon's army had been incarcerated, and many of them had died there.

Edna stopped the car. At the nearest granite fence, we lunched on cucumber and watercress sandwiches. We drank milk. Then we wandered about for a few hours, holding hands, passing brooks, fields, bushes, until we reached a wooded place. Edna suggested that we rest a bit in a clearing that was blanketed with soft, green moss. After a few minutes of relaxation, I looked at her in a certain way, and she said, "Let's light a fire."

"It is forbidden," I said, taking her in my arms.

"No one will see the fire. Besides, I don't like to make love with all this heavy clothing on."

"We could catch cold all naked," I said. "Also, someone might see us."

"They would have much more fun seeing us make love nude than dressed. That would be unexpected at this time of year."

Edna gathered branches and pieces of dry wood, while I stayed seated and refused to help. When she asked me to light the fire, I handed the matches to her. In a few minutes, the fire began to warm us, and we sat and watched it in silence. The burning fir twigs spread their special scent and the reddish flame flickered in the wind. I looked into Edna's eyes, the color of a mountain spring reflecting the glow of the fire. I kissed her and she responded eagerly.

I hoped that in her passion she might forget her demand that I undress, but my hopes were not fulfilled. While we were still united by a kiss, Edna began to unbutton my jacket. To keep warm, I moved closer to the fire, took off my flannel pants, and dropped them to the ground.

"Your clothes will look terrible," Edna said, folding the pants and jacket with care. She hung up her dress and her loden overcoat on collapsible hangers that she took out of her purse.

"May I keep my socks on?" I asked.

"That would be unesthetic," she said, taking off her bra and hanging it on a dried fir twig. "You can spread them between these two branches. And put your boots below them."

The aroma of burning fir tree twigs mingled with the scent of the fresh fir trees and filled the air around us. Her body had never looked so beautiful as on that late afternoon, when she approached me in the glow of the fire and in the light of the last rays of the sun that had begun to sink behind a rocky peak.

The contact of her skin, as I took her in my arms, made me shiver with desire. I started to kiss her neck and each of the freckles there.

"I know now why I love you so much, Jan. From the day I first met you, it was clear you desperately needed me. First, no seat belt, then different kinds of pepper that you wanted for the stew, and now you leave your pants on the wet ground. How you need me!"

The aroma of acacias in full bloom on a sunny June midday emanated from Edna, and I felt a great surge of love.

Delicately, she drew me down onto the soft moss.

In our embrace, we were oblivious of the fir trees around us, of the granite tors above us, of the gust of wind that struck our fire and made it spread. Edna was the first to notice the flames reaching my clothing. Moving like lightning, she seized her loden coat and began beating at the flames.

At that very moment, the image of another fire came to my mind. Flames and . . . boys. Zdzislaw, Romek, Kurt, Michal, Bogdan.

There had been no formal nursery school in our town, so our parents had engaged a teacher, Pani Zofia, to meet with us once a week in our parents' homes. Such arrangements were called *komplety*; I loved to participate in them. I especially liked Pani Zofia. She was young, always had a smile, and spoke to us in a sweet and gentle voice.

I would never have been able to remember my own mother with the pleasure and precision that I did Pani Zofia in that split second. My teacher had in some ways reciprocated my special feeling for her. When we had cake, she always selected the largest or the most decorated piece for me. She praised my answers to her questions with an encouraging smile. At the end of each session she hugged all of us, but she always held me longer in her arms. I didn't know much then about heaven, but at that moment when I felt her warmth, inhaled her perfume, was aware of the touch of her skin, the fabric of her dress, her hair, I realized I was in the very heart of paradise.

The images and impressions of that evening rushed through my mind as if I were watching a movie running at four times the standard speed. I was oblivious to the granite rocks of Dartmoor, to the chill—even to Edna.

It had been a few days after Christmas that the fire broke out. A branch of our fir Christmas tree caught fire from a beeswax candle. It had happened when we were all gathered in the salon of Romek's parents' home. All of us children sat in what had seemed to me enormous gilded antique chairs, covered in silk. Some of our parents were there with us, but they clustered in the dining room, having tea with our hosts.

As the teacher talked to us about the Christmas tree decorations, we watched the yellow, green, red, blue, and purple candles, all of them burning, the papier-mâché angels in silvery dresses with golden hair and wings floating joyfully in the air. Small glass bells and balloons in all colors of the rainbow and paper clowns with red, round laughing faces peered out at us from the pine needles.

Pani Zofia began to tell us about the circus: about clowns, Harlequins, acrobats, magicians, and lion tamers. She began to draw the outline of a lion on a green board. Precisely while she was doing that, the fire started. We watched as a branch of our Christmas tree caught fire, we watched as the flames spread to the top of the tree. We were silent at first, unable to utter a sound. Suddenly, as if on signal, we shouted "Fire!" and I loudest of all: "Fire, fire, *fire*!"

"My darling, I know it's fire," Edna said, jumping about and beating at the flames.

"It started from a candle, a yellow beeswax candle," I said.

"*I* started the fire," she said, still working to extinguish it. "There was no candle here."

Pani Zofia turned to face us and saw the tree in flames. An expression of horror rippled across her face. At once she started to beat at the fire with her woolen scarf.

None of us moved or tried to run away. I watched as the light of the fire danced across her freckled neck, as her arms and her delicate fingers flailed away at the tree.

But her beating at the flames with her scarf only caused the fire to burn with new force. And instead of retreating, Pani Zofia went forward. Her auburn, shoulder-length hair caught fire. It all went up in flames. I gasped. She looked beautiful like that—triumphant even. Then her blouse and skirt began to burn. At that moment, several adults rushed in. They herded us out of the room. Two of them tried to help our teacher. Another pushed the burning tree onto the snow-covered balcony. I heard the sound of broken glass, and my last glimpse of the room showed me Pani Zofia slumped down on her knees, her hair and clothing still smouldering. There was no expression of horror on her face now. She appeared to smile.

I wanted to free myself, to run toward her, but a man's strong arms held me firmly and swept me away to another room.

All of the other boys were here, and a maid was watching over them. The smell of burning was in the air, and despite the frost outside, someone opened a window. Snow was falling heavily. The sounds of people running and shouting reached us through the closed door.

A short while later, Romek's mother came into the room. She was crying. After she saw that we were all right, she left hurriedly. Other parents came into the room, kissed us, and then were gone.

Some time later, a doctor in a white smock, accompanied by Romek's parents, came into the room, looked carefully for a few minutes at each of us, and then whispered something to the other adults.

My father came also, still wearing his overcoat, his fur collar covered with snow. He took me in his arms and kissed my forehead. "We must go home, Janeczku!"

"Forgive me, forgive me! It was all my idea." Edna's words brought me back to reality. She had managed to beat the fire out, and slid down next to me, exhausted. Her body was warm from the fire and the struggle.

I looked up. "It was not your fault. The wind spread the fire," I said.

"That fire . . ." I stopped. There was no reason to explain.

Edna looked tired. I helped her lie back on the soft moss and covered her with her loden coat.

"Do you feel all right?"

"Yes, just a little tired." Then, after a moment of silence, she asked, "Was it something terrible? There was such an expression in your face."

I nodded.

"Do you still love me, Jan?"

I was surprised by her question and, from somewhere, I summoned the energy to spring to my feet. "I love everything about you," I said. "Your life past and future, your children, your husband. I love the scarf you touch, the cup you drink from. If you left me tomorrow, I'd go on loving you forever."

I kissed her lips.

We dressed quickly and began walking down the path toward our car. When we reached a clearing in the woods, I stepped back to have a good look at her. With her head thrown back and the sunset dancing on her hair, she was the very picture on the poster I had discovered so long ago in Paris.

"Back to Ipswich!" she shouted to me, and gave her scarf a flick. "We have a lot to do."

Her command shot through me like an infusion of warmth, and I felt my whole being rise. I took her hand and let her lead me from among the trees. I had found my Lady.